Murder at Monticello

Books by Rita Mae Brown

THE HAND THAT CRADLES THE ROCK

SONGS TO A HANDSOME WOMAN

THE PLAIN BROWN RAPPER

RUBYFRUIT JUNGLE

IN HER DAY

SIX OF ONE

SOUTHERN DISCOMFORT

SUDDEN DEATH

HIGH HEARTS

STARTING FROM SCRATCH:
A DIFFERENT KIND OF WRITERS' MANUAL

BINGO

VENUS ENVY

DOLLEY:
A NOVEL OF DOLLEY MADISON IN LOVE AND WAR

And with Sneaky Pie Brown

WISH YOU WERE HERE

REST IN PIECES

Murder at Monticello

or Old Sins

RITA MAE BROWN

& SNEAKY PIE BROWN

ILLUSTRATIONS BY WENDY WRAY

BANTAM BOOKS NEW YORK · TORONTO · LONDON · SYDNEY · AUCKLAND

During colonial times there were fewer people inhabiting the great state of Virginia and therefore fewer family names. Many of those early names are with us today, and to be true to the time, I have used them here.

Thomas Jefferson's grandson, James Madison Randolph, had no children, so "his branch" of the Randolph family used for this novel is entirely fictitious, as are the present-day characters and all events of the novel.

MURDER AT MONTICELLO

A Bantam Book / December 1994

All rights reserved.

Copyright © 1994 by American Artists, Inc.

No part of this book may be reproduced or transmitted in any form or by any means, electronic or mechanical, including photocopying, recording, or by any information storage and retrieval system, without permission in writing from the publisher.

For information address: Bantam Books.

Library of Congress Cataloging-in-Publication Data

Brown, Rita Mae.
  Murder at Monticello, or, Old sins / Sneaky Pie
Brown, Rita Mae Brown ; illustrations by Wendy
Wray.
      p.   cm.
  ISBN 0-553-08140-3
  I. Title.   II. Title: Murder at Monticello.
III. Title: Old sins.
PS3552.R698M87   1994
813'.54—dc20   94-16711
                                           CIP

Published simultaneously in the United States and Canada

Bantam Books are published by Bantam Books, a division of Bantam Doubleday Dell Publishing Group, Inc. Its trademark, consisting of the words "Bantam Books" and the portrayal of a rooster, is Registered in U.S. Patent and Trademark Office and in other countries. Marca Registrada. Bantam Books, 1540 Broadway, New York, New York 10036.

PRINTED IN THE UNITED STATES OF AMERICA

BVG   0 9 8 7 6 5 4 3 2

For Gordon Reistrup
because he makes us laugh.

Cast of Characters

Mary Minor Haristeen (Harry), the young postmistress of Crozet, whose curiosity almost kills the cat and herself

Mrs. Murphy, Harry's gray tiger cat, who bears an uncanny resemblance to authoress Sneaky Pie and who is wonderfully intelligent!

Tee Tucker, Harry's Welsh corgi, Mrs. Murphy's friend and confidant; a buoyant soul

Pharamond Haristeen (Fair), veterinarian, formerly married to Harry

Mrs. George Hogendobber (Miranda), a widow who thumps her own Bible!

Market Shiflett, owner of Shiflett's Market, next to the post office

Pewter, Market's fat gray cat, who, when need be, can be pulled away from the food bowl

Susan Tucker, Harry's best friend, who doesn't take life too seriously until her neighbors get murdered

Big Marilyn Sanburne (Mim), queen of Crozet

Oliver Zeve, the exuberant director of Monticello, to whom reputation means a lot

Kimball Haynes, energetic young head of archaeology at Monticello. He is a workaholic who believes in digging deeper

Wesley Randolph, owner of Eagle's Rest, a passionate Thoroughbred man

Warren Randolph, Wesley's son. He's trying to step into the old man's shoes

Ansley Randolph, Warren's pretty wife, who is smarter than people think

Samson Coles, a well-born realtor who has his eyes on more than property

Lucinda Payne Coles, Samson's bored wife

Heike Holtz, one of the assistant archaeologists at Monticello

Rick Shaw, Albemarle sheriff

Cynthia Cooper, police officer

Paddy, Mrs. Murphy's ex-husband, a saucy tom

Simon, an opossum with a low opinion of humanity

Author's Note

Monticello is a national treasure well served by its current executive director, Daniel P. Jordan. Some of you will recall Mr. Jordan and his wife, Lou, opening Thomas Jefferson's home to then–President-elect Clinton.

The architectural and landscape descriptions are as accurate as I could make them. The humans are made up, of course, and Oliver Zeve, Monticello's director in this novel, is not based on Mr. Jordan.

One eerie event took place while I was writing this mystery. In the book, a potsherd of good china is unearthed in a slave cabin. On October 18, 1992, four days after I sent off the first draft of this book to my publisher, an article appeared in *The Daily Progress*, the newspaper of Charlottesville, Virginia. This article described how William Kelso, Monticello's director of archaeology, found some fine china in the slave quarters believed to have been inhabited by Sally Hemings. These quarters were close to Jefferson's home. Often slave quarters were distant from the master's house, so the location of Miss Hemings's cabin is in itself worthy of note. Finding the china bits was life imitating fiction. Who knows, but it fluffed my fur.

My only quibble with Mr. Jordan and the wonderful staff at Monticello is that they aren't paying attention to the feline contributions to Mr. Jefferson's life. Who do you think kept the mice from eating all the parchment that Mr. Jefferson used? Then again, my ancestors drove the moles from the garden and the rodents from the stables too. No doubt when the great man wrote the Declaration of Independence he was inspired by a cat. Who is more independent than a cat?

Human Americans are having a fit and falling in it over multiculturalism. Well, how about multispecies-ism? You think the world centers around humans? When history is taught, Americans really ought to give full attention to the contributions of cats, dogs, horses, cattle, sheep, hens—why, just about any kind of domesticated animal and some of the wild too. Where would our Founding Fathers and Mothers be if they hadn't had wild turkeys to eat? So abandon that human-centric point of view.

For my part, my feline ancestors arrived on Tidewater shores in 1640. The first Americat was a tabby, one Tabitha Buckingham. I am, therefore, F.F.V.—First Felines of Virginia. Of course, I take pride in my heritage, but I believe any kitty who comes to this country is as much an Americat as I am. We're all lucky to be here.

As for the human concept of the past, let me just say that history is scandal hallowed by time. Fortunately, human beans (I think of you as beans) being what they are, every nation, every country, produces sufficient scandal. If you all ever behaved reasonably, what would I have to write about?

Always,

SNEAKY PIE

Thomas Jefferson
(April 13, 1743 -
July 4, 1826)

and

Martha Wayles Skelton
(Oct. 19(?), 1748 -
Sept. 6, 1782)

Children:

Martha ("Patsy")
(Sept. 27, 1772 -
d. 1836)
m.
Feb. 23, 1790

Thomas Mann Randolph

Jane Randolph
(April 3, 1774 -
Sept. 1775)

Son
(May 28, 1777 -
June 14, 1777)

Maria ("Polly")
(Aug. 1, 1778 -
April 17, 1804)
m.
Oct. 13, 1797

John Wayles Eppes

Lucy Elizabeth
(Nov. 30, 1780 -
April 15, 1781)

Lucy Elizabeth
(May 8, 1782 -
Oct. 13, 1784)

Children of Maria ("Polly") and John Wayles Eppes:

Infant
(Dec. 31, 1799 -
Jan. 25, 1800)

Francis
(Sept. 20, 1801 -
May 30, 1881)

Maria
(Feb. 15, 1804 -
July 1807)

Children of Martha ("Patsy") and Thomas Mann Randolph:

Anne Cary
(Jan. 23, 1791 -
Feb. 11, 1826)

Thomas Jefferson
(Sept. 12, 1792 -
Oct. 8, 1875)

Ellen Wayles
(Aug. 30, 1794 -
July 26, 1795)

Ellen Wayles
(Oct. 13, 1796 -
April 21, 1876)

Cornelia Jefferson
(July 26, 1799 -
Feb. 24, 1871)

Virginia Jefferson
(Aug. 22, 1801 -
April 26, 1882)

Mary Jefferson
(Nov. 2, 1803 -
Mar. 29, 1876)

James Madison
(Jan. 17, 1806 -
Jan. 23, 1834)

Benjamin Franklin
(July 14, 1808 -
Feb. 18, 1871)

Meriwether Lewis
(Jan. 31, 1810 -
Sept. 24, 1837)

Septimia Anne
(Jan. 3, 1814 -
Sept. 14, 1887)

George Wythe
(March 10, 1818 -
April 13, 1867)

Murder at
Monticello

Laughing, Mary Minor Haristeen studied the nickel in her up-turned palm. Over the likeness of Monticello was inscribed our nation's motto, E Pluribus Unum. She handed the nickel to her older friend, Mrs. Miranda Hogendobber. "What do you think?"

"That nickel isn't worth a red cent." Mrs. Hogendobber pursed her melon-tinted lips. "And the nickel makes Monticello appear so big and impersonal when it's quite the reverse, if you'll forgive the pun."

The two women, one in her mid-thirties and the other at an age she refused to disclose, glanced up from the coin to Monti-cello's west portico, its windows aglow with candlelight from the parlor behind as the last rays of the early spring sun dipped be-hind the Blue Ridge Mountains.

If the friends had strolled to the front door of Thomas Jefferson's house, centered in the east portico, and then walked to the edge of the lawn, they would have viewed a sea of green, the ever-flattening topography to Richmond and ultimately to the Atlantic Ocean.

Like most born residents of central Virginia's Albemarle County, Harry Haristeen, as she was known, and Miranda Hogendobber could provide a fascinating tour of Monticello. Miranda would admit to being familiar with the estate since before World War II, but that was all she would admit. Over the decades increasing restoration work on the house itself, the dependencies, and gardens, both food and flowering, had progressed to the point where Monticello was the pride of the entire United States. Over a million out-of-town visitors a year drove up the tricky mountain road to pay their eight dollars, board a jitney bus, and swirl around an even twistier road to the top of the hill and thence the red brick structure—each brick fashioned by hand, each hinge pounded out in a smithy, each pane of glass painstakingly blown by a glassmaker, sweating and puffing. Everything about the house suggested individual contribution, imagination, simplicity.

As the tulips braved the quickening western winds, Harry and Mrs. Hogendobber, shivering, walked around the south side of the grounds by the raised terrace. A graceful silver maple anchored the corner where they turned. When they reached the front they paused by the large doors.

"I'm not sure I can stand this." Harry took a deep breath.

"Oh, we have to give the devil his due, or should I say her due?" Mrs. Hogendobber smirked. "She's been preparing for this for six decades. She'll say four, but I've known Mim Sanburne since the earth was cooling."

"Isn't this supposed to be the advantage of living in a small town? We know everyone and everyone knows us?" Harry rubbed her tight shoulder muscles. The temperature had dropped dramatically. "Well, okay, let's brave Mim, the Jefferson expert."

They opened the door, slipping in just as the huge clock

perched over the entrance notched up seven P.M. The day, noted by a weight to the right as one faced the door, read Wednesday. The Great Clock was one of Jefferson's many clever innovations in the design of his home. Even great minds err, however. Jefferson miscalculated the weight and pulley system and ran out of room to register all the days of the week in the hall. Each Friday the day weight slipped through a hole in the floor to the basement, where it marked Friday afternoon and Saturday. The weight then reappeared in the hall on Sunday morning, when the clock was wound.

Harry and Mrs. Hogendobber had arrived for a small gathering of Albemarle's "best," which is to say those whose families had been in Virginia since before the Revolution, those who were glamorous and recently arrived from Hollywood, which Harry dubbed Hollyweird, and those who were rich. Harry fell into the first category, as did Mrs. Hogendobber. As the postmaster— Harry preferred the term postmistress—of the small town of Crozet, Mary Minor Haristeen would never be mistaken for rich.

Marilyn Sanburne, known as Mim or Big Marilyn, clasped and unclasped her perfectly manicured hands. The wife of Crozet's mayor and one of Albemarle's richer citizens, she should have been cool as a cucumber. But a slight case of nerves rattled her as she cast her eyes over the august audience, which included the director of Monticello, the exuberant and fun-loving Oliver Zeve. The head of archaeology, Kimball Haynes, at thirty quite young for such a post, stood at the back of the room.

"Ladies and gentlemen"—Mim cleared her throat while her daughter, Little Marilyn, thirty-two, viewed her mother with a skillful show of rapt attention—"thank you all for taking time out from your busy schedules to gather with us tonight on this important occasion for our beloved Monticello."

"So far so good," Mrs. Hogendobber whispered to Harry.

"With the help of each one of you, we have raised five hundred thousand dollars for the purpose of excavating and ultimately restoring the servant's quarters on Mulberry Row."

As Mim extolled the value of the new project, Harry reflected on the continued duplicity that existed in her part of the world. Servants. Ah, yes, servants—not slaves. Well, no doubt some of them were cherished, beloved even, but the term lent a nice gloss to an ugly reality—Mr. Jefferson's Achilles' heel. He was so tremendously advanced in most ways, perhaps it was churlish to wish he had been more advanced about his source of labor. Then again, Harry wondered what would happen if the shoe were on her foot: Would she be able to refuse a skilled labor force? She would need to house them, clothe them, feed them, and provide medical care. Not that any of that was cheap, and maybe in today's dollars it would add up to more than a living wage. Still, the moral dilemma if one was white, and Harry was white, nagged at her.

Nonetheless, Mim had provided the driving energy behind this project, and its progress was a great personal victory for her. She had also made the largest financial contribution to it. Her adored only son had sped away from Crozet to marry a sophisticated model, a flashy New York lady who happened to be the color of café au lait. For years Mim refused her son entry to the ancestral mansion, but two years ago, thanks to a family crisis and the soft words of people like Miranda Hogendobber, Big Marilyn had consented to let Stafford and Brenda come home for a visit. Confronting one's own prejudices is never easy, especially for a person as prideful as Mim, but she was trying, and her efforts to unearth this portion of Monticello's buried history were commendable.

Harry's eyes swept the room. A few Jefferson descendants were in attendance. His daughters, Martha and Maria, or Patsy and Polly as they were called within the family, had provided T.J. with fifteen grandchildren. Those surviving out of that generation in turn provided forty-eight great-grandchildren. The names of Cary, Coles, Randolph, Eppes, Wayles, Bankhead, Coolidge, Trist, Meikleham, and Carr were carrying various dilutions of Jefferson blood into the twentieth century and, soon, the twenty-first.

Tracing one's bloodlines back to the original red-haired resident of Monticello was a bit like tracing every Thoroughbred's history back to the great sires: Eclipse, 1764; Herod, 1758; and Matchem, 1748.

Nonetheless, people did it. Mim Sanburne herself adamantly believed she was related to the great man on her mother's side through the Wayles/Coolidge line. Given Mim's wealth and imperious temperament, no one challenged her slender claim in the great Virginia game of ancestor worship.

Harry's people had lurched onto Virginia's shores in 1640, but no intertwining with Mr. Jefferson's line was ever claimed. In fact, both her mother's family, the Hepworths, and her father's seemed content to emphasize hard work in the here and the now as opposed to dwelling on a glorious past.

Having fought in every conflict from the French and Indian War to the Gulf crisis, the family believed its contributions would speak for themselves. If anything, her people were guilty of reverse snobbery and Harry daily fought the urge to deflate Mim and her kind.

Once she had overcome her nerves, commanding the spotlight proved so intoxicating to Big Marilyn that she was loath to relinquish it. Finally, Oliver Zeve began the applause, which drowned out Mim's oratory, although she continued to speak until the noise overwhelmed her. She smiled a tight smile, nodded her appreciation—not a hair out of place—and sat down.

Mim's major fund-raising victims, Wesley Randolph and his son Warren, Samson Coles, and Center Berryman, applauded vigorously. Wesley, a direct descendant of Thomas Jefferson through Thomas's beloved older daughter, Martha, had been consistently generous over the decades. Samson Coles, related to Jefferson through his mother, Jane Randolph, gave intermittently, according to the fluctuations of his real estate business.

Wesley Randolph, fighting leukemia for the last year, felt a strong need for continuity, for bloodlines. Being a Thoroughbred breeder, this was probably natural for him. Although the cancer was in remission, the old man knew the sands in the hourglass were spinning through the tiny passage to the bottom. He wanted his nation's past, Jefferson's past, preserved. Perhaps this was Wesley's slender grasp on immortality.

After the ceremony Harry and Mrs. Hogendobber returned to Oliver Zeve's house, where Mrs. Murphy and Tee Tucker, Harry's tiger cat and Welsh corgi respectively, awaited her. Oliver owned a fluffy white Persian, one Archduke Ferdinand, who used to accompany him to Monticello to work. However, children visiting the shrine sometimes pestered Archduke Ferdinand until he spit and scratched them. Although the archduke was within his feline rights, Oliver thought it best to keep him home. This was a great pity, because a cat will see a national shrine with a sharper eye than a human.

Then, too, Archduke Ferdinand believed in a hereditary nobility that was quite at odds with Jefferson's point of view.

As of this moment the archduke was watching Mrs. Murphy from a vantage point at the top of the huge ficus tree in Oliver's living room.

Kimball, who accompanied them, exclaimed, "The female pursues the male. Now, I like that idea."

Mrs. Murphy turned her head. "*Oh, please. Archduke Ferdinand is not my type.*"

The Archduke growled, "*Oh, and Paddy is your type? He's as worthless as tits on a boar hog.*"

Mrs. Murphy, conversant with her ex-husband's faults, nonetheless defended him. "*We were very young. He's a different cat now.*"

"*Ha!*" the Archduke exploded.

"Come on, Mrs. Murphy, I think you're wearing out your welcome." Harry leaned over and scooped up the reluctant tiger cat who was relishing the archduke's discomfort.

Oliver patted Harry on the back. "Glad you could attend the ceremony."

"Well, I'm not. We didn't see a single thing!" Harry's little dog grumbled.

Mrs. Hogendobber slung her ponderous purse over her left forearm and was already out the door.

"A lot of good will come from Mim's check." Kimball smiled as Harry and Mrs. H. climbed into the older woman's pristine Ford Falcon.

Kimball would have occasion to repent that remark.

2

One of the things that fascinated Harry about the four distinct seasons in central Virginia was the quality of the light. With the advent of spring the world glowed yet retained some of the softness of the extraordinary winter light. By the spring equinox the diffuse quality would disappear and brightness would take its place.

Harry often walked to the post office from her farm on Yellow Mountain Road. Her old Superman-blue pickup, nursed throughout the years, needed the rest. The early morning walk awakened her not just to the day but to the marvelous detail of everyday life, to what motorists only glimpse as they speed by, if they notice at all. The swelling of a maple bud, the dormant gray hornet's nest as big as a football, the brazen cries of the ravens, the sweet smell of the earth as the sun warmed her; these precious assaults on the senses kept Harry sane. She never could understand how people could walk with pavement under their feet, smog in their eyes, horns blaring, boom boxes blasting, their daily encounters with other human beings fraught with rudeness if not outright danger.

Considered a failure by her classmates at Smith College, Harry felt no need to judge herself or them by external standards. She had reached a crisis at twenty-seven when she heard her peers murmur incessantly about career moves, leveraged debt, and, if they were married, producing the firstborn. Well, at that time she was married to her high school sweetheart, Pharamond Haristeen, D.V.M., and it was good for a while. She never did figure out if the temptations of those rich, beautiful women on those huge Albemarle County farms had weakened her big blond husband's resolve, or if over time they would have grown apart anyway. They had divorced. The first year was painful, the second year less so, and now, moving into the third year of life without Fair, she felt they were becoming friends. Indeed, she confided to her best girlfriend, Susan Tucker, she liked him more now than when they were married.

Mrs. Hogendobber originally blew smoke rings around Harry's head over the divorce. She finally calmed down and took up the task of matchmaking, trying to set up Harry with Blair Bainbridge, a divinely handsome man who had moved next door to Harry's farm. Blair, however, was on a fashion shoot in Africa these days. As a model he was in hot demand. Blair's absence drew Fair back into Harry's orbit, not that he was ever far from it. Crozet, Virginia, provided her citizens with the never-ending spectacle of love found, love won, love lost, and love found again. Life was never dull.

Maybe that's why Harry didn't feel like a failure, no matter how many potentially embarrassing questions she was asked at those Smith College reunions. Lots of squealing around the daisy chain was how she thought of them. But she jumped out of bed every morning eager for another day, happy with her friends, and contented with her job at the post office. Small though the P.O. was, everybody dropped in to pick up their mail and have a chat, and she enjoyed being at the center of activity.

Mrs. Murphy and Tee Tucker worked there too. Harry couldn't imagine spending eight to ten hours each day away from her animals. They were too much fun.

As she walked down Railroad Avenue, she noticed that Reverend Herb Jones's truck was squatting in front of the Lutheran church with a flat. She walked over.

"No spare," she said to herself.

"*They don't pay him enough money,*" Mrs. Murphy stated with authority.

"*How do you know that, smarty-pants?*" Tucker replied.

"*I've got my ways.*"

"*Your ways? You've been gossiping with Lucy Fur, and all she does is eat communion wafers.*" Tucker said this gleefully, thrilled to prove that Herbie's new second cat desecrated the sacrament.

"*She does not. That's Cazenovia over at St. Paul's. You think every church cat eats communion wafers. Cats don't like bread.*"

"*Oh, yeah? What about Pewter? I've seen her eat a doughnut. 'Course, I've also seen her eat asparagus.*" Tucker marveled at the gargantuan appetite of Market Shiflett's cat. Since she worked in the grocery store next to the post office, the gray animal was constantly indulged. Pewter resembled a furry cannonball with legs.

Mrs. Murphy leapt on the running board of the old stepside truck as Harry continued to examine the flat. "*Doesn't count. That cat will eat anything.*"

"*Bet you she's munching away in the window when we pass the store.*"

"*You think I'm stupid?*" Mrs. Murphy refused the bet. "*But I will bet you that I can climb that tree faster than you can run to it.*" With that she was off and Tucker hesitated for a second, then tore toward the tree as Mrs. Murphy was already halfway up it. "*Told you I'd win.*"

"*You have to back down.*" Tucker waited underneath with her jaws open for full effect, her white fangs gleaming.

"Oh." Mrs. Murphy's eyes widened. Her whiskers swept forward and back. She looked afraid, and the dog puffed up with victory. That fast Mrs. Murphy somersaulted off the tree over the back of the dog and raced to the truck, leaving a furious Tucker barking her head off.

"Tucker, enough." Harry reprimanded her as she continued toward the P.O. while making a mental note to call Herb at home.

"*Get me in trouble! You started it.*" The dog blamed the cat. "*Don't yell at me,*" Tucker whined to Harry.

"*Dogs are dumb. Dumb. Dumb. Dumb,*" the cat sang out, tail hoisted to the vertical, then ran in front of Tucker, who, of course, chased her.

Murphy flipped in the air to land behind Tucker. Harry laughed so hard, she had to stop walking. "You two are crazy."

"*She's crazy. I am perfectly sane.*" Tucker, put out, sat down.

"*Ha.*" Mrs. Murphy again sailed into the air. She was filled with spring, with the hope that always attends that season.

Harry wiped her feet off at the front door of the post office, took the brass keys out of her pocket, and unlocked the door just as Mrs. Hogendobber was performing the same ritual at the back door.

"Well, hello." They both called to each other as they heard the doors close in opposite ends of the small frame building.

"Seven-thirty on the dot," Miranda called out, pleased with her punctuality. Miranda's husband had run the Crozet post office for decades. Upon his death, Harry had won the job.

Never a government employee, Miranda nonetheless had helped George since his first day on the job, August 7, 1952. At first she mourned him, which was natural. Then she said she liked retirement. Finally she admitted she was bored stiff, so Harry politely invited her to drop in from time to time. Harry had no idea that Miranda would relentlessly drop in at seven-thirty each morning. The two discovered over time and a few grumbles that it was quite pleasant to have company.

The mail truck beeped outside. Rob Collier tipped his Orioles baseball cap and tossed the bags through the front door. He delivered mail from the main post office on Seminole Trail in Charlottesville. "Late" was all he said.

"Rob's hardly ever late," Miranda noted. "Well, let's get to it." She opened the canvas bag and began sorting the mail into the slots.

Harry also sifted through the morass of printed material, a tidal wave of temptations to spend money, since half of what she plucked out of her canvas bag were mail-order catalogues.

"Ahhh!" Miranda screamed, withdrawing her hand from a box.

Mrs. Murphy immediately rushed over to inspect the offending box. She placed her paw in and fished around.

"*Got anything?*" Tucker asked.

"*Yeah.*" Mrs. Murphy threw a large spider on the floor. Tucker jumped back as did the two humans, then barked, which the humans did not.

"*Rubber.*" Mrs. Murphy laughed.

"Whose box was that?" Harry wanted to know.

"Ned Tucker's." Mrs. Hogendobber frowned. "This is the work of Danny Tucker. I tell you, young people today have no respect. Why, I could have suffered a heart attack or hyperventilated at the very least. Wait until I get my hands on that boy."

"Boys will be boys." Harry picked up the spider and wiggled it in front of Tucker, who feigned indifference. "Oops, first customer and we're not halfway finished."

Mim Sanburne swept through the door. A pale yellow cashmere shawl completed her Bergdorf-Goodman ensemble.

"Mim, we're behind," Miranda informed her.

"Oh, I know," Mim airily said. "I passed Rob on the way into town. I wanted to know what you thought of the ceremony at Monticello. I know you told me you liked it, but among us girls, what did you really think?"

Harry and Miranda had no need to glance at each other. They knew that Mim needed both praise and gossip. Miranda, better at the latter than the former, was the lead batter. "You made a good speech. I think Oliver Zeve and Kimball Haynes were just thrilled, mind you, thrilled. I did think that Lucinda Coles had her nose out of joint, and I can't for the life of me figure out why."

Seizing the bait like a rockfish, or small-mouthed bass, Mim lowered her voice. "She flounced around. It's not as if I didn't ask her to be on my committee, Miranda. She was my second call. My first was Wesley Randolph. He's just too ancient, poor dear. But when I asked Lucinda, she said she was worn out by good causes even if it did involve sanitized ancestors. I didn't say anything to her husband, but I was tempted. You know how Samson Coles feels. The more times his name gets in the paper, the more people will be drawn to his real estate office, although not much is selling now, is it?"

"We've seen good times and we've seen bad times. This will pass," Miranda sagely advised.

"I'm not so sure," Harry piped up. "I think we'll pay for the eighties for a long, long time."

"Fiddlesticks." Mim dismissed her.

Harry prudently dropped the subject and switched to that of Lucinda Payne Coles, who could claim no special bloodlines other than being married to Samson Coles, descended from Jane Randolph, mother to Thomas Jefferson. "I'm sorry to hear that Lucinda backed off from your wonderful project. It truly is one of the best things you've ever done, Mrs. Sanburne, and you've done so much in our community." Despite Harry's mild antipathy toward the snobbish older woman, she was genuine in her praise.

"You think so? Oh, I am so glad." Big Marilyn clasped her hands together like a child at a birthday party excited over all those unwrapped presents. "I like to work, you know."

Mrs. Hogendobber recalled her Scripture. " 'Each man's work will become manifest; for the Day will disclose it, because it will be revealed with fire, and the fire will test what sort of work each one has done. If the work which any man has built on the foundation survives, he will receive a reward.' " She nodded wisely and then added, "First Corinthians, 3:13–14."

Mim liked the outward appearance of Christianity; the reality of it held far less appeal. She particularly disliked the passage about it being easier for a camel to pass through the eye of a needle than for a rich man to enter the kingdom of heaven. After all, Mim was as rich as Croesus.

"Miranda, your biblical knowledge never ceases to amaze me." Mim wanted to say, "to bore me," but she didn't. "And what an appropriate quotation, considering that Kimball will be digging up the foundations of the servants' quarters. I'm just so excited. There's so much to discover. Oh, I wish I had been alive during the eighteenth century and had known Mr. Jefferson."

"I'd rather have known his cat," Mrs. Murphy chimed in.

"Jefferson was a hound man," Tee Tucker hastened to add.

"How do you know?" The tiger cat swished her tail and tiptoed along the ledge under the boxes.

"Rational. He was a rational man. Intuitive people prefer cats."

"Tucker?" Mrs. Murphy, astonished at the corgi's insight, could only exclaim her name.

The humans continued on, blithely unaware of the animal conversation which was more interesting than their own.

"Maybe you did know him. Maybe that's why you're so impassioned about Monticello." Harry almost tossed a clutch of mail-order catalogues in the trash, then caught herself.

"You don't believe that stuff," Mrs. Hogendobber pooh-poohed.

"Well, I do, for one." Mim's jaw was set.

"You?" Miranda appeared incredulous.

"Yes, haven't you ever known something without being told it, or walked into a room in Europe and felt sure you'd been there before?"

"I've never been to Europe," came the dry reply.

"Well, Miranda, it's high time. High time, indeed," Mim chided her.

"I backpacked over there my junior year in college." Harry smiled, remembering the kind people she had met in Germany and how excited she was at getting into what was then a communist country, Hungary. Everywhere she traveled, people proved kind and helpful. She used sign language and somehow everyone understood everyone else. She thought to herself that she wanted to return someday, to meet again old friends with whom she continued to correspond.

"How adventuresome," Big Marilyn said dryly. She couldn't imagine walking about, or, worse, sleeping in hostels. When she had sent her daughter to the old countries, Little Marilyn had gone on a grand tour, even though she would have given anything to have backpacked with Harry and her friend Susan Tucker.

"Will you be keeping an eye on the excavations?" Miranda inquired.

"If Kimball will tolerate me. Do you know how they do it? It's so meticulous. They lay out a grid and they photograph everything and also draw it on graph paper—just to be sure. Anyway, they painstakingly sift through these grids and anything, absolutely anything, that can be salvaged is. I mean, potsherds and belt buckles and rusted nails. Oh, I really can't believe I am part of this. You know, life was better then. I am convinced of it."

"Me too." Harry and Miranda sounded like a chorus.

"Ha!" Mrs. Murphy yowled. "Ever notice when humans drift back in history they imagine they were rich and healthy. Get a toothache in the eighteenth century and find out how much you like it." She glared down at Tucker. "How's that for rational?"

"You can be a real sourpuss sometimes. Just because I said that Jefferson preferred dogs to cats."

"But you don't know that."

"Well, have you read any references to cats? Everything that man ever wrote or said is known by rote around here. Not a peep about cats."

"*You think you're so smart. I suppose you happen to have a list of his favorite canines?*"

Tucker sheepishly hung her head. "*Well, no—but Thomas Jefferson liked big bay horses.*"

"*Fine, tell that to Tomahawk and Gin Fizz back home. They'll be overwhelmed with pride.*" Mrs. Murphy referred to Harry's horses, whom the tiger cat liked very much. She stoutly maintained that cats and horses had an affinity for one another.

"Do you think from time to time we might check out the dig?" Harry leaned over the counter.

"I don't see why not," Mim replied. "I'll call Oliver Zeve to make sure it's all right. You young people need to get involved."

"What I wouldn't give to be your age again, Harry." Miranda grew wistful. "My George would have still had hair."

"George had hair?" Harry giggled.

"Don't be smart," Miranda warned, but her voice carried affection.

"Want a man with a head full of hair? Take my husband." Mim drummed her fingers on the table. "Everyone else has."

"Now, Mim."

"Oh, Miranda, I don't even care anymore. All those years that I put a good face on my marriage—I just plain don't care. Takes too much effort. I've decided that I am living for me. Monticello!" With that she waved and left.

"I declare, I do declare." Miranda shook her head. "What got into her?"

"*Who* got into her?"

"Harry, that's rude."

"I know." Harry tried to keep her lip buttoned around Mrs. Hogendobber, but sometimes things slipped out. "Something's happened. Or maybe she was like this when she was a child."

"She was never a child." Miranda's voice dropped. "Her mother made her attend the public schools and Mim wanted to go away to Miss Porter's. She wore outfits every day that would have bankrupted an average man, and this was at the end of the Depression and the beginning of World War Two, remember. By the time we got to Crozet High, there were two classes of students. Marilyn, and the rest of us."

"Well—any ideas?"

"Not a one. Not a single one."

"*I've got an idea*," Tucker barked. The humans looked at her. "*Spring fever.*"

3

Fair Haristeen, a blond giant, studied the image on the small TV screen. He was taking an ultrasound of an unborn foal in the broodmare barn at Wesley Randolph's estate, Eagle's Rest. Using sound waves to scan the position and health of the fetus was becoming increasingly valuable to veterinarian and breeder alike. This practice, relatively new in human medicine, was even more recent in the equine world. Fair centered the image he wanted, pressed a small button, and the machine spat out the picture of the incubating foal.

"Here he is, Wesley." Fair handed the printout to the breeder.

Wesley Randolph, his son Warren, and Warren's diminutive but gorgeous wife, Ansley, hung on the veterinarian's every word.

"Well, this colt's healthy in the womb. Let's keep our fingers crossed."

Wesley handed the picture to Warren and folded his arms across his thin chest. "This mare's in foal to Mr. Prospector. I want this baby!"

"You can't do much better than to breed to Claiborne Farm's stock. It's hard to make a mistake when you work with such good people."

Warren, ever eager to please his domineering father, said, "Dad wants blinding speed married to endurance. I think this might be our best foal yet."

"Dark Windows—she was a great one," Wesley reminisced. "Damn filly put her leg over a divider when we were hauling her to Churchill Downs. Got a big knee and never raced after that. She was a special filly—like Ruffian."

"I'll never forget that day. When Ruffian took that moment's hesitation in her stride—it was a bird or something on the track that made her pause—and shattered the sesamoid bones in her fetlock. God, it was awful." Warren recalled the fateful day when Thoroughbred racing lost one of its greatest fillies to date, and perhaps one of the greatest runners ever seen, during her match race with Kentucky Derby–winner Foolish Pleasure at Belmont Park.

"Too game to stay down after her leg was set. Broke it a second time coming out of the anesthesia and only would have done it a third time if they'd tried to set the break again. It was the best thing to do, to save her any more pain, putting her down." Fair added his veterinary expertise to their memory of the black filly's trauma.

Wesley shook his head. "Damn shame. Damn shame. Would've made one hell of a brood mare. Her owners might even have tried to breed her to that colt she was racing against when it happened. Foolish Pleasure. Better racehorse than sire, though, now that we've seen his get."

"I'll never forget how the general public reacted to Ruffian's death. The beautiful black filly with the giant heart—she gave two hundred percent, every time. When they put her down, the whole country mourned, even people who had never paid attention to racing. It was a sad, sad day." Ansley was visibly moved by this recollection. She changed the subject.

"You got some wonderful stakes winners out of Dark Windows. She was a remarkable filly too." Ansley praised her father-in-law. He needed attention like a fish needs water.

"A few, a few." He smiled.

"I'll be back around next week. Call me if anything comes up." Fair headed for his truck and his next call.

Wesley followed him out of the barn while his son and daughter-in-law stayed inside. Behind the track, over a small knoll, was a lake. Wesley thought he'd go sit there later with his binoculars and bird-watch. Eased his mind, bird-watching. "Want some unsolicited advice?"

"Looks like I'm going to get it whether I want it or not." Fair opened the back of his customized truck-bed, which housed his veterinary supplies.

"Win back Mary Minor Haristeen."

Fair placed his equipment in the truck. "Since when are you playing Cupid?"

Wesley, gruff, bellowed, "Cupid? That little fat fellow with the quiver, bow, and arrows, and the little wings on his shoulders? Him? Give me some time and I'll be a real angel—unless I'm going downtown in the afterlife."

"Wesley, only the good die young. You'll be here forever." Fair liked teasing him.

"Ha! I believe you're right." Wesley appreciated references to his wild youth. "I'm old. I can say what I want when I want." He breathed in. " 'Course, I always did. The advantage of being stinking rich. So I'm telling you, go get that little girl you so foolishly, and I emphasize foolishly, cast aside. She's the winning ticket."

"Do I look that bad?" Fair wondered, the teasing fading out of him.

"You look like a ship without a rudder's what you look like. And running around with Boom Boom Craycroft. . . . big tits and not an easy keeper." Wesley likened Boom Boom to a horse that was expensive to feed, hard to put weight on, and often the victim of a breakdown of one sort or another. This couldn't have been a truer comparison, except in Boom Boom's case the weight referred to carats. She could gobble up more precious stones than a pasha. "Women like Boom Boom love to drive a man crazy. Harry's got some fire and some brains."

Fair rubbed the blond stubble on his cheek. He'd known Wesley all his life and liked the man. For all his arrogance and bluntness, Wesley was loyal, called it like he saw it, and was truly generous, a trait he passed on to Warren. "I think about it sometimes—and I think she'd have to be crazy to take me back."

Wesley put his arm around Fair's broad shoulders. "Listen to me. There's not a man out there who hasn't strayed off the reservation. And most of us feel rotten about it. Diana looked the other way when I did it. We were a team. The team came first, and once I grew up some I didn't need those—ah, adventures. I came clean. I told her what I'd done. I asked her to forgive me. Screwing around hurts a woman in ways we don't understand. Diana was in my corner two hundred percent. Heart like Ruffian. Always giving. Sometimes I wonder how a little poontang could get me off the track, make me hurt the person I loved most in this world." He paused. "Women are more forgiving than we are. Kinder too. Maybe we need them to civilize us, son. You think about what I'm saying."

Fair closed the lid over his equipment. "You aren't the first person to tell me to win back Harry. Mrs. Hogendobber works me over every now and then."

"Miranda. I can hear her now." Wesley laughed.

"I'm not saying you're wrong. Harry was a good wife and I was a fool, but how do you get over that guilt? I don't want to be with a woman and feel like a heel, even if I was."

"That's where love works its miracles. Love's not about sex, although that's where we all start. Diana taught me about love. It's as gossamer as a spiderweb and just as strong. Winds don't blow down a web. Ever watch 'em?" His hand moved back and forth. "That woman knew me, knew my every fault, and she loved me for me. And I learned to love her for her. The only thing that pleases me about my condition is when I get to the other side, I'm going to see my girl."

"Wesley, you look better than I've seen you look in the last eight months."

"Remission. Damn grateful for it. I do feel good. Only thing that gets me down is the stock market." He shivered to make his point. "And Warren. I don't know if he's strong enough to take over. He and Ansley don't pull together. Worries me."

"Maybe you ought to talk to them like you talked to me."

Wesley blinked beneath his bushy gray eyebrows. "I try. Warren evades me. Ansley's polite and listens, but it's in one ear, out t'other." He shook his head. "I've spent my whole life developing bloodlines, yet I can hardly talk to my own blood."

Fair leaned against the big truck. "I think a lot of people feel that way . . . and I don't have any answers." He checked his watch. "I'm due at Brookhill Farm. You call me about that mare and—and I promise to think about what you said."

Fair stepped into the truck, turned the ignition, and slowly traveled down the winding drive lined with linden trees. He waved, and Wesley waved back.

4

The old Ford truck chugged up Monticello Mountain. A light drizzle kept Harry alert at the wheel, for this road could be treacherous no matter what the weather. She wondered how the colonists had hauled up and down this mountain using wagons pulled by horses, or perhaps oxen, with no disc brakes. Unpaved during Thomas Jefferson's time, the road must have turned into a quagmire in the rains and a killer sheet of ice in the winter.

Susan Tucker fastened her seat belt.

"Think my driving's that bad?"

"No." Susan ran her thumb under the belt. "I should have done this when we left Crozet."

"Oh, I forgot to tell you. Mrs. H. pitched a major hissy when she reached into your mailbox and touched that rubber spider that Danny must have stuck in there. Mrs. Murphy pulled it out onto the floor finally."

"Did she throw her hands in the air?" Susan innocently inquired.

"You bet."

"A deep, throaty scream."

"Moderate, I'd say. The dog barked."

Susan smiled a Cheshire smile. "Wish I'd been there."

Harry turned to glance at her best friend. "Susan—"

"Keep your eyes on the road."

"Oh, yeah. Susan, did you put that spider in the mailbox?"

"Uh-huh."

"Now, why would you want to go and do a thing like that?"

"Devil made me do it."

Harry laughed. Every now and then Susan would do something, disrupt something, and you never knew when or where. She'd been that way since they first met in kindergarten. Harry hoped she'd never change.

The parking lot wasn't as full as usual for a weekend. Harry and Susan rode in the jitney up the mountain, which became more fog-enshrouded with every rising foot. By the time they reached the Big House, as locals called it, they could barely see their hands in front of their faces.

"Think Kimball will be out there?" Susan asked.

"One way to find out." Harry walked down to the south side of the house, picking up the straight road that was called Mulberry Row. Here the work of the plantation was carried out in a smithy as well as in eighteen other buildings dedicated to the various crafts: carpentry, nail making, weaving, and possibly even harness making and repair. Those buildings vanished over the decades after Jefferson's death when, a quarter of a million dollars in debt—roughly two and a half million dollars today—his heirs were forced to sell the place he loved.

Slave quarters also were located along Mulberry Row. Like

the other buildings, these were usually constructed of logs; sometimes even the chimneys were made of logs, which would occasionally catch fire, so that the whole building was engulfed in
flames within minutes. The bucket brigade was the only means of
firefighting.

As Harry and Susan walked through the fog, their feet
squished in the moist earth.

"If you feel a descent, you know we've keeled over into the
food garden." Harry stopped for a moment.

"We can stay on the path and go slow. Harry, Kimball isn't
going to be out here in this muck."

But he was. Wearing a green oilskin Barbour coat, a necessity
in this part of the world, big Wellies on his feet, and a water-
repellent baseball hat on his head, Kimball resembled any other
Virginia gentleman or gentlewoman on a misty day.

"Kimball!" Harry called out.

"A fine, soft day," he jubilantly replied. "Come closer, I
can't see who's with you."

"Me," Susan answered.

"Ah, I'm in for a double treat." He walked up to greet
them.

"How can you work in this?" Susan wondered.

"I can't, really, but I can walk around and think. This place
had to function independently of the world, in a sense. I mean, it
was its own little world, so I try to put myself back in time and
imagine what was needed, when and why. It helps me understand
why some of these buildings and the gardens were placed as they
are. Of course, the people working under the boardwalks—that's
what I call the terraces—had a better deal, I think. Would you two
damsels like a stroll?"

"Love it." Harry beamed.

"Kimball, how did you come to archaeology?" Susan asked.
Most men Kimball's age graduating from an Ivy League college
were investment bankers, commodities brokers, stockbrokers, or
numbers crunchers.

"I liked to play in the dirt as a child. This seemed a natural progression." He grinned.

"It wasn't one of those quirks of fate?" Harry wiped a raindrop off her nose.

"Actually, it was. I was studying history at Brown and I had this glorious professor, Del Kolve, and he kept saying, 'Go back to the physical reality, go back to the physical reality.' So I happened to notice a yellow sheet of paper on the department bulletin board —isn't it odd that I can still see the color of the flyer?—announcing a dig in Colonial Williamsburg. I never imagined that. You see, I always thought that archaeology meant you had to be digging up columns in Rome, that sort of thing. So I came down for the summer and I was hooked. Hooked on the period too. Come on, let me show you something."

He led them to his office at the back of the attractive gift shop. They shook off the water before entering and hung their coats on the wooden pegs on the wall.

"Cramped," Susan observed. "Is this temporary?"

He shook his head. "We can't go about building anything, you know, and some of what has been added over the years— well, the damage has been done. Anyway, I'm in the field most of the time, so this suffices, and I've also stashed some books in the second floor of the Big House, so I've a bit more room than it appears. Here, look at this." He reached into a pile of horseshoes on the floor and handed an enormous shoe to Harry.

She carefully turned the rusted artifact over in her hands. "A toe grab. I can't make out if there were any grabs on the back, but possibly. This horse had to do a lot of pulling. Draft horse, of course."

"Okay, look at this one." He handed her another.

Harry and Susan exclaimed at this shoe. Lighter, made for a smaller horse, it had a bar across the heel area, joining the two arms of the shoe.

"What do you think, Susan?" Harry placed the shoe in her friend's hands.

"We need Steve O'Grady." Susan referred to an equine vet in the county, an expert on hoof development and problems and strategies to overcome those problems. He was a colleague of Fair Haristeen, whose specialty was the equine reproductive system. "But I'd say this belonged to a fancy horse, a riding horse, anyway. It's a bar shoe . . ."

"Because the horse had a problem. Navicular maybe." Harry suggested a degenerative condition of the navicular bone, just behind the main bone of the foot, the coffin bone, often requiring special shoeing to alleviate the discomfort.

"Perhaps, but the blacksmith decided to give the animal more striking area in the back. He moved the point of contact behind the normal heel area." Kimball placed his hand on his desk, using his fingers as the front of the hoof and his palm as the back and showed how this particular shoe could alter the point of impact.

"I didn't know you rode horses." Harry admired his detective work on the horseshoe.

"I don't. They're too big for me." Kimball smiled.

"So how'd you know this? I mean, most of the people who do ride don't care that much about shoeing. They don't learn anything." Susan, a devout horsewoman, meaning she believed in knowing all phases of equine care and not just hopping on the animal's back, was intensely curious.

"I asked an expert." He held out his palms.

"Who?"

"Dr. O'Grady." Kimball laughed. "But still, I had to call around, dig in the libraries, and find out if horseshoeing has changed that much over the centuries. See, that's what I love about this kind of work. Well, it's not work, it's a magical kind of living in the past and the present at the same time. I mean, the past is ever informing the present, ever with us, for good or for ill. To work at what you love—a heaping up of joys."

"It is wonderful," Harry agreed. "I don't mean to imply that what I do is anything as exalted as your own profession, but I like my job, I like the people, and most of all, I love Crozet."

"We're the lucky ones." Susan understood only too well the toll unhappiness takes on people. She had watched her father drag himself to a job he hated. She had watched him dry up. He worried so much about providing for his family that he forgot to be with his family. She could have done with fewer things and more dad. "Being a housewife and mother may not seem like much, but it's what I wanted to do. I wouldn't trade a minute of those early years when the kids were tiny. Not one second."

"Then they're the lucky ones," Harry said.

Kimball, content in agreement, pulled open a drawer and plucked out a bit of china with a grayish background and a bit of faded blue design. "Found this last week in what I'm calling Cabin Four." He flipped it over, a light number showing on its reverse side. "I've been keeping it here to play with it. What was this bit of good china doing in a slave cabin? Was it already broken? Did the inhabitant of the little cabin break it herself—we know who lived in Cabin Four—and take it out of the Big House to cover up the misdeed? Or did the servants, forgive the euphemism, go straight to the master, confess the breakage, and get awarded the pieces? Then again, what if the slave just plain took it to have something pretty to look at, to own something that a rich white person would own, to feel for a moment part of the ruling class instead of the ruled? So many questions. So many questions."

"I've got one you can answer." Susan put her hand up.

"Shoot."

"Where's the bathroom?"

5

Larry Johnson intended to retire on his sixty-fifth birthday. He even took in a partner, Hayden McIntire, M.D., three years before his retirement age so Crozet's residents might become accustomed to a new doctor. At seventy-one, Larry continued to see patients. He said it was because he couldn't face the boredom of not working. Like most doctors trained in another era, he was one of the community, not some highly trained outsider come to impose his superior knowledge on the natives. Larry also knew the secrets: who had abortions before they were legal, what upstanding citizens once had syphilis, who drank on the sly, what families carried a disposition to alcoholism, diabetes, insanity, even violence. He'd seen so much over the years that he trusted his instincts. He didn't much care if it made scientific sense, and one of the lessons Larry learned is that there really is such a thing as bad blood.

"You ever read these magazines before you put them in our slot?" The good doctor perused the *New England Journal of Medicine* he'd just pulled out of his mailbox.

Harry laughed. "I'm tempted, but I haven't got the time."

"We need a thirty-six-hour day." He removed his porkpie hat and shook off the raindrops. "We're all trying to do too much in too little time. It's all about money. It'll kill us. It'll kill America."

"You know, I was up at Monticello yesterday with Susan—"

Larry interrupted her. "She's due for a checkup."

"I'll be sure to tell her."

"I'm sorry, I didn't mean to interrupt." He shrugged his shoulders in resignation. "But if I don't say what's on my mind when it pops into my head, I forget. Whoosh, it's gone." He paused. "I'm getting old."

"Ha," Mrs. Murphy declared. *"Harry's not even thirty-five and she forgets stuff all the time. Like the truck keys."*

"She only did that once." Tucker defended her mother.

"You two are bright-eyed and bushy-tailed." Larry knelt down to pet Tucker while Mrs. Murphy prowled on the counter. "Now, what were you telling me about Monticello?"

"Oh, we drove up to see how the Mulberry Row dig is coming along. Well, you were talking about money and I guess I was thinking how Jefferson died in hideous debt and how an intense concern with money seems to be part of who and what we are as a nation. I mean, look at Light-Horse Harry Lee. Lost his shirt, poor fellow."

"Yes, yes, and being the hero, mind you, the beau ideal of the Revolutionary War. Left us a wonderful son."

"Yankees don't think so." The corner of Harry's mouth turned upward.

"I liken Yankees to hemorrhoids . . . they slip down and hang around. Once they see how good life is around here, they don't go back. Ah, well, different people, different ways. I'll have to think about what you said—about money—which I am spending at a rapid clip as Hayden and I expand the office. Since Jefferson never stopped building, I can't decide if he possessed great stamina or great foolishness. I find the whole process nerve-racking."

Lucinda Payne Coles opened the door, stepped inside, then turned around and shook her umbrella out over the stoop. She closed the door and leaned the dripping object next to it. "Low pressure. All up and down the East Coast. The Weather Channel says we've got two more days of this. Well, my tulips will be grateful but my floors will not."

"Read where you and others"—Larry cocked his head in the direction of Harry—"attended Big Marilyn's do."

"Which one? She has so many." Lucinda's frosted pageboy shimmied as she tossed her head. Little droplets spun off the blunt ends of her hair.

"Monticello."

"Oh, yes. Samson was in Richmond, so he couldn't attend. Ansley and Warren Randolph were there. Wesley too. Carys, Eppes, oh, I can't remember." Lucinda displayed little enthusiasm for the topic.

Miranda puffed in the back door. "I've got lunch." She saw Larry and Lucinda. "Hello there. I'm buying water wings if this keeps up."

"You've already got angel wings." Larry beamed.

"Hush, now." Mrs. H. blushed.

"What'd she do?" Mrs. Murphy wanted to know.

"What'd she do?" Lucinda echoed the cat.

"She's been visiting the terminally ill children down at the hospital and she's organized her church folks to join in."

"Larry, I do it because I want to be useful. Don't fuss over me." Mrs. Hogendobber meant it, but being human, she also enjoyed the approval.

A loud meow at the back diverted the slightly overweight

lady's attention, and she opened the door. A wet, definitely over-weight Pewter straggled in. The cat and human oddly mirrored each other.

"*Fat mouse! Fat mouse!*" Mrs. Murphy taunted the gray cat.

"What does that man do over there? Force-feed her?" Lucinda stared at the cat.

"*It's all her own work.*" Mrs. Murphy's meow carried her dry wit.

"*Shut up. If I had as many acres to run around as you do, I'd be slender too,*" Pewter spat out.

"*You'd sit in a trance in front of the refrigerator door, waiting for it to open. Open Sesame.*" The tiger's voice was musical.

"*You two are being ugly.*" Tucker padded over to the front door and sniffed Lucinda's umbrella. She smelled the faint hint of oregano on the handle. Lucinda must have been cooking before she headed to the P.O.

Lucinda sauntered over to her postbox, opened it with the round brass key, and pulled out envelopes. She sorted them at the ledge along one side of the front room. The flutter of mail hitting the wastebasket drew Larry's attention.

Mrs. Hogendobber also observed Lucinda's filing system. "You're smart, Lucinda. Don't even open the envelopes."

"I have enough bills to pay. I'm not going to answer a form letter appealing for money. If a charity wants money, they can damn well ask me in person." She gathered up what was left of her mail, picked up her umbrella, and pushed open the door. She forgot to say good-bye.

"She's not doing too good, is she?" Harry blurted out.

Larry shook his head. "I can sometimes heal the body. Can't do much for the heart."

"She's not the first woman whose husband has had an affair. I ought to know." Harry watched Lucinda Coles open her car door, hop in while holding the umbrella out, then shake the umbrella, throw it over the back seat of the Grand Wagoneer, slam the door, and drive off.

"She's from another generation, Mary Minor Haristeen. 'Let marriage be held in honor among all, and let the marriage bed be undefiled; for God will judge the immoral and adulterous.' Hebrews 13:4."

"I'm going to let you girls fight this one out." Larry slapped his porkpie hat back on his head and left. What he knew that he didn't tell them was with whom Samson Coles was carrying on his affair.

"Miranda, are you implying that my generation does not honor the vows of marriage? That just frosts me!" Harry shoved a mail cart. It clattered across the floor, the canvas swaying a bit.

"I said no such thing, Missy. Now, you just calm yourself. She's older than you by a good fifteen years. A woman in middle age has fears you can't understand but you will—you will. Lucinda Payne was raised to be an ornament. She lives in a world of charities, luncheons with the girls, and black-tie fund-raisers. You work. You expect to work, and if you marry again your life isn't going to change but so much. Of course you honored your marriage vows. The pity is that Fair Haristeen didn't."

"I kept remembering what Susan used to say about Ned. He'd make her so mad she'd say, 'Divorce, never. Murder, yes.' There were a few vile moments when I wonder how I managed not to kill Fair. They passed. I don't think he could help it. We married too young."

"Too young? You married Fair the summer he graduated from Auburn Veterinary College. In my day you would have been an old maid at that age. You were twenty-four, as I recall."

"Memory like a wizard." Harry smiled, then sighed. "I guess I know what you mean about Lucinda. It's sad really."

"For her it's a tragedy."

"*Humans take marriage too seriously.*" Pewter licked her paw and began smoothing down her fur. "*My mother used to say, 'Don't worry about tomcats. There's one coming around every corner like a streetcar.' *"

"*Your mother lived to a ripe old age, so she must have known something,*" Mrs. Murphy recalled.

"Maybe Lucinda should go to a therapist or something," Harry thought out loud.

"She ought to try her minister first." Mrs. Hogendobber walked over to the window and watched the huge raindrops splash on the brick walkway.

"You know what I can't figure?" Harry joined her.

"What?"

"Who in the world would want Samson Coles?"

6

The steady rain played havoc with Kimball's work. His staff stretched a bright blue plastic sheet onto four poles which helped keep off the worst of the rain, but it trickled down into the earthen pit as they had cut down a good five feet.

A young German woman, Heike Holtz, carefully brushed away the soil. Her knees were mud-soaked, her hands also, but she didn't care. She'd come to America specifically to work with Kimball Haynes. Her long-range goal was to return to Germany and begin similar excavations and reconstruction at Sans Souci. Since this beautiful palace was in Potsdam, in the former East Germany, she suffered few illusions about raising money or generating interest for the task. But she was sure that sooner or later her countrymen would try to save what they could before it fell down about their ears. As an archaeologist, she deplored the Russians' callous disregard for the majority of the fabulous architecture under their control. At least they had preserved the Kremlin. As to how they treated her people, she wisely kept silent. Americans, so fortunate for the most part, would never understand that kind of systematic oppression.

"Heike, go on and take a break. You've been in this chill since early this morning." Kimball's light blue eyes radiated sympathy.

She spoke in an engaging accent, musical and very seductive. She didn't need the accent. Heike was a knockout. "No, no, Professor Haynes. I'm learning too much to leave."

He patted her on the back. "You're going to be here for a year, and Heike, if the gods smile down upon me, I think I can get you an appointment at the university so you can stay longer than that. You're good."

She bent her head closer to her task, too shy to accept the praise by looking him in the eye. "Thank you."

"Go on, take a break."

"This will sound bizarre," she accented the bi heavily, "but I feel something."

"I'm sure you do," he laughed. "Chilblains."

He stepped out of the hearth where Heike was working. The fireplace had been one of the wooden fireplaces which caught fire. Charred bits studded one layer of earth, and they were just now getting below that. Whoever cleaned up after the fire removed as much ash as they could. Two other students worked also.

Heike pawed with her hands, carefully but with remarkable intensity. "Professor."

Kimball returned to her and quickly knelt down. He was working alongside her now. Each of them laboring with swift precision.

"*Mein Gott!*" Heike exclaimed.

"We got more than we bargained for, kiddo." Kimball wiped his hand across his jaw, forgetting the mud. He called to

Sylvia and Joe, his other two students working in this section. "Joe, go on up and get Oliver Zeve."

Joe and Sylvia peered at the find.

"Joe?"

"Yes, Professor."

"Not a word to anyone, you hear? That's an order," he remarked to the others as Joe ran toward the Big House.

"The last thing we want is for the papers to get hold of this before we've had time to prepare a statement."

7

"Why wasn't I told first?" Mim jammed the receiver of the telephone back on the cradle. She put it back cockeyed so the device beeped. Furious, she smashed the receiver on correctly.

Her husband, Jim Sanburne, mayor of Crozet, six feet four and close to three hundred pounds, was possessed of an easygoing nature. He needed it with Mim. "Now, darlin', if you will reflect upon the delicate nature of Kimball Haynes's discovery, you will realize you had to be the second call, not the first."

Her voice lowered. "Think I was the second call?"

"Of course. You've been the driving force behind the Mulberry Row restorations."

"And I can tell you I'm enduring jealous huffs from Wesley Randolph, Samson Coles, and Center Berryman too. Wait until they find out about this—actually, I'd better call them all." She paced into the library, her soft suede slippers barely making any sound at all.

"Wesley Randolph? The only reason you and Wesley cross swords is that he wants to run the show. Just arrange a few photo opportunities for his son. Warren is running for state senate this fall."

"How do you know that?"

"I'm not the mayor of Crozet for nothing." His broad smile revealed huge square teeth. Despite his size and girth, Jim exuded a rough-and-tumble masculine appeal. "Now, sit down here by the fire and let's review the facts."

Mim dropped into the inviting wing chair covered in an expensive MacLeod tartan fabric. Her navy cashmere robe piped in camel harmonized perfectly. Mim's aesthetic sensibilities were highly developed. She was one hundred eighty degrees from Harry, who had little sense of interior design but could create a working farm environment in a heartbeat. It all came down to what was important to each of them.

Mim folded her hands. "As I understand it from Oliver, Kimball Haynes and his staff have found a skeleton in the plot he's calling Cabin Four. They've worked most of the day and into the night to uncover the remains. Sheriff Shaw is there too, although I can't see that it matters at this point."

Jim crossed his feet on the hassock. "Do they have any idea when the person died or even what sex the body is?"

"No. Well, yes, they're sure it's a man, and Oliver said an odd thing—he said the man must have been rich. I was so shocked, I didn't pursue it. We're to keep a tight lip. Guess I'd better wait to call the others but, oh, Jim, they'll be so put out, and I can't lie. This could cost contributions. You know how easy it is for that crew to get their noses out of joint."

"Loose lips sink ships." Jim, who had been a skinny eighteen-year-old fighting in Korea, remembered one of the phrases World War II veterans used to say. He tried to forget some of the other things he'd experienced in that conflict, but he vowed never to be so cold again in his entire life. As soon as the frosts came, Jim would break out his wired socks with the batteries attached.

"Jim, he's been dead for a hundred seventy-five to two hundred years. You're as bad as Oliver. Who cares if the press knows? It will bring more attention to the project and possibly even more money from new contributors. And if I can present this find to the Randolphs, Coleses, and Berrymans as an historic event, perhaps all will yet be well."

"Well, sugar, how he died might affect that."

8

Bright yellow tape cordoned off Cabin Four. Rick Shaw puffed on a cigarette. As sheriff of Albemarle County, he'd viewed more than his share of corpses: shotgun suicides, drownings, car accident after car accident, killings by knife, pistol, poison, ax—even a piano bench. People used whatever came to hand. However, this was the oldest body he'd studied.

His assistant, Cynthia Cooper, recently promoted to deputy, scribbled in her small notebook, her ball-point pen zipping over the blue lines. A photographer for the department snapped photos.

Rick, sensitive to the situation, arrived at six-thirty P.M., well after five P.M., when Monticello closed its doors for the night, allowing for the departure of straggling tourists. Oliver Zeve, arms folded across his chest, chatted with Heike Holtz. Kimball looked up with relief when Harry and Mrs. Hogendobber walked down Mulberry Row. Mrs. Murphy and Tucker trailed behind.

Oliver excused himself from Heike and walked over to Kimball. "What in the hell are they doing here?"

Kimball, nonplused, stuck his hands in his back pockets. "We're going to be here some time, people need to be fed."

"We're perfectly capable of calling a catering service." Oliver snapped.

"Yes," Kimball smoothly replied, "and they're perfectly capable of babbling this all over town as well as picking up the phone to The Washington Post or, God forbid, The Enquirer. Harry and Miranda can keep their mouths shut. Remember Donny Ensign?"

Kimball referred to an incident four years past when Mrs. Hogendobber served as secretary for the Friends of Restoration. She happened one night to check Donny Ensign's books. She always did George's books and she enjoyed the task. As treasurer, Donny was entrusted with the money, obviously. Mrs. H. had a hunch, she never did say what set her off, but she quickly realized that Mr. Ensign was cooking the books. She immediately notified Oliver and the situation was discreetly handled. Donny resigned and he continued to pay back a portion of what he had siphoned off until the sum, $4,559.12, was cleared. In exchange, no one reported him to Rick Shaw nor was his name destroyed in the community.

"Yes." Oliver drew out the word even as he smiled and trotted over to the two women. "Here, let me relieve you lovely ladies of this burden. I can't tell you how grateful I am that you're bringing us food. Kimball thinks of everything, doesn't he?"

Rick felt a rub against his leg. He beheld Mrs. Murphy. "What are you doing here?"

"Offering my services." She sat on the toe of the sheriff's shoe.

"Harry and Mrs. Hogendobber, what a surprise." A hint of sarcasm entered Rick's voice.

"Don't sound so enthusiastic, Sheriff." Miranda chided him.

"We aren't going to interfere in your case. We're merely offering nourishment."

Cynthia hopped out of the site. "Bless you." She scratched Tucker's head and motioned for Harry to follow her. Tucker followed also. "What do you make of this?"

Harry peered down at the skeleton lying facedown in the dirt. The back of his skull was crushed. Coins lay where his pockets must have been, and a heavy, crested ring still circled the bones of the third finger on his left hand. Tatters of fabric clung to the bones, a piece of heavily embroidered waistcoat. A bit more of the outer coat remained; the now-faded color must have once been a rich teal. The brass buttons were intact, as were the buckles on his shoes, again quite ornate.

"Mrs. H., come here," Harry called.

"I don't want to see it." Mrs. Hogendobber busily served sandwiches and cold chicken.

"It's not so bad. You've seen far worse at the butcher shop." Harry deviled her.

"That isn't funny."

Mrs. Murphy and Tucker shouldn't have been in the site, but so much was going on, no one really noticed.

"*Smell anything?*" The cat asked her companion.

"*Old smoke. A cold trail—this fellow's been dead too long for scenting.*" The corgi wrinkled her black nose.

Mrs. Murphy pawed a piece of the skull. "*Pretty weird.*"

"*What?*"

"*Well, the guy's had his head bashed, but someone put this big piece of skull back in place.*"

"Yeah." The dog was fascinated with the bones, but then, any bones fascinated Tucker.

"Hey, hey, you two, get out of here!" Harry commanded.

Tucker obediently left, but Mrs. Murphy didn't. She batted at the skull. "*Look, you dummies.*"

"She thinks everything is a toy." Harry scooped up the cat.

"*I do not!*" Mrs. Murphy puffed her tail in fury, squirmed out of Harry's arms, and jumped back to the ground to pat the skull piece again.

"I'm sorry, Cynthia, I'll put her back in the truck. Wonder if I could put her in Monticello? The truck's a ways off."

"*She'll shred Mr. Jefferson's bedspread,*" Tucker warned. "*If it has historic value, she can't wait to get her claws in it. Think what she'll say to Pewter, 'I tore up Thomas Jefferson's silk bedspread.' If it has tassles on it, forget it. There won't be any left.*"

"*And you wouldn't chew the furniture legs?*" the cat shot back.

"*Not if they give me one of those bones, I won't.*" The corgi laughed.

"*Stop being an ass, Tucker, and help me get these two nincompoops to really look at what they're seeing.*"

Tucker hopped into the dig and walked over to the skeleton. She sniffed the large skull fragment, a triangular-shaped piece perhaps four inches across at the base.

"What's going on here?" Harry, frustrated, tried to reach for the cat and the dog simultaneously. They both evaded her with ease.

Cynthia, trained as an observer, watched the cat jump sideways as though playing and return each time to repeatedly touch the same piece of the skull. Each time she would twist away from an exasperated Harry. "Wait a minute, Harry." She hunkered down in the earth, still soft from the rains. "Sheriff, come back here a minute, will you?" Cynthia stared at Mrs. Murphy, who sat opposite her and stared back, relieved that someone got the message.

"That Miranda makes mean chicken." He waved his drumstick like a baton. "What could tear me away from fried chicken, cold greens, potato salad, and did you see the apple pie?"

"There'd better be some left when I get out of here." Cynthia called up to Mrs. Hogendobber. "Mrs. H., save some for me."

"Of course I will, Cynthia. Even though you're our new deputy, you're still a growing girl." Miranda, who'd known

Cynthia since the day she was born, was delighted that she'd received the promotion.

"Okay, what is it?" Rick eyed the cat, who eyed him back.

For good measure, Mrs. Murphy stuck out one mighty claw and tapped the triangular skull piece.

He did notice. "Strange."

Mrs. Murphy sighed. "No shit, Sherlock."

Cynthia whispered, "Oliver's deflected us a bit, you know what I mean? We should have noticed the odd shape of this piece, but his mouth hasn't stopped running."

Rick grunted in affirmation. They'd confer about Oliver later. Rick took his index finger and nudged the piece of bone.

Harry, mesmerized, knelt down on the other side of the skeleton. "Are you surprised that there isn't more damage to the cranium?"

Rick blinked for a moment. He had been lost in thought. "Uh, no, actually. Harry, this man was killed with one whacking-good blow to the back of the head with perhaps an ax or a wedge or some heavy iron tool. The break is too clean for a blunt instrument—but the large piece here is strange. I wonder if the back of an ax could do that?"

"Do what?" Harry asked.

"The large, roughly triangular piece may have been placed back in the skull," Cynthia answered for him, "or at the time of death it could have been partially attached, but the shape of the break is what's unusual. Usually when someone takes a crack to the head, it's more of a mess—pulverized."

"Thank, you, thank you, thank you!" Mrs. Murphy crowed. "Not that I'll get any credit."

"I'd settle for some of Mrs. Hogendobber's chicken instead of thanks," Tucker admitted.

"How can you be sure, especially with a body—or what's left of it—this old, that one person killed him? Couldn't it have been two or three?" Harry's curiosity was rising with each moment.

"I can't be sure of anything, Harry." Rick was quizzical. "But I see what you're getting at. One person could have pinned him while the second struck the blow."

Tucker, now completely focused on Mrs. H.'s chicken, saucily yipped, *"So the killer scooped the brains out and fed them to the dog."*

"Gross, Tucker." Mrs. Murphy flattened her ears for an instant. *"You've come up with worse."*

"Tucker, go on up to Mrs. Hogendobber and beg. You're just making noise. I need to think," the cat complained.

"Mrs. Hogendobber has a heart of steel when it comes to handing out goodies."

"Bet Kimball doesn't."

"Good idea." The dog followed Mrs. Murphy's advice.

Harry grimaced slightly at the thought. "A neat killer. Those old fireplaces were big enough to stand in. One smash and that was it." Her mind raced. "But whoever did it had to dig deep into the fireplace, arrange the body, cover it up. It must have taken all night."

"Why night?" Cynthia questioned.

"These are slave quarters. Wouldn't the occupant be working during the day?"

"Harry, you have a point there." Rick stood up, his knees creaking. "Kimball, who lived here?"

"Before the fire it was Medley Orion. We don't know too much about her except that she was perhaps twenty at the time of the fire," came the swift reply.

"After the fire?" Rick continued his questioning.

"We're not sure if Medley came back to this site to live. We know she was still, uh, employed here because her name shows up in the records," Kimball said.

"Know what she did, her line of work?" Cynthia asked.

"Apparently a seamstress of some talent." Kimball joined them in the pit, but only after being suckered out of a tidbit by Tucker. "Ladies who came to visit often left behind fabrics for

Medley to transform. We have mention of her skills in letters visitors wrote back to Mr. Jefferson.''

''Was Jefferson paid?'' Rick innocently asked.

''Good heavens, no!'' Oliver called from the food baskets. ''Medley would have been paid directly either in coin or in kind.''

''Slaves could earn money independently of their masters?'' Cynthia inquired. This notion shed new light on the workings of a plantation.

''Yes, indeed, they could and that coin was coveted. A few very industrious or very fortunate slaves bought their way to freedom. Not Medley, I'm afraid, but she seems to have had quite a good life,'' Oliver said soothingly.

''Any idea when this fellow bit the dust, literally?'' Harry couldn't resist.

Kimball leaned down and picked up a few of the coins. ''Don't worry, we've photographed everything, from numerous different angles and heights, drawn the initial positions on our grids—everything is in order.'' Kimball reassured everyone that the investigation was not jeopardizing the progress of his archaeological work. ''The nearest date we can come to is 1803. That's the date of a coin in the dead man's pocket.''

''The Louisiana Purchase,'' Mrs. Hogendobber sang out.

''Maybe this guy was opposed to the purchase. A political enemy of T.J.'s,'' Rick jested.

''Don't even think that. Not for an instant. And especially not on hallowed ground.'' Oliver sucked in his breath. ''Whatever happened here, I am certain that Mr. Jefferson had no idea, no idea whatsoever. Why else would the murderer have gone to such pains to dispose of the body?''

''Most murderers do,'' Cynthia explained.

''Sorry, Oliver, I didn't mean to imply . . .'' Rick apologized.

''Quite all right, quite all right.'' Oliver smiled again. ''We're just wrought up, you see, because this April thirteenth will be the two hundred fiftieth anniversary of Mr. Jefferson's birth, and we don't want anything to spoil it, to bleed attention away from his achievements and vision. Something like this could, well, imbalance the celebration, shall we say?"

"I understand." Rick did too. "But I am elected sheriff to keep the peace, if you will, and the peace was disturbed here, perhaps in 1803 or thereabouts. We'll carbon-date the body, of course. Oliver, it's my responsibility to solve this crime. When it was committed is irrelevant to me."

"Surely, no one is in danger today. They're all"—he swept his hand outward—"dead."

"I'd like to think the architect of this place would not find me remiss in my duties." Rick's jaw was set.

A chill shivered down Harry's spine. She knew the sheriff to be a strong man, a dedicated public servant, but when he said that, when he acknowledged his debt to the man who wrote the Declaration of Independence, the man who elevated America's sense of architecture and the living arts, the man who endured the presidency and advanced the nation, she recognized that she, too, all of them, in fact, even Heike, were tied to the redheaded man born in 1743. But if they really thought about it, they owed honor to all who came before them, all who tried to improve conditions.

As Oliver Zeve could concoct no glib reply, he returned to the food baskets. But he muttered under his breath, "Murder at Monticello. Good God."

9

Riding back to Crozet in Mrs. Hogendobber's Falcon, Mrs. Murphy asleep in her lap, Tucker zonked on the back seat, Harry's mind churned like an electric blender.

"I'm waiting."

"Huh?"

"Harry, I've known you since little on up. What's going on?" Mrs. Hogendobber tapped her temple.

"Oliver. He ought to work for a public relations firm. You know, the kind of people who can make Sherman's March look like trespassing."

"I can understand his position. I'm not sure it's as bad as he thinks, but then, I'm not responsible for making sure there's enough money to pay the bills for putting a new roof on Monticello either. He's got to think of image."

"Okay, a man was murdered on Mulberry Row. He had money in his pockets, I wonder how much by today's standards. . . ."

"Kimball will figure that out."

"He wore a big gold ring. Not too shabby. What in the hell was he doing in Medley Orion's cabin?"

"Picking up a dress for his wife."

"Or worse." Harry frowned. "That's why Oliver is so fussy. Another slave wouldn't have a brocaded vest or a gold ring on his finger. The victim was white and well-to-do. If I think of that, so will others when this gets reported. . . ."

"Soon, I should think."

"Mim will fry." Harry couldn't help smiling.

"She already knows," Mrs. Hogendobber informed her.

"Damn, you know everything."

"No. Everybody." Mrs. H. smiled. "Kimball mentioned it to me when I said, sotto voce, mind you, that Mim must be told."

"Oh." Harry's voice trailed off, then picked up steam. "Well, what I'm getting at is if I think about white men in slaves' cabins, so will other people. Not that the victim was carrying on with Medley, but who knows? People jump to conclusions. And that will bring up the whole Sally Hemings mess again. Poor Thomas Jefferson. They won't let that rest."

"His so-called affair with the beautiful slave, Sally, was invented by the Federalists. They loathed and feared him. The last thing they wanted was Jefferson as president. Not a word of truth in it."

Harry, not so sure, moved on. "Funny, isn't it? A man was killed one hundred ninety years ago, if 1803 was the year, and we're disturbed by it. It's like an echo from the past."

"Yes, it is." Miranda's brow furrowed. "It is because for one human being to murder another is a terrible, terrible thing. Whoever killed that man knew him. Was it hate, love, love turned to hate, fear of some punishment? What could have driven someone to kill this man, who must have been powerful? I can tell you one thing.''

"What?"

"The devil's deep claws tore at both of them, killer and killed.''

10

"I told Marilyn Sanburne no good would come of her Mulberry Row project." Disgusted, Wesley Randolph slapped the morning newspaper down on the dining table. The coffee rolled precariously in the Royal Doulton cup. He had just finished reading the account of the find, obviously influenced by Oliver Zeve's statement. "Let sleeping dogs lie," he growled.

"Don't exercise yourself," Ansley drawled. Her father-in-law's recitation of pedigree had amused her when Warren was courting her, but now, after eighteen years of marriage, she could recite them as well as Wesley could. Her two sons, Breton and Stuart, aged fourteen and sixteen, knew them also. She was tired of his addiction to the past.

Warren picked up the paper his father had slapped down and read the article.

"Big Daddy, a skeleton was unearthed in a slave's cabin. Probably more dust than bone. Oliver Zeve has issued what I think is a sensible report to the press. Interest will swell for a day or two and then subside. If you're so worked up about it, go see the mortal coil for yourself." Ansley half smiled when she stole the description from *Hamlet*.

Warren still responded to Ansley's beauty, but he detected her disaffection for him. Not that she overtly showed it. Far too discreet for that, Ansley had settled into the rigors of propriety as regarded her husband. "You take history too lightly, Ansley." This statement should please the old man, he thought.

"Dearest, I don't take it at all. History is dead. I'm alive today and I'd like to be alive tomorrow—and I think our family's contributions to Monticello are good for today. Let's keep Albemarle's greatest attraction growing."

Wesley shook his head. "This archaeology in the servants' quarters"—he puffed out his ruddy cheeks—"stirs up the pot. The next thing you know, some council of Negroes—"

"African Americans," Ansley purred.

"I don't give a damn what you call them!" Wesley raised his voice. "I still think 'colored' is the most polite term yet! Whatever you want to call them, they'll get themselves organized, they'll camp in a room underneath a terrace at Monticello, and before you know it, all of Jefferson's achievements will be nullified. They'll declare that *they* did them."

"Well, they certainly performed most of the work. Didn't he have something like close to two hundred slaves on his various properties?" Ansley challenged her father-in-law while Warren held his breath.

"Depends on the year," Wesley waffled. "And how do you know that?"

"Mim's lecture."

"Mim Sanburne is the biggest pain in the ass this county has suffered since the seventeenth century. Before this is all over, Jefferson will be besmirched, dragged in the dirt, made out to be a scoundrel. Mim and her Mulberry Row. Leave the servant question alone! Damn, I wish I'd never written her a check."

"But it's part of history." Ansley was positively enjoying this.

"Whose history?"

"America's history, Big Daddy."

"Oh, balls!" He glared at her, then laughed. She was the only person in his life who dared stand up to him—and he loved it.

Warren, worry turning to boredom, drank his orange juice and turned to the sports page.

"Have you any opinion?" Wesley's bushy eyebrows knitted together.

"Huh?"

"Warren, Big Daddy wants to know what you think about this body at Monticello stuff."

"I—uh—what can I say? Hopefully this discovery will lead us to a better understanding of life at Monticello, the rigors and pressures of the time."

"We aren't your constituency. I'm your father! Do you mean to tell me a corpse in the garden, or wherever the hell it was"—he grabbed at the front page to double-check—"in Cabin Four, can be anything but bad news?"

Warren, long accustomed to his father's fluctuating opinion of his abilities and behavior, drawled, "Well, Poppa, it sure was bad news for the corpse."

Ansley heard Warren's Porsche 911 roar out of the garage. She knew Big Daddy was at the stable. She picked up the phone and dialed.

"Lucinda," she said with surprise before continuing, "have you read the paper?"

"Yes. The queen of Crozet has her tit in the wringer this time," Lucinda pungently put it.

"Really, Lulu, it's not that bad."

"It's not that good."

"I never will understand why being related to T.J. by blood, no matter how thinned out, is so important," said Ansley, who understood only too well.

Lucinda drew deeply on her cheroot. "What else have our respective husbands got? I don't think Warren's half so besotted with the blood stuff, but I mean, Samson makes money from it. Look at his real estate ads in *The New York Times*. He wiggles in his relation to Jefferson every way he can. 'See Jefferson country from his umpty-ump descendant.' " She took another drag. "I suppose he has to make a living somehow. Samson isn't the brightest man God ever put on earth."

"One of the best-looking though," Ansley said. "You always did have the best taste in men, Lulu."

"Thank you—at this point it doesn't matter. I'm a golf widow."

"Count your blessings, sister. I wish I could get Warren interested in something besides his so-called practice. Big Daddy keeps him busy reading real estate contracts, lawsuits, syndication proposals—I'd go blind."

"Boom time for lawyers," Lulu said. "The economy is in the toilet, everybody's blaming everybody else, and the lawsuits are flying like confetti. Too bad we don't use that energy to work together."

"Well, right now, honey, we've got a tempest in a teapot. Every old biddy and crank scholar in central Virginia will pass out opinions like gas."

"Mim wanted attention for her project." Lulu didn't hide her sarcasm. She'd grown tired of taking orders from Mim over the years.

"She's got it now." Ansley walked over to the sink and began to run the water. "What papers did you read this morning?"

"Local and Richmond."

"Lulu, did the Richmond paper say anything about the cause of death?"

"No."

"Or who it is? The *Courier* was pretty sparse on the facts."

"Richmond too. They probably don't know anything, but we'll find out as soon as they do, I guess. You know, I've half a mind to call Mim and just bitch her out." Lucinda stubbed out her cheroot.

"You won't." An edge crept into Ansley's voice.

A long silence followed. "I know—but maybe someday I will."

"I want to be there. I'd pay good money to see the queen get her comeuppance."

"As she does a lot of business with both of our husbands, about all I can do is dream—you too." Lucinda bid Ansley good-bye, hung up the phone, and reflected for a moment on her precarious position.

Mim Sanburne firmly held the reins of Crozet social life. She paid back old scores, never forgot a slight, but by the same token, she never forgot a favor. Mim could use her wealth as a crowbar, a carrot, or even as a wreath to toss over settled differences—settled in her favor. Mim never minded spending money. What she minded was not getting her way.

11

The gray of dawn yielded to rose, which surrendered to the sun. The horses fed and turned out, the stalls mucked, and the opossum fed his treat of sweet feed and molasses, Harry happily trotted inside to make herself breakfast.

Harry started each morning with a cup of coffee, moved her great-grandmother's cast-iron iron away from the back door—her security measure—jogged to the barn, and got the morning chores out of the way. Then she usually indulged herself in hot oatmeal or fried eggs or sometimes even fluffy pancakes drenched in Lyon's Golden Syrup from England.

The possum, Simon, a bright and curious fellow, would sometimes venture close to the house, but she could never coax him inside. She marveled at how Mrs. Murphy and Tucker accepted the gray creature. Mrs. Murphy displayed an unusual

tolerance for other animals. Often it took Tucker a bit
longer.

"All right, you guys. You already had breakfast, but if you're
real good to me, I might, I just might, fry an egg for you."

"I'll be good, I'll be good." Tucker wagged her rear end since she
had no tail.

"If you'd learn to play hard to get, you'd have more dignity." Mrs.
Murphy jumped onto a kitchen chair.

"I don't want dignity, I want eggs."

Harry pulled out the number five skillet, old and heavy cast
iron. She rubbed it with Crisco after every washing to help preserve its longevity. She dropped a chunk of butter into the middle
of the pan, which she placed on low heat. She fetched a mixing
bowl and cracked open four eggs, diced a bit of cheese, some
olives, and even threw in a few capers. As the skillet reached the
correct temperature, the butter beginning to sizzle, she placed the
eggs in it. She folded them over once, turned it off, and quickly
put the eggs on a big plate. Then she divided the booty.

Tucker ate out of her ceramic bowl, which Harry placed on
the floor.

Mrs. Murphy's bowl, "Upholstery Destroyer" emblazoned
on its side, sat on the table. She ate with Harry.

"This is delicious." The cat licked her lips.

"Yeah." Tucker could barely speak, she was eating so fast.

The tiger cat enjoyed the olives. Seeing her pick them out
and eat them first made Harry laugh every time she did it.

"You're too much, Mrs. Murphy."

"I like to savor my food," the cat rejoined.

"Got any more?" Tucker sat down beside her empty bowl, her
neck craned upward, should any morsel fall off the table.

"You're as bad as Pewter."

"Thanks."

"You two are chatty this morning." Harry cheerfully drank
her second cup of coffee as she thought out loud to the animals.
"Guess being up at Monticello has made me think. What would

we be doing if this were 1803? I suppose, getting up at the same time and feeding the horses wouldn't have changed. Mucking stalls hasn't changed. But someone would have had to stoke a fire in an open hearth. If a person lived alone, it would have been a lot harder than today. How could anyone perform her chores, cook for herself, butcher meat—well, I guess you could have bought your meat, but only a day at a time unless you had a smokehouse or the meat was salted down. Think about it. And you two, no worm medicine or rabies shots, but then, no vaccines for me either. Clothing must have been itchy and heavy in the winter. Summer wouldn't have been too bad because the women could have worn linen dresses. Men could take off their shirts. And I resent that. If I can't take off my shirt, I don't see why they can." She carried on this conversation with her two friends as they hung on every word and every mouthful of egg that was shoveled into Harry's mouth. "You two aren't really listening, are you?"

"We are!"

"Here." Harry handed Mrs. Murphy an extra olive and gave Tucker a nibble of egg. "I don't know why I spoil you all. Look at how much you've had to eat this morning."

"We love you, Mom." Mrs. Murphy emitted a major purr.

Harry scratched the tiger cat's ears with one hand and reached down to perform the same service for Tucker. "I don't know what I'd do without you two. It's so easy to love animals and so hard to love people. Men anyway. Your mom is striking out with the opposite sex."

"No, you're not." Tucker consoled her and was very frustrated that Harry couldn't understand. *"You haven't met the right guy yet."*

"I still think Blair is the right guy." Mrs. Murphy put in her two cents.

"Blair is off on some modeling job. Anyway, I don't think Mom needs a man who's that pretty."

"What do you mean by that?" the cat asked.

"She needs the outdoor type. You know, a lineman or a farmer or a vet."

Mrs. Murphy thought about that as Harry rubbed her ears. *"You still miss Fair?"*

"Sometimes I do," the little dog replied honestly. *"He's big and strong, he could do a lot of farmwork, and he could protect Mom if something went wrong, you know."*

"She can protect herself." True as this was, the cat also worried occasionally about Harry being alone. No matter how you cut it, most men were stronger than most women. It was good to have a man around the farm.

"Yeah—but still," came the weak reply.

Harry stood up and took the dishes to the porcelain sink. She meticulously washed each one, dried them, and put them away. Coming home to dirty dishes in the sink drove Harry to despair. She turned off the coffeepot. "Looks like a Mary Minor Haristeen day." This meant it was sunny.

She paused for a moment to watch the horses groom one another. Then her mind drifted off for a moment and she spoke to her animal friends. "How could Medley Orion live with a body under her fireplace—if she knew? She may not have known a single thing, but if she did, how could she make her coffee, eat her breakfast, and go about her business—knowing? I don't think I could do it."

"If you were scared enough, you could," Mrs. Murphy wisely noted.

12

The old walnut countertop gleamed as Mrs. Hogendobber polished it with beeswax. Harry, using a stiff broom, swept out the back of the post office. The clock read two-thirty, a time for chores and a lull between people stopping in at lunchtime and on their way home from work. Mrs. Murphy, sound asleep in the mail cart, flicked her tail and cackled, dreaming of mice. Tucker lay on her side on the floor, made shiny from the decades of treading feet. She, too, was out cold.

"Hey, did I tell you that Fair asked me to the movies next week?" Harry attacked a corner.

"He wants you back."

"Mrs. H., you've been saying that since the day we separated. He sure didn't want me back when he was cavorting with Boom Boom Craycroft, she of the pontoon bosoms."

Mrs. Hogendobber waved her dust cloth over her head like a small flag. "A passing fancy. He had to get it out of his system."

"And so he did," came Harry's clipped reply.

"You must forgive and forget."

"Easy for you to say. It wasn't your husband."

"You've got me there."

Harry, surprised that Mrs. Hogendobber agreed with her so readily, paused a moment, her broom held off the ground. A knock at the back door brought the broom down again.

"Me," Market Shiflett called.

"Hi." Harry opened the door and Market, who owned the grocery store next door, came in, followed by Pewter.

"Haven't seen you today. What have you been up to?" Miranda kept polishing.

"This and that and who shot the cat." He smiled, looked down at Pewter, and apologized. "Sorry, Pewter."

Pewter, far too subtle to push the dog awake, flicked her fat little tail over Tucker's nose until the dog opened her eyes.

"I was dead to the world." Tucker blinked.

"Where's herself?" Pewter inquired.

"Mail cart, last time I saw her."

A gleam in her eye betrayed Pewter's intentions. She walked to the mail cart and halted. She scrunched down and wiggled her rear end, then with a mighty leap she catapulted herself into the mail cart. A holy howl attended this action. Had Mrs. Murphy not been a cat in the prime of her life, had she been, say, an older feline, she surely would have lost her bladder control at such a rude awakening. A great hissing and spitting filled the bin, which was beginning to roll just a bit.

"Now, that's enough." Market hurried over to the mail cart, where he beheld the spectacle of his beloved cat, claws out, rolling around the heavy canvas bag with Mrs. Murphy in the same posture. Tufts of fur floated in the air.

Harry dashed over. "I don't know what gets into these two.

They're either the best of friends or like Muslims versus Christians." Harry reached in to separate the two, receiving a scratch for her concern.

"*You fat pig!*" Mrs. Murphy bellowed.

"*Scaredy-cat, scaredy-cat,*" Pewter taunted.

"You ought not to make light of religious differences," Mrs. Hogendobber, faithful to the Church of the Holy Light, admonished Harry. "Cats aren't religious anyway."

"*Who says?*" Two little heads popped over the side of the cart.

This moment of peace lasted a millisecond before they dropped back in the cart and rolled over each other again.

Harry laughed. "I'm not reaching in there. They're bound to get tired of this sooner or later."

"Guess you're right." Market thought the hissing was awful. "I wanted to tell you I've got a special on cat food today. You want me to save you a case?"

"Oh, thanks. How about a nice, fresh chicken too."

"Harry, don't tell me you're going to cook a chicken?" Mrs. Hogendobber held her heart as though this was too much. "What's this world coming to?"

"Speaking of that, how about them finding a body up at Monticello?"

Before either woman could respond, Samson Coles blustered in the front door, so Market repeated his question.

Samson shook his leonine head. "Damn shame. I guarantee you that by tomorrow the television crews will be camped out at Mulberry Row and this unfortunate event will be blown out of all proportion."

"Well, I don't know. It does seem strange that a body would be buried under a cabin. If the death was, uh, legitimate, wouldn't the body be in a cemetery? Even slaves had cemeteries." Market said.

Both Harry and Mrs. H. knew the body didn't belong to a slave. So did Mrs. Murphy, who said so loudly to Pewter. They had exhausted themselves and lay together in the bottom of the cart.

"*How do you know that?*" the gray cat wondered.

"*Because I saw the corpse,*" Mrs. Murphy bragged. "*The back of the skull was caved in like a big triangle.*"

"*You aren't supposed to give out the details,*" Tucker chided.

"*Oh, bull, Tucker. The humans can't understand a word I'm saying. They think Pewter and I are in here meowing and you're over there whining at us.*"

"*Then get out of the cart so we can all talk,*" Tucker called up. "*I saw the body too, Pewter.*"

"*Did you now?*" Pewter grasped the edge of the cart with her chubby paws and peered over the side.

"*Don't listen to him. All he wanted was Mrs. Hogendobber's chicken.*"

"*I saw the body as plain as you did, bigmouth. It was lying facedown under the hearth, maybe two feet under where the floor must have been at the time of death. So there.*"

"*You don't say!*" Pewter's eyes widened into big black balls. "*A murder!*"

"Good point, Market." Samson cupped his chin in his hand for a moment. "Why would a body be buried—what did they say, under the fireplace?"

"*Hearth,*" the dog called out, but they didn't pay attention.

"Maybe the man died in the winter and they couldn't dig up the frozen ground. But the ground wouldn't be frozen under the hearth, would it?" Market threw this out. He didn't necessarily believe it.

"I thought the people at that time had mausoleums, or something like mausoleums anyway, dug into rock where they'd store bodies until the spring thaws. Then they'd dig the grave," Miranda added.

"Did they really?" Market shivered at the thought of bodies being stacked up somewhere like cordwood.

"Well, they were frozen, I suspect," Miranda answered.

"Gruesome." Samson grimaced. "Has Lucinda come in today?"

"No," Harry answered.

"I can't keep track of my own wife's schedule." His affable tone belied the truth—he didn't want Lucinda tailing him. He liked to know her whereabouts because he didn't want her to know his.

"What'd she think of the Monticello discovery?" Mrs. Hogendobber asked politely.

"Lucinda? Oh, she didn't think it would be positive publicity, but she can't see that it has anything to do with us today." Samson tapped the countertop, admiring Mrs. Hogendobber's handiwork. "I hear Wesley Randolph doesn't like this one bit. He's overreacting, but then, he always does. Lulu's interest in history isn't as deep as mine," he sighed, "but then, she doesn't have my connections to Mr. Jefferson. A direct line from his mother, Jane, you know, and then, of course, on my father's side I'm related to Dolley Madison. Naturally, my interest is keen and Lulu's people were new. I don't think they got over here until the 1780s." He stopped for a second, realized he was unrolling his pedigree to people who could recite it as well as he could. "I digress. Anyway, Lulu reads a good amount. Like me, she'll be glad when this episode is behind us. We don't want the wrong kind of attention here in Albemarle County."

"Samson, we're talking about almost two centuries between then and now." Market chuckled.

"The past lives on in Virginia, the mother of presidents." Samson beamed a Chamber of Commerce smile. He couldn't have known how true was that pronouncement, or how tragic.

As Samson left, Danny Tucker and Stuart and Breton Randolph boisterously rushed into the post office. Danny looked like his mother, Susan. Stuart and Breton also strongly resembled their mother, Ansley. Every mouth jabbered simultaneously as the teenage boys reached into the mailboxes.

"Eii—" Danny let out a yell and jerked back his hand.

"Mousetrap?" Stuart's sandy eyebrows shot upward.

"No such luck," Danny sarcastically replied.

Breton peeped in the mailbox. "Gross." He reached in and pulled out a fake eyeball.

Harry whispered to Mrs. Hogendobber. "Did you do that?"

"I won't say I did and I won't say I didn't."

"Harry, did you put this eyeball in the mailbox?" Danny, accompanied by his buddies, leaned on the counter.

"No."

"Mother's not fond of rubber eyeballs," Mrs. Murphy disclosed.

Reverend Herb Jones walked into the hubbub. "A prayer meeting?"

"Hi, Rev." Stuart adored the pastor.

"Stuart, address Reverend Jones properly," Miranda ordered.

"I'm sorry. Hello, Reverend Jones."

"I always do what Mrs. H. tells me." Reverend Jones put his arm around Stuart's shoulders. "I'd be scared not to."

"Now, Herbie . . ." Miranda began to protest.

Breton, a sweet kid, chimed in. "Mrs. Hogendobber, we all do what you tell us because you're usually right."

"Well . . ." A long, breathless pause followed. "I'm glad you all realize that." She exploded in laughter and everyone joined in, including the animals.

"Harry." Herb put his hand on the counter as he laughed. "Thanks for calling me the other day about my flat tire. Fixed it— now just got another one."

"Oh, no," Harry responded.

"You need a new truck," Market Shiflett suggested.

"Yes, but I need the money, and so far—"

"No pennies from heaven." Harry couldn't resist. This set everyone off again.

"Reverend Jones, I'll help you change your tire," Danny volunteered.

"Me too." Breton jumped in.

"Me three." Stuart was already out the door.

As they bounded out, Danny flashed his rubber eye back at Harry, who made a cross with her fingers.

"Good kids. I miss Courtney. She's loving her first year at college. Still hard to let go." Market, a widower, sighed.

"You did a wonderful job with that girl," Miranda praised him.

"Too bad you didn't do better with Lardguts," Mrs. Murphy called out.

"Thanks," Market replied.

"I resent that," Pewter growled.

"Well, back to the salt mines." Market paused. "Pewter?"

"I'm coming. I'm not staying here to be insulted by a—a string bean."

"Oh, Pewter, where's your sense of humor?" Tucker padded over to her and gave her a nudge.

"How do you stand her?" Pewter liked the corgi.

"I tear up her catnip toys when she's not looking."

Pewter, at Market's heels, gaily sprang out the door as she thought of a catnip sock shredded to bits.

Harry and Miranda returned to their chores.

"You are the culprit. I know it." Harry giggled.

"An eye for an eye . . ." Mrs. H. quoted her Old Testament.

"Yeah, but it was Susan who put the rubber spider in the box, not Danny."

"Oh, darn." The older woman clapped her hands together. She thought, "Well, help me get even."

Harry tipped back her head and roared. Miranda laughed too, as did Mrs. Murphy and Tucker, whose laughter sounded like little snorts.

13

Samson Coles's bright red Grand Wagoneer stuck out like a sore thumb on the country roads. The big eight-cylinder engine harnessed to a four-wheel drive was essential to his business. He'd hauled prospective buyers through fields, forded rivers, and rumbled down old farm roads. The roominess inside pleased people, and he was disappointed when Jeep discontinued the boxy vehicle to replace it with a smaller, sleeker model, the Grand Cherokee. The Grand Cherokee suffered from a Roman nose and too much resemblance to the rest of the Jeep line, he thought. The wonderful thing about the old Wagoneer was that no other car looked like it. Samson craved standing apart from the crowd.

However, he didn't much crave it today. He parked behind a huge bank barn, pulled on his galoshes, and stomped through over a mile of slush to Blair Bainbridge's farm next to Harry's place.

He knew Harry was keeping an eye on the farm in Blair's absence. The great thing about a small town is that most people know your schedule. It was also the bad thing about a small town.

Harry usually sorted Blair's mail at work and put it in an international packet so he'd get it within a few days unless Blair happened to be on a shoot in a very remote area or in a political hot spot. She'd stop by Blair's Foxden Farm on her way home from work.

The squish of mud dragged him down. Hard to run in galoshes, and Samson was in a hurry. He had a two o'clock appointment at Midale. That listing, once the property sold, meant a healthy commission for Samson. He needed the money. He was listing the estate at $2.2 million. He thought Midale would sell between $1.5 and $1.8 million. He'd work that out with his client later. The important thing was to get the listing. He'd learned a long time ago that in the real estate business if you give the client a high price, you usually win the listing. Occasionally, he would sell a property for the listing price. More often than not, the place would sell for twenty to thirty percent less and he covered himself by elaborately explaining that the market had dipped, interest rates varied, whatever soothed the waters. After all, he didn't want a reputation for being an unrealistic agent.

He checked his watch. Eleven-fifteen. Damn, not much time. Two o'clock would roll around before he knew it.

The lovely symmetrical frame house came into view. He hurried on. At the back screen door he lifted the lid of the old milk box. The key dangled inside on a small brass hook.

He put the key in the door, but it was already unlocked. He opened and closed the door behind him.

Ansley rushed out from the living room, where she'd been waiting. "Darling." She threw her arms around his neck.

"Where'd you park your car?" Samson asked.

"In the barn, out of sight. Now, is that a romantic thing to say?"

He squeezed her tight. "I'll show you my romantic side in other ways, sweet thing."

14

The County of Albemarle wasted little money on the offices of the sheriff's department. Presumably they saw fit to waste the taxpayers' money in other ways. Rick Shaw felt fortunate that he and his field staff had bulletproof vests and new cars at regular intervals. The walls, once painted 1950s grade-school-green, had at least graduated to real-estate-white. So much for improvements. Spring hadn't really sprung. Rick was grateful. Every spring the incidence of drunkenness, domestic violence, and general silliness rose. Cynthia Cooper attributed it to spring fever. Rick attributed it to the inherent vile qualities of the human animal.

"Now, see here, Sheriff, is this really necessary?" Oliver Zeve's lips narrowed to a slit. A note of authority and class superiority slithered into his deep voice.

Rick, long accustomed to people of higher social position trying to browbeat him, politely but firmly said, "Yes."

During this discussion Deputy Cooper marched back and forth, occasionally catching Rick's eye. She knew her boss really wanted to pick up the director of Monticello by the seat of his tailored pants and toss him out the front door. Rick's expression changed when he spoke to Kimball Haynes. "Mr. Haynes, have you found anything else?"

"I'm pretty sure that the body was buried before the fire. There's no ash or cinder below the line where we discovered him —uh, the corpse."

"Couldn't the fire have been set to cover the evidence?" Rick doodled on his desk pad.

"Actually, Sheriff, that would have jeopardized the murderer if the murderer lived at Cabin Four or worked on the estate. You see, these fires were woefully common. Once the fire burned itself out and people could walk in the ruins, they would shovel up the cold ash and scrape the ground back down to the hard earth underneath."

"Why?" The sheriff stopped doodling and made notes.

"Courtesy more than anything. Every time it rained, whoever had lived in the cabin would smell that smoke and ash. Also, what if after the fire they used the opportunity to enlarge the cabin or to make some improvement? You'd want to start on a good, flat surface. . . ."

"True."

"Burning the cabin would only have served the purpose of making it appear the victim had died in the fire. Given the obvious status of the victim, that would be peculiar, wouldn't it? Why would a well-to-do white man be in a slave's cabin fire? Unless he was asleep and died of smoke inhalation, and you know what that would mean," Kimball offered.

Oliver's temper flared. "Kimball, I vigorously protest this specious line of reasoning. This is all conjecture. Very imaginative and certainly makes a good story but has little to do with the facts at hand. Namely, a skeleton, presumably almost two hundred years old, is found underneath the hearth. Spinning theories doesn't get us anywhere. We need facts."

Rick nodded gravely, then stung quickly. "That's exactly why the remains must go to the lab in Washington."

Caught, Oliver fought back. "As director of Monticello, I protest the removal of any object, animate or inanimate, human or otherwise, found on the grounds of Mr. Jefferson's home."

Kimball, exasperated, couldn't restrain his barbed humor. "Oliver, what are we going to do with a skeleton?"

"Give it a decent burial," Oliver replied through clenched teeth.

"Mr. Zeve, your protest is duly noted, but these remains are going to Washington and hopefully they'll be able to give us some boundaries concerning time, if nothing else, sex, and race," the sheriff stated flatly.

"We know it's a man." Oliver crossed his arms over his chest.

"What if it's a woman in a man's clothing? What if a slave had stolen an expensive vest—"

"Waistcoat," Oliver corrected him.

"Well, what if? What if she wanted to make a dress out of it or something? Now, I am not in the habit of theorizing, and I can't accept anything until I have a lab report. Do I think the skeleton is that of a male? Yes, I do. The pelvis in a male skeleton is smaller than that in a female. I've seen enough of them to know that. But as for the rest of it—I don't know much."

"Then may I ask you to please not theorize about the possibility of the victim's dying by smoke inhalation? Let's wait on that too."

"Oliver, that was my, uh, moment of imagination." Kimball

shouldered the blame since Oliver wanted to assign it. "Miscegenation is an old word and an ugly word, but it would have been the word and the law at the time. I understand your squeamishness."

"Squeamish?"

"Okay, wrong word. It's a delicate issue. But I return to my original scenario, and being an archaeologist, I have some authority here. In the process of preparing the burned cabin for a new building, the killer would run the very real risk that a spade would turn up the corpse. That is one strong reason against a fire having been set to cover up the evidence. The other, far more convincing data is that the layer of charred earth—again, scraped back as best they could—was roughly two feet above the corpse, allowing for the slight difference between the actual floor of the cabin and the floor of the hearth."

"Is there any record of this cabin burning?" Rick listened to the slow glide as the soft lead crossed the white page. He found it a consoling sound.

"If the murder occurred in 1803, as it would appear, Jefferson was in his first term as president. We have no record in his own hand of such an event, and he was a compulsive record-keeper. He'd even count out beans, nails—just compulsive. So, if he were home at the time, or visiting home from Washington, we can be certain he would have made a note of it. I'm sorry to say that the overseer lacked Mr. Jefferson's meticulous habits," Kimball replied.

"Unless the overseer was in on it and wanted no attention called to the cabin." Rick stopped writing.

An edge crept into Oliver's tone. "I guess after years on the job you would naturally think like that, Sheriff."

"Mr. Zeve, I understand that at this moment we seem to be in an adversarial position. In as plain a language as I can find: A man was murdered and it was covered up, forgive the pun, for nigh onto two hundred years. I am not the expert that you are on the end of the eighteenth century, the beginning of the nineteenth, but I would hazard a guess that our forefathers were more civilized and less prone to violence than we are today. I would especially think this is true of anyone who would have worked at Monticello, or visited the estate. So, whoever killed our victim had a powerful motive.''

15

In the parking lot the cool, clammy evening air caused Kimball to shudder. Oliver added to his discomfort.

"You weren't helpful in there." Oliver tried to sound more disappointed than angry.

"Usually you and I work easily together. Your position is far more political than mine, Oliver, and I appreciate that. It's not enough for you to be an outstanding scholar on Thomas Jefferson, you've got to play footsie with the people who write the checks, the National Historic Trust in D.C., and the descendants of the man. I'm sure I've left out other pressures."

"The people and artisans who work at Monticello." Oliver supplied this omission.

"Of course," Kimball agreed. "My one concern is discovering as much as we can about Mulberry Row and preserving the architectural and even landscaping integrity of Monticello at the time of Mr. Jefferson's peak. My interpretation of peak, naturally."

"Then don't offer up theories for the good sheriff. Let him find out whatever there is to find out. I don't want this turned into a three-ring circus and certainly not before the two hundred fiftieth birthday celebration. We need to make sure that celebration has the correct focus." He inhaled and whispered, "Money, Kimball, money. The media will turn somersaults on April thirteenth, and the attention will be a godsend to all our efforts to preserve, maintain, and extend Monticello."

"I know."

"Then, please, let's not give anyone ideas about white men sleeping in slave cabins, or with slave women. *Smoke inhalation.*" Oliver pronounced the two words as though they were a sentence of doom.

Kimball waited, turning this over in his mind. "All right, but I can't turn away the opportunity to help Sheriff Shaw."

"Of course not." Oliver intoned, "I know you well enough to know that. I'm in an optimistic frame of mind and I think whatever comes back from the lab will put this to rest. Then we can put the remains to rest in a Christian burial."

After saying good-night, Kimball hopped into his car. He watched Oliver's taillights as he backed out behind him and then sped away. A moment of darkness enveloped him, a premonition perhaps or a sense of sorrow over his disagreement with Oliver, who could bounce him right out of a job. Then again, maybe thinking about murder and death, no matter how far distant, casts a brooding spell over people. Evil knows no time. Kimball shuddered again and chalked it up to the cool, cloying dampness.

16

The biting wind on Monticello Mountain made the forty-five-degree temperature feel like thirty-five. Mim huddled in her down jacket. She wanted to wear her sable, but Oliver Zeve warned her that wouldn't look good for the Friends of Restoration. The antifur people would kick up a fuss. Made her spit. Furs had been keeping the human race warm for millennia. She did admit that the down jacket also kept her warm and was much lighter.

Montalto, the green spherical anchor at the northern end of Carter's Ridge, drifted in and out of view. Ground clouds snaked through the lowlands, and they were slowly rising with the advent of the sun.

Mim admired Thomas Jefferson. She read voraciously what he himself had written and what had been written about him by others. She knew that he had purchased Montalto on October 14,

1777. Jefferson drew several observatory designs, for he wished to build one on Montalto. There was no end to his ideas, his drawings. He would return to projects years later and complete them. He needed little sleep, so he could accomplish more than most people.

Mim, greedy for sleep, wondered how he managed with so little. Perhaps his schemes held loneliness at bay when he sat at his desk at five in the morning. Or perhaps his mind raced so fast he couldn't shut it off—might as well let it be productive. Another man might have gone on the prowl for trouble.

Not that Thomas Jefferson lacked his share of trouble or heartache. His father died when he was fourteen. His beloved tomboy older sister, Jane, died when he was twenty-two. His wife died on September 6, 1782, when he was thirty-nine, after he stayed home to nurse her for the last four painful months of her life. He sequestered himself in his room for three weeks following her death. After that he rode and rode and rode as if his horse could carry him away from death, from the burden of his crushing sorrow.

Mim felt she knew the man. Her sorrows, while not equal to Jefferson's, nonetheless provided her with a sense that she could understand his losses. She understood his passion for architecture and landscaping. Politics proved harder for her to grasp. As the wife of Crozet's mayor, she glad-handed, fed, and smiled at every soul in the community . . . and everybody wanted something.

How could this brilliant man participate in such a low profession?

A sound check in the background brought her out of her reverie. Little Marilyn pulled out a mirror for her mother. Mim scrutinized her appearance. Not bad. She cleared her throat. Then she stood up as she saw a production assistant walking her way.

Mim, Kimball, and Oliver would be discussing the corpse on *Wake-up Call*, the national network morning show.

She was to deflect any suggestions of miscegenation, as Samson Coles put it to her on the phone. Wesley Randolph, when she called on him, advised her to emphasize that Jefferson was probably in Washington at the time of the unfortunate man's demise. When Mim said that perhaps they'd have to wait for the pathology report from D.C., her rival and friend harrumphed. "Wait nothing. Don't be honest, Mim. This is politics even if centuries have passed. In politics your virtues will be used against you. There's private morality and public morality. I keep telling Warren that. Ansley understands, but my son sure doesn't. You get up there and say whatever you want so long as it sounds good—and remember, the best defense is a good offense."

Mim, poised at the edge of the lights behind the camera, watched as Kimball Haynes pointed to the site of the body.

Little Marilyn watched the monitor. A photo of the skeleton flashed on the screen. "Indecent." Mim fumed. "You shouldn't show a body until the next of kin are notified."

A hand gripped her elbow, guiding her to her mark. The sound technician placed a tiny microphone on the lapel of her cashmere sweater. She shed her jacket. Her perfect three strands of pearls gleamed against the hunter-green sweater.

The host glided over to her, flashed his famous smile, and held out his right hand, "Mrs. Sanburne, Kyle Kottner, so pleased you could be with us this morning."

He paused, listened to his earphone, and swiveled to face the camera with the red light. "I'm here now with Mrs. James Sanburne, president of the Friends of Restoration and the moving force behind the Mulberry Row project. Tell us, Mrs. Sanburne, about slave life during Thomas Jefferson's time."

"Mr. Jefferson would have called his people servants. Many of them were treasured as family members and many servants were highly skilled. His servants were devoted to him because he was devoted to them."

"But isn't it a contradiction, Mrs. Sanburne, that one of the fathers of liberty should own slaves?"

Mim, prepared, appeared grave and thoughtful. "Mr. Kottner, when Thomas Jefferson was a young man at the House of Burgesses before the Revolutionary War, he said that he made an effort at emancipation which failed. I think that the war diverted his attention from this subject, and as you know, he was sent to France, where his presence was crucial to our war efforts. France was the best friend we had." Kyle started to cut her off, but Mim smiled brightly. "And after the war Americans faced the herculean labor of forming a new kind of government. Had he been born later, I do believe he would have successfully tackled this thorny problem."

Amazed that a woman from a place he assumed was the Styx had gotten the better of him, Kyle shifted gears. "Have you any theories about the body found in Cabin Four?"

"Yes. I believe he was a violent opponent of Mr. Jefferson's. What we would call a stalker today. And I believe one of the servants killed him to protect the great man's life."

Pandemonium. Everyone started talking at once. Mim stifled a broad smile.

Harry, Mrs. Hogendobber, Susan, and Market were watching on the portable TV Susan had brought to the post office. Mrs. Murphy, Tucker, and Pewter stared at the tube as well.

"Slick as an eel." Harry clapped her hands in admiration.

"Stalker theory! Where does she come up with this stuff?" Market scratched his balding head.

"The newspapers," Susan answered. "You've got to hand it to her. She turned the issue of slavery on its head. She controlled the interviewer instead of vice versa. Until the real story surfaces, if it ever does, she's got the media chasing their tails."

"The real story will surface." Miranda spoke with conviction. "It always does."

Pewter flicked her whiskers fore and aft. *"Does anyone have a glazed doughnut? I'm hungry."*

"No," Tucker replied. *"Pewter, you have no sense of mystery."*

"That's not true," she defended herself. *"But I see Mim on a daily*

basis. Watching her on television is no big deal." Pewter, waiting for a comeback from Mrs. Murphy, was disappointed when none was forthcoming. "*What planet are you on?*"

The gorgeous eyes widened, the tiger cat hunched forward and whispered, "*I've got a funny feeling about this. I can't put my paw on it.*"

"*Oh, you're hungry, that's all.*" Pewter dismissed Mrs. Murphy's premonition.

17

Harry and Warren Randolph grunted as they picked up the York rake and put it on the back of her truck.

"Either this thing is getting heavier or I'm getting weaker," Warren joked.

"It's getting heavier."

"Hey, come on for a minute. I want to show you something."

Harry opened the door to the truck so Tucker and Mrs. Murphy could leap out to freedom. They followed Harry to the Randolphs' beautiful racing barn, built in 1892. Behind the white frame structure with the green standing-seam tin roof lay the mile-long oval track. Warren bred Thoroughbreds. That, too, like this property, had been in the family since the eighteenth century. The Randolphs loved blooded horses. The impressive walnut-paneled foyer at the manor house, hung with equine paintings spanning the centuries, attested to that fact.

The generous twelve-by-twelve-foot stalls were back to back in the center line of the barn. The tack room, wash stalls, and feed room were located in the center of the stall block. Circling the outside of the stalls was a large covered aisle that doubled as an exercise track during inclement weather. Since many windows circled the outside wall, enough light shone on the track so that even on a blizzardy day a rider could work a horse.

Kentucky possessed more of these glorified shed-row barns than Virginia, so Warren naturally prized his barn, built by his paternal grandfather. Colonel Randolph had put his money in the Chesapeake and Ohio Railway as well as the Union Pacific.

"What do you think?" His hazel eyes danced.

"Beautiful!" Harry exclaimed.

"What do you think?" Mrs. Murphy asked Tucker.

Tucker tentatively put one paw on the Pavesafe rubber bricks. The dull reddish surface of interlocking bricks could expand and contract within itself, so no matter what the weather or temperature, the surface remained nonskid. The bricks were also specially treated to resist bacteria.

The tailless dog took a few gingery steps, then raced to the other curved end of the massive barn. *"Yahoo! This is like running on cushions."*

"Hey, hey, wait for me!" The cat bolted after her companion.

"Your cat and dog approve." Warren jammed his hands into his pockets like a proud father.

Harry knelt down and touched the surface. "This stuff is right out of paradise."

"No, right out of Lexington, Kentucky." He led her down the row of stalls. "Honey, they're so far ahead of us in Kentucky that it hurts my pride sometimes."

"I guess we have to expect that. It is the center of the Thoroughbred industry." Harry's toes tingled with the velvety feel underneath.

"Well, you know me, I think Virginia should lead the nation in every respect. We've provided more presidents than any other state. We provided the leadership to form this nation—"

Warren sang out the paean of Virginia's greatness, practicing perhaps for many speeches to follow. Harry, a native of the Old Dominion, didn't disagree, but she thought the other twelve colonies had assisted in the break from the mother country. Only New York approximated the original Virginia in size before the break from West Virginia, and it was natural that a territory that big would throw up something or someone important. Then, too, the perfect location of Virginia, in the center of the coastline, and its topography, created by three great rivers, formed an environment hospitable to agriculture and the civilizing arts. Good ports and the Chesapeake Bay completed the rich natural aspects of the state. Prideful as Harry felt, she thought bragging on it was a little shy of good manners or good sense. People not fortunate enough to have been born in Virginia nor wise enough to remove themselves to the Old Dominion hardly needed this dolorous truth pointed out to them. It made outsiders surly.

When Warren finished, Harry returned to the flooring. "Mind if I ask how much this stuff costs?"

"Eight dollars a square foot and nine fifty for the antistumble edge."

Harry calculated, roughly, the square footage before her and arrived at the staggering sum of forty-five thousand dollars. She gulped. "Oh" squeaked out of her.

"That's what I said, but I tell you, Harry, I haven't any worries about big knees or injuries of any sort on this stuff. Before, I used cedar shavings. Well, what a whistling bitch to keep hauling shavings in with the dump truck, plus there's the man-hours to fetch it, replenish the supply in the aisle, rake it out, and clean it three times a day. I about wore out myself and my boys. And the dust when we had to work the horses inside—not good for the horses in their stalls or the ones being exercised, so then you spend time sprinkling it down. Still use the cedar for the stalls though. I grind it up a bit, mix it in with regular shavings. I like a sweet-smelling barn."

"Most beautiful barn in Virginia." Harry admired the place.

"*Mouse alert!*" Mrs. Murphy screeched to a stop, fishtailed into the feed room, and pounced at a hole in the corner to which the offending rodent had repaired.

Tucker stuck her nose in the feed room. "*Where?*"

"*Here,*" called Mrs. Murphy from the corner.

Tucker crouched down, putting her head between her paws. She whispered, "*Should I stay motionless like you?*"

"*Nah, the little bugger knows we're here. He'll wait until we're gone. You know a mouse can eat a quart of grain a week? You'd think that Warren would have barn cats.*"

"*Probably does. They smelled you coming and took off.*" Tucker laughed as the tiger grumbled. "*Let's find Mom.*"

"*Not yet.*" Mrs. Murphy stuck her paw in the mouse hole and fished around. She withdrew a wad of fuzzy fabric, the result of eating a hole in a shirt hanging in the stable, no doubt. "*Ah, I feel something else.*"

A piece of paper stuck to Mrs. Murphy's left forefinger claw as she slid it out of the hole. "*Damn, if I could just grab him.*"

Tucker peered down at the high-quality vellum scrap. "*Goes through the garbage too.*"

"*So do you.*"

"*Not often.*" The dog sat down. "*Hey, there's a little bit of writing here.*"

Mrs. Murphy withdrew her paw from her third attempt at the mouse hole. "*So there is. 'Dearest darling.' Ugh. Love letters make me ill.*" The cat studied it again. "*Too chewed up. Looks like a man's writing, doesn't it?*"

Tucker looked closely at the shred. "*Well, it's not very pretty. Guess there are lovers at the barn. Come on.*"

"*Okay.*"

They joined Harry as she inspected a young mare Warren and his father had purchased at the January sale at Keeneland.

Since this was an auction for Thoroughbreds of any age, unlike the sales specifically for yearlings or two-year-olds, one could sometimes find a bargain. The yearling auctions were the ones where the gavel fell and people's pockets suddenly became lighter than air.

"I'm trying to breed in staying power. She's got the bloodlines." He thought for a moment, then continued. "Do you ever wonder, Harry, what it's like to be a person who has no blood? A person who shuffled through Ellis Island—one's ancestors, I mean. Would you ever feel that you belong, or would there be some vague romantic attachment, perhaps, to the old country? I mean, it must be dislocating to be a new American."

"Ever attend the citizenship ceremony at Monticello? They do it every Fourth of July."

"No, can't say that I have, but I'd better do it if I'm going to run for the state Senate."

"I have. Standing out there on the lawn are Vietnamese, Poles, Ecuadorians, Nigerians, Scots, you name it. They raise their hands, and this is after they've demonstrated a knowledge of the Constitution, mind you, and they swear allegiance to this nation. I figure after that they're as American as we are."

"You are a generous soul, Harry." Warren slapped her on the back. "Here, I've got something for you." He handed her a carton of the rubber paving bricks. It was heavy.

"Thank you, Warren, these will come in handy." She was thrilled with the gift.

"Oh, here. What kind of a gentleman am I? Let me carry this to the truck."

"We could carry it together," Harry offered. "And, by the bye, I think you should run for the state Senate."

Warren spied a wheelbarrow and placed the carton in it. "You do? Well, thank you." He picked up the arms of the wheelbarrow. "Might as well use the wheel. Just think if the guy who invented it got royalties!"

"How do you know a woman didn't invent the wheel?"

"You got me there." Warren enjoyed Harry. Unlike his wife, Ansley, Harry was relaxed. He couldn't imagine her wearing nail polish or fretting over clothes. He rather wished he weren't a married man when he was around Harry.

"Warren, why don't you let me come on out here and bush-hog a field or two? These bricks are so expensive, I feel guilty accepting them."

"Hey, I'm not on food stamps. Besides, these are an overflow and I've got nowhere else to use them. You love your horses, so I bet you could use them in your wash rack . . . put them in the center and then put rubber mats like you have in the trailer around that. Not a bad compromise."

"Great idea."

Ansley pulled into the driveway, her bronzed Jaguar as sleek and as sexy as herself. Stuart and Breton were with her. She saw Harry and Warren pushing the wheelbarrow and drove over to them instead of heading for the house.

"Harry," she called from inside the car, "how good to see you."

"Your husband is playing Santa Claus." Harry pointed to the carton.

"Hi, Harry." The boys called out. Harry returned their greeting with a wave.

Ansley parked and elegantly disembarked from the Jag. Stuart and Breton ran up to the house. "You know Warren. He has to have a new project. But I must admit the barn looks fabulous and the stuff couldn't be safer. Now, you come on up to the house and have a drink. Big Daddy's up there, and he loves a pretty lady."

"Thanks, I'd love to, but I'd better push on home."

"Oh, I ran into Mim," Ansley mentioned to her husband. "She now wants you on the Greater Crozet Committee."

Warren winced. "Poppa just gave her a bushel of money for her Mulberry Row project—she's working over our family one by one."

"She knows that, and she said to my face how 'responsible' the Randolphs are. Now she wants your stores of wisdom. Exact words. She'll ask you for money another time."

"Stores of wisdom." The left side of Harry's mouth twitched in a suppressed giggle as she looked at Warren. At forty-one, he remained a handsome man.

Warren grunted as he lifted the heavy carton onto the tailgate. "Is it possible for a woman to have a Napoleon complex?"

The human mouth is a wonderful creation, except that it can rarely remain shut. The jaw, hinged on each side of the face, opens and closes in a rhythm that allows the tongue to waggle in a staggering variety of languages. Gossip fuels all of them. Who did what to whom. Who said what to whom. Who didn't say a word. Who has how much money and who spends it or doesn't. Who sleeps with whom. Those topics form the foundation of human discourse. Occasionally the human can discuss work, profit and loss, and what's for supper. Sometimes a question or two regarding the arts will pass although sports as a subject is a better bet. Rare moments bring forth a meditation on spirituality, philosophy, and the meaning of life. But the backbeat, the pulse, the percussion of exchange, was, is, and ever shall be gossip.

Today gossip reached a crescendo.

Mrs. Hogendobber picked up her paper the minute the paperboy left it in the cylindrical plastic container. That was at six A.M. She knew that Harry's fading red mailbox, nailed to an old fence post, sat half a mile from her house. She usually scooped out the paper on her way to work, so she wouldn't have read it yet.

Mrs. H. grabbed the black telephone that had served her well since 1954. The click, click, click as the rotary dial turned would allow a sharp-eared person to identify the number being called.

"Harry, Wesley Randolph died last night."

"What? I thought Wesley was so much better."

"Heart attack." She sounded matter-of-fact. By this time she'd seen enough people leave this life to bear it with grace. One positive thing about Wesley's death was that he'd been fighting leukemia for years. At least he wouldn't die a lingering, painful death. "Someone from the farm must have given the information to the press the minute it happened."

"I just saw Warren Sunday afternoon. Thanks for telling me. I'll have to pay my respects after work. See you in a little bit."

Now, telling a friend of another friend's passing doesn't fall under the heading of gossip, but that day at work Harry sloshed around in it.

The first person to alert Harry and Mrs. Hogendobber to the real story was Lucinda Coles. Luckily Mim Sanburne was picking up her mail, so they could cross-fertilize, as it were.

"—everywhere." Lucinda gulped a breath in the middle of her story about Ansley Randolph. "Warren, in a state of great distress, naturally, was finally reduced to calling merchants to see if by chance Ansley had stopped by on her rounds. Well, he couldn't find her. He called me and I said I didn't know where she was. Of course, I had no idea the poor man's father had dropped dead in the library."

Mim laid a trump card on the table. "Yes, he called me too, and like you, Lulu, I hadn't a clue, but I had seen Ansley at about five that afternoon at Foods of All Nations. Buying a bottle of expensive red wine: Medoc, 1970, Château le Trelion. She seemed surprised to see me"—Mim paused—"almost as if I had caught her out . . . you know."

"Uh-huh." Lucinda nodded in the customary manner of a woman affirming whatever another woman has said. Of course, the other woman's comment usually has to do with emotions, which could never actually be qualified or quantified—that being the appeal of emotions. They both acknowledged a tyranny of correct feelings.

"She's running around on Warren."

"Uh-huh." Lucinda's voice grew in resonance, since she, as a victim of infidelity, was also an expert on its aftermath. "No good will come of it. No good ever does."

After those two left, Boom Boom Craycroft dashed in for her mail. Her comment, after a lengthy discussion of the slight fracture of her tibia, was that everybody screws around on everybody, and so what?

The men approached the subject differently. Mr. Randolph's demise was characterized by Market as a response to his dwindling finances and the leukemia. It was hard for Harry to believe a man would have a heart attack because his estate had diminished, thanks to his own efforts, from $250 million to $100 million, but anything was possible. Perhaps he felt poor.

Fair Haristeen lingered over the counter, chatting. His idea was that a life of trying to control everybody and everything had ruined Wesley Randolph's health. Sad, of course, because Randolph was an engaging man. Mostly, Fair wanted Harry to pick which movie they would see Friday night.

Ned Tucker, Susan's husband, took the view that we die when we want to, therefore Père Randolph was ready to go and nobody should feel too bad about it.

By the end of the workday speculation had run the gamut. The last word on Wesley Randolph's passing, from Rob Collier as he picked up the afternoon mail, was that the old man was fooling around with his son's wife. The new medication Larry Johnson had prescribed for his illness had revved up his sex drive.

Warren walked in on the tryst and his father died of a heart attack from the shock.

As Harry and Mrs. Hogendobber locked up, they reviewed the day's gossip. Mrs. Hogendobber dropped the key in her pocket, inhaled deeply, and said to Harry, "I wonder what they say about us?"

"Gossip lends to death a new terror." Harry smirked.

$$\boxed{19}$$

"You know, if I ever get tired of home, I'll come live in your barn," Paddy promised.

"No, you won't," Simon, the possum, called down from the hayloft. "You'll steal my treasures. You're no good, Paddy. You were born no good and you'll die no good."

"Quit flapping your gums, you overgrown rat. When I want your opinion, I'll ask for it." Paddy washed one of his white spats.

A large black cat permanently wearing a tuxedo and spats, Paddy was handsome and knew it. His white bib gleamed, and despite his propensity for fighting, he always cleaned himself up.

Mrs. Murphy sat on a director's chair in the tack room. Paddy sat in the chair opposite her while Tucker sprawled on the floor. Simon wouldn't come down. He hated strange animals.

The last light of day cast a peachy-pink glow through the outside window. The horses chatted to one another in their stalls.

"I wish Mom would come home," Tucker said.

"She'll be at Eagle's Rest a long time." Mrs. Murphy knew that calling upon the bereaved took time, plus everyone else in Crozet would be there.

"Funny how the old man dropped." Paddy started cleaning his other forepaw. *"They're already digging his grave at the cemetery. I walked through there on my rounds. His plot's next to the Berrymans on one side and the Craigs on the other."*

Tucker walked to the end of the barn, then returned. *"The sky's bloodred over the mountains."*

"Another deep frost tonight too," Paddy remarked. *"Just when you think spring is here."*

"Days are warming up," Mrs. Murphy noted. *"Dr. Craig. Wasn't that Larry Johnson's partner?"*

Paddy replied, *"Long before any of us were born."*

"Let me think."

"Murph." Tucker wistfully stood on her hind legs, putting her front paws on the chair. *"Ask Herbie Jones, he remembers everything."*

"If only humans could understand." Mrs. Murphy frowned, then brightened. *"Dr. Jim Craig. Killed in 1948. He took Larry into his practice just like Larry took in Hayden McIntire."*

Paddy stared at his former wife. When she got a bee in her bonnet, it was best to let her go on. She evidenced more interest in humans than he did.

"What set you off?"

The tiger cat glanced down at her canine companion. *"Paddy said he walked through the cemetery. The Randolphs are buried between the Berrymans and the Craigs."*

Tucker wandered around restlessly. *"Another unsolved murder."*

"Ah, one of those spook tales they tell you when you're a kitten to scare you," Paddy pooh-poohed. *"Old Dr. Craig is found in his Pontiac, motor running. Found at the cemetery gates. Yeah, I remember now. His grandson, Jim Craig II, tried to reopen the case years back, but nothing came of it."*

"*Shot between the eyes,*" Mrs. Murphy said. "His medical bag stolen but no money."

"*Well, this town is filled with weirdos. Somebody really wanted to play doctor.*" Paddy giggled.

"In 1948." Mrs. Murphy triumphantly recalled the details told to her long ago by her own mother, Skippy. "*The town smothered in shock because everyone loved Dr. Craig.*"

"*Not everyone,*" Paddy said.

"Hooray!" Tucker jumped up as she heard the truck coming down the driveway. "Mom's home."

"*Paddy, come on in. Harry likes you.*"

"*Yeah, get out of here, useless,*" Simon called down from the loft.

The owl poked her head out from under her wing, then stuck it back. She rarely joined in these discussions with the other animals since she worked the night shift.

The dog bounded ahead of them.

The tuxedo cat and the tiger strolled at a leisurely pace to the front door. It wouldn't do to appear too excited.

"*Ever wish we were still together?*" Paddy asked. "*I do.*"

"*Paddy, being in a relationship with you was like putting Miracle-Gro on my character defects.*" Her tail whisked to the vertical when Harry called her name.

"*Does that mean you don't like me?*"

"*No. It means I didn't like me in that situation. Now, come on, let's get some supper.*"

20

The upper two floors of Monticello, not open to the public, served as a haven and study for the long-legged Kimball Haynes. While most of the valuable materials relating to Mr. Jefferson and his homes reposed in the rare books section of the Alderman Library at the University of Virginia, the Library of Congress, or the Virginia State Library in Richmond, only a small library existed upstairs at Monticello.

One of Kimball's pleasures consisted of sitting in the rectangular room above the south piazza, or greenhouse, which connects the octagonal library to Jefferson's cabinet, the room he used as his private study. Kimball kept a comfortable wing chair there and a private library, which included copies of records that Jefferson or his white employees kept in their own hand. He pored over account books, visitors' logs, and weather reports for the year 1803. As Mr. Jefferson was serving his first term as president during that year, the records lacked the fullness of the great man's attention. Peas, tomatoes, and corn were planted as always. A coach broke an axle. The repairs were costly. The livestock demanded constant care. A visitor assigned to a third-floor room in November complained of being frightfully cold, a reasonable complaint, since there were no fireplaces up there.

As the night wore on, Kimball heard the first peepers of spring. He loved that sound better than Mozart. He thumbed the copies blackened by the soil on his hands. Ground-in dirt was an occupational hazard for an archaeologist. He had used these references for years, returning to the rare books collection at the University of Virginia only when he'd scrubbed his hands until they felt raw.

After absorbing those figures, Kimball dropped the pages on the floor and leaned back in the old chair. He flung one leg over a chair arm. Facts, facts, facts, and not a single clue. Whoever was buried in the dirt at Cabin Four wasn't a tradesman. A tinker or wheelwright or purveyor of fresh fish, even a jeweler, wouldn't have had such expensive clothing on his back.

The corpse belonged to a gentleman. Someone of the president's own class. 1803.

Now, Kimball knew that might not be the year of the man's death, but it couldn't have been far off. Whatever happened politically that year might have some bearing on the murder, but Kimball's understanding of human nature suggested that in America people rarely killed each other over politics. Murder was closer to the skin.

He recalled a scandal the year before, 1802, that cut Thomas Jefferson to the quick. His friend from childhood, John Walker, accused Jefferson of making improper advances to his wife. According to John Walker, this affair started in 1768, when Thomas Jefferson was not yet married, but Walker maintained that it continued until 1779, seven years after Jefferson had married Martha Wayles Skelton, on January 1, 1772. The curious aspect of this scandal was that Mrs. Walker saw fit to burden her husband with the disclosure of her infidelity only some time after 1784, when Jefferson was in France.

Kimball also remembered that upon Jefferson's return from France, he and John Walker began to move on separate political paths. Light-Horse Harry Lee, father of Robert E. Lee, later volunteered to mediate between the two former friends. As Light-Horse Harry loathed Thomas Jefferson, the result of this effort was a foregone conclusion. Things went from bad to worse with James Thomson Callender, a vicious tattletale, fanning the flames. It was at this time that the infamous allegations against Jefferson for sleeping with his slave, Sally Hemings, began to make the rounds.

By January of 1805 these stories gained enough currency to cause the *New-England Palladium* to castigate Mr. Jefferson's morals. Apparently, Mr. Jefferson did not stand for family values.

The fur flew. Few cocktails are more potent than politics mixed with sex. Drinks were on the house, literally. Congress wallowed in the gossip. Things haven't changed, Kimball thought to himself.

To make matters murkier, Jefferson admitted to making a pass at Mrs. Walker. Acting as a true gentleman, Jefferson shouldered all the blame for the affair, which he carefully noted as occurring before his marriage. In those days, the fellow accepted the stigma, no matter what had really happened. To blame the lady meant you weren't a man.

Thanks to Jefferson's virile stance, even his political enemies let the Walker affair go. Everyone let it go but John Walker. Only as Walker lay dying at his estate in Keswick, called Belvoir, did he acknowledge that Jefferson was as much sinned against as sinner. By then it was too late.

The Sally Hemings story, however, did damage the president. A white man sleeping with a black woman created a spectacular conundrum for everyone. A gentleman couldn't admit such a thing. It would destroy his wife and generate endless jokes at his expense. Let there be one red-haired African American at Monticello and the jig was up, literally. That little word-play ran from Maine to South Carolina in the early 1800s. Oh, how they must have laughed in the pubs. "The jig is up."

It did not help Mr. Jefferson's case that some fair-skinned African Americans did appear at Monticello bearing striking resemblance to the master. However, as Kimball recalled, Thomas wasn't the only male around with Jefferson blood.

So what if a cousin had had an affair with Sally? Bound by the aristocratic code of honor, Jefferson still must remain silent or he would cause tremendous suffering to the rake's wife. A gentleman always protects a lady regardless of her relation to him. A gentleman could also try to protect a woman of color by remaining silent and giving her money and other favors. Silence was the key.

One thing was certain about the master sleeping with a slave: The woman had no choice but to say yes. In that truth lay lyric heartache sung from generation to generation of black women. Broke the hearts of white women too.

Stars glittered in the sky, the Milky Way smeared in an arc over the buildings as it had centuries ago. Kimball realized this murder might or might not have something to do with Thomas Jefferson's personal life, but it surely had something to do with a violent and close relationship between a white man and a black woman.

He would go over the slave roster tomorrow. He was too sleepy tonight.

21

The Crozet Lutheran Church overflowed with people who had come to pay their last respects to Wesley Randolph. The deceased's family, Warren, Ansley, Stuart, and Breton, sat in the front pew. Kimball Haynes, his assistant Heike Holtz, Oliver Zeve and his wife, and the other staff at Monticello came to say good-bye to a man who had supported the cause for over fifty of his seventy-three years.

Marilyn and Jim Sanburne sat in the second pew on the right along with their daughter Marilyn Sanburne Hamilton, alluring in black and available thanks to a recent divorce. Big Mim would apply herself to arranging a more suitable match sometime in the future.

The entire town of Crozet must have been there, plus the

out-of-towners who had occasion to know Wesley from business dealings, as well as friends from all over the South.

The Reverend Herbert Jones, his deep voice filling the church, read the Scriptures.

Somber but impressive, the funeral would have been remembered in proportion to Wesley's services to the community. However, this funeral stuck in people's memories for another reason.

Right in the middle of Reverend Jones's fervent denial of death, "For if we believe we are risen in Christ," Lucinda Payne Coles whispered loud enough for those around her to hear, "You sorry son of a bitch." Red in the face, she slid out of the pew and walked down the aisle. The usher swung the door open for her. Samson, glued to his seat, didn't even swivel his head to follow his wife's glowering progress.

As the people filed out of the church, Mim cornered Samson in the vestibule. "What in the world was that all about?"

Samson shrugged, "She loved Wesley, and I think her emotions got the better of her."

"If she loved Wesley, she wouldn't have marred his funeral. I'm not stupid, Samson. What are you doing to her?" Mim took the position that men wronged women more often than women wronged men. In this particular case she was right.

Samson hissed, "Mim, this is none of your business." He stalked off, knowing full well she'd never refer a customer to him again. At that moment he didn't care. He was too confused to care.

Harry, Susan, and Ned observed this exchange, as did everyone else.

"You're going to get a call tonight." Susan squeezed her husband's forearm. "That's the price of being such a good divorce lawyer."

"Funny thing is, I hate divorce." Ned shook his head.

"Don't we all?" Harry agreed as the source of her former discontent, Fair, joined them.

"Damn."

"Fair, you always were a man of few words." Ned nodded a greeting.

"My patients don't talk," Fair replied. "You know, something's really wrong. That's not like Lulu. She knows her place."

"It's going to be a much poorer place now," Susan wryly noted.

"Mim will wreak vengeance on Samson. Bad enough he told her to bugger off, he did it in public. He'll have to crawl on his belly over hot coals—publicly—to atone for his sin." Ned knew how Mim worked. She used her money and her vast real estate holdings as leverage if she felt a pinch in the pocketbook would suffice. When her target was a woman, she generally preferred to cast her into social limbo. But the human is an animal nonetheless, and harsh lessons were learned faster than mild ones. Had Mim been a man, she would have been called a hard-ass, but she'd have been lauded as a good businessman. Since she was a woman, the term bitch seemed to cover it. Unfair, but that was life. Then again, had Mim been a man, she might not have had to teach people quite so many lessons. They would have feared her from the get-go.

Larry Johnson, physician to Wesley and the family, climbed into his car to follow the funeral procession to the family cemetery.

"Hear Warren wouldn't let anyone sign the death certificate but Larry," Fair mentioned. "Heard it over at Sharkey Loomis's stable."

"That must have been a sad task for Larry. They'd been friends for years." Harry wondered how it would feel to know someone for fifty, sixty years and then lose them.

"Come on, or we'll be last in line." Susan shepherded them to their cars.

22

A hard-driving rain assisted Kimball Haynes. The slashing of the drops against the windowpane helped him to concentrate. It was long past midnight, and he was still bent over the records of births and deaths from 1800 to 1812.

He cast wide his research net, then slowly drew it toward him. Medley Orion, born around 1785, was reported to be a beautiful woman. Her extraordinary color was noted twice in the records; her lovely cast of features must have been delicious. White people rarely noted the physiognomy of black people unless it was to make fun of them. But an early note in a lady's hand, quite possibly that of Martha, Jefferson's eldest daughter, stated these qualities.

Martha married when Medley was five or six. She would have seen the woman as a child and as she grew. Usually Martha kept good accounts, but this reference was on a scrap of paper on the reverse of a list penned in tiny, tiny handwriting about different types of grapes.

A flash of lightning seared across the night sky. A crackle, then a pop, sounded out in the yard. The electricity went off.

Kimball had no flashlight. He was wearing his down vest, since it was cold in the room. His hands fingered a square box of matches. He struck one. He hadn't placed any candles in the room, but then, why would he? He rarely worked late into the night at Monticello.

The rain pounded the windows and drummed on the roof, a hard spring storm. Even in this age of telephones and ambulances, this would be a hateful night in which to fall ill, give birth, or be caught outside on horseback.

The match fizzled. Kimball declined to strike another. He could have felt his way down the narrow stairway, a mere twenty-four inches wide, to the first floor, the public floor of Monticello. There were beeswax candles down there. But he decided to peer out the window. A rush of water and occasional glimpses of trees bending in the wind were all he could make out.

The house creaked and moaned. The day you see, the night you hear. Kimball heard the door hinges rasp in the slight air current sent up by the winds outside. The windows upstairs were not airtight, so a swish of wind snuck inside. The windows themselves rattled in protest at the driving rains. The winds howled, circled, then swept back up in the flues. Occasionally a raindrop or two would trickle down into the fireplace, bringing with it the memory of fires over two hundred years ago. Floorboards popped.

Perhaps in such a hard storm a wealthy person would light a candle to bring some cheer into the room. A fire would struggle in the fireplace because the downdraft was fierce, despite the flue. Still, a bit of light and good cheer would fill the room, and frightened children could be told stories of the Norse and Greek gods, Thor tossing his mighty hammer or Zeus hurtling a bolt of lightning to earth like a blue javelin.

"What would such a storm have been like in Cabin Four?" Kimball wondered. The door would be closed. Perhaps Medley might have had tallow candles. No evidence of such had been found in her cabin, but tallow candles had been found in other digs and certainly the smithy and joinery had them for people who worked after dark. A quilt wrapped around one's body would help. The fireplaces in the servants' quarters lacked the refinement of the fireplaces in the Big House, so more rain and wind would funnel down the chimneys, sending dust and debris over the room. At least Medley had a wooden floor. Some cabins had packed-earth floors, which meant on the cold mornings your bare feet would hit frost on the ground. Maybe Medley Orion would hop into bed and pull the covers up on such a night.

Kimball feverishly worked to piece together the bits of her life. This was archaeology of a different sort. The more he knew about the woman, the closer he would come to a solution, he thought. Then he'd double-think and wonder if she might be innocent. Someone was killed in her cabin, but maybe she knew nothing. No. Impossible. The body had to have been buried at night. She knew, all right.

The rain wrapped around Monticello like a swirling silver curtain. Kimball, grateful for the time to sit and cogitate, a man's word for dream, knew he'd have to keep pressing on. He did realize he needed advice from a woman friend or friends. Compared to men, women rarely killed. What would compel a slave woman to take a man's life, and a white man's at that?

23

Imbued with the seriousness of her task, Mim invited Lucinda Coles, Miranda Hogendobber, Port Haffner, Ellie Wood Baxter, and Susan Tucker and Mary Minor Haristeen for youth. Little Marilyn was also present in the capacity of acolyte to Mim in her own role as social priestess. Ansley Randolph would have been invited, but given that Wesley Randolph lay in the ground but a scant three days, that would never do.

When Kimball Haynes asked for assistance, he suffered an embarrassment of riches. Although not as politically canny as Oliver, Kimball possessed a scrap of shrewdness. One doesn't advance in this world without it. After his night at Monticello in the rainstorm, he thought the wisest policy would be to call Mim Sanburne. After all, she, too, felt some of the heat over what was happening at Monticello. She squeezed money out of turnips. She never turned down a hard job. She knew everybody, which was worth more than knowing everything. To top it off, Mim adored being at the center of activities.

Mim swooned when Kimball called saying that he wanted to get together with her because he thought she might have the key to the problem. He assured her that she had great insight into the female mind. That did it. Mim couldn't bear having great insight into the female mind without her friends knowing. Hence to-night.

Although furious at Samson, Mim bore no animosity toward Lulu other than that she should not have lost her temper in the middle of a funeral service. Then again, Mim felt some kinship with Lucinda since she was certain Samson was up to no good. Not that Mim wouldn't use Lucinda to bring Samson to heel if the occasion presented itself. She'd wait and see.

Caviar, chopped eggs and onions, fresh salmon, eleven different kinds of cheese and crackers, sliced carrots, snow peas stuffed with cream cheese, crisp cauliflower, and endive with bacon grease dribbled over it completed the warm-ups, as Mim called them. Lunch dazzled everyone. Mim found a divine recipe for lobster ravioli which proved so enticing, no one even mentioned her diet. Arugula salad and a sliver of melon balanced the palate. Those wishing megacalorie desserts gorged on a raspberry cobbler with a vanilla cream sauce or good old devil's food cake for the chocolate lovers.

Mim had the fruits flown down from New York City, as she kept an account there with a posh food emporium. Finally, everyone's mood elevated to the stratosphere. Should anyone require a revitalizing liquid after luncheon, a vast array of spirits awaited them.

Susan chose a dry sherry. She declared that the raw wind cut into her very bones. She knew perfectly well that someone had to stampede for the crystal decanters on the silver trays. Lucinda would die before she'd take the first drink, so Susan figured she'd be the one to save Lulu's life. Miranda declined alcohol, as did Harry and Ellie Wood, a septuagenarian in splendid health.

"I always feel prosperous on a full stomach." Mrs. Hogendobber accepted a cup of piping coffee from the maid dressed in black with a starched white apron and cap.

"Mim, you've outdone yourself. Hear! Hear!" Lulu held up her glass as the other ladies and Kimball did likewise or tapped their spoons to china cups from Cartier.

"A trifle." Mim acknowledged the praise. It might have been a trifle to her, but it damn near killed the cook. It wasn't a trifle to Mim either, but by making light of her accomplishments she added to her formidable reputation. She knew not one lady in the room could have pulled off a luncheon like that, much less at the last minute.

"You know Ansley is comatose with grief." Port, another dear friend of Mim's, paused as the maid handed her a brandy the color of dark topaz.

"Really?" Ellie Wood leaned forward. "I had no idea she was that fond of Wesley. I thought they were usually at sixes and sevens."

"They were," Port crisply agreed. "She's comatose with grief because she had to stay home. She made me swear that I would call her the instant we finished and tell her everything, including, of course, what we wore."

"Oh, dear," Harry blurted out honestly.

"You have youth, Harry, and youth needs no adornment." Miranda came to her rescue. Harry lacked all clothes sense. If she had an important date, Susan and Miranda would force her into something suitable. Harry's idea of dressing up was ironing a crease in her Levi 501s.

"I don't know." Susan kidded her schoolmate. "We're thirty-something, you know."

"Babies." Port kicked off one shoe.

"Time to have some." Mim glared at her daughter. Little Marilyn evaded her mother's demand.

Kimball rubbed his hands together. "Ladies, once again we are indebted to Mrs. Sanburne. I do believe she's the glue that holds us together. I knew we couldn't proceed at Mulberry Row without her leadership in the community."

"Hear. Hear." More toasts and teaspoons on china cups.

Kimball continued. "I'm not sure what Mim has told you. I called needing her wisdom once again and she has provided me with you. I must ask your indulgence as I review the facts. The body of a man was found facedown in Cabin Four. The back of his skull bore testimony to one mighty blow with a heavy, sharp object like an ax but probably not an ax, or else the bone fragment would have been differently smashed—or so Sheriff Shaw believes. The victim wore expensive clothes, a large gold ring, and his pockets were full of money. I counted out the coins and he had about fifty dollars in his pockets. In today's money that would be about five hundred. The remains are in Washington now. We will know when he died, his age, his race, and possibly even something about his health. It's amazing what they can tell these days. He was found under the hearth—two feet under. And that is all we know. Oh, yes, the cabin was inhabited by Medley Orion, a woman in her early twenties. Her birth year isn't clearly recorded. The first mention of her is as a child, so we can speculate. But she was young. A seamstress. Now, I want you to cast your minds back, back to 1803, since our victim was killed then or shortly thereafter. The most recent coin in his pocket was 1803. What happened?"

This stark question created a heavy silence.

Lucinda spoke first. "Kimball, we didn't know that a man was murdered. The papers said only a skeleton was unearthed. This is quite a shock. I mean, people speculated but . . ."

"He was killed by a ferocious blow to the head." Kimball directed his gaze toward Lucinda. "Naturally, Oliver didn't, and won't, want to attest to the fact that the person was murdered until the report comes back from Washington. It will give all of us at Monticello a bit more time to prepare."

"I see." Lucinda cupped her chin in her hand. In her late forties, she was handsome rather than beautiful, stately rather than sweet.

Ellie Wood, a logical soul, speculated. "If he was hit hard, the person would have had to be strong. Was the wound in the front of the skull or the back?"

"The back," Kimball replied.

"Then whoever did it wanted no struggle. No noise either." Ellie Wood quickly grasped the possibilities.

"Might this man have been killed by Medley's lover?" Port inquired. "Do you know if she had a lover?"

"No. I don't. I do know she bore a child in August of 1803, but that doesn't mean she had a lover as we understand the concept." Kimball crossed his arms over his chest.

"Surely you don't think Thomas Jefferson instituted a breeding program?" Lucinda was shocked.

"No, no." Kimball reached for the brandy. "He tried not to break up families, but I haven't found any records to indicate Medley ever had a permanent partner."

"Did she bear more children?" Little Marilyn finally joined in the conversation.

"Apparently not," he said.

"That's very odd." Puzzlement shone over Susan's face. "Birth control consisted of next to nothing."

"Sheepskin. A primitive form of condom." Kimball sipped the brandy, the best he had ever tasted. "However, the chance of a slave having access to anything that sophisticated is out of the question."

"Who said her partner was a slave?" Harry threw down the joker.

Mim, not wanting to appear old-fashioned, picked it up. "Was she beautiful, Kimball? If she was, then her partners may indeed have had access to sheep membrane." Mim implied that Medley therefore would have attracted the white men.

"By what few accounts I can find, yes, she was beautiful."

Lucinda scowled. "Oh, I hope we can just slide by this. I think we're opening a can of worms."

"We are, but somebody's got to open it." Mim stood her ground. "We've swept this sort of thing under the rug for centuries. Not that I enjoy the process, I don't, but miscegenation may be a motive for murder."

"I don't think a black woman would have killed a man merely because he was white," Ellie Wood said. "But if she had a black lover, he might be driven to it out of jealousy if nothing else."

"But what if it was Medley herself?" Kimball's voice rose with suppressed excitement. "What would drive a slave to kill a rich white man? What would drive a woman of any color to kill a man? I think you all know far better than I."

Catching his enthusiasm, Port jumped up. "Love. Love can run anyone crazy."

"Okay, say she loved the victim. Not that I think too many slaves loved the white men who snuck into their cabins." Harry grew bold. "Even at her most irrational, would she kill him because he walked out on her? How could she? White men walked out on black women every morning. They just turned their backs and poof, they were gone. Wouldn't she have been used to it? Wouldn't an older slave have prepared her and said something like, 'This is your lot in life'?"

"Probably would have said 'This is your cross to bear.' " Miranda furrowed her brow.

Unsettled as Lucinda was by Samson's infidelity, and she was getting closer and closer to the real truth, she recognized as the afternoon continued that her unhappiness at least had a front door. She could walk out. Medley Orion couldn't. "Perhaps he humiliated her in some secret place, some deep way, and she snapped."

"Not humiliated, threatened." Susan's eyes lit up. "She was a slave. She'd learned to mask her feelings. Don't we all, ladies?" This idea rippled across the room. "Whoever this was, he had a hold on her. He was going to do something terrible to her or to someone she loved, and she fought back. My God, where did she get the courage?"

"I don't know if I can agree." Miranda folded her hands together. "Does it take courage to kill? God forbids us to take another human life."

"That's it!" Mim spoke up. "He must have threatened to take someone else's life—or hers. What if he threatened to kill Mr. Jefferson—not my stalker theory, mind you, but an explosive rage on the dead man's part—something erratic?"

"I doubt she'd kill to save her master," Little Marilyn countered her mother. "Jefferson was an extraordinary human being, but he was still the master."

"Some slaves loved their masters." Lucinda backed up Mim.

"Not as many as white folks want to believe." Harry laughed. She couldn't help but laugh. While bonds of affection surely existed, it was difficult for her to grasp that the oppressed could love the oppressor.

"Well, then what?" Ellie Wood's patience, never her strong point, ebbed.

"She killed to protect her true lover." Port savored her brandy.

"Or her child," Susan quietly added.

An electric current shot around the room. Was there a mother anywhere in the world who wouldn't kill for her child?

"The child was born in August 1803." Kimball twirled the crystal glass. "If the victim were killed after August, he might have known the child."

"But he might have known the child even before it was born." Mim's eyes narrowed.

"What?" Kimball seemed temporarily befuddled.

"What if it were his?" Mim's voice rang out.

A silence followed this.

Harry then said, "Most men, or perhaps I should say some men, who have enjoyed the favors of a woman who becomes pregnant declare they don't know if the baby is theirs. Of course they can't get away with that now thanks to this DNA testing stuff. They sure could get away with it then."

"Good point, Harry. I say the child was born before he was killed." Susan held them spellbound. "The child was born and it looked like him."

"Good God, Susan, I hope you're wrong." Lucinda blinked. "How could a man kill his own child to—to save his face?"

"People do terrible things," Port flatly stated, for she didn't understand it either, but then, she didn't refute it.

"Well, he paid for his intentions, if that's what they were." Ellie Wood felt rough justice had been done. "If that's true, he paid for it, and done is done."

" 'Vengeance is mine, and recompense, for the time when their foot shall slip; for the day of their calamity is at hand and their doom comes swiftly.' Deuteronomy 32:35," Miranda intoned.

But done was not done. The past was coming undone, and the day of calamity was at hand.

24

"I thought it would take some of the burden off you. You don't need people at you right now." Ansley Randolph leaned on the white fence and watched the horses breeze through their morning workout around the track—the Fibar and sand mix kept the footing good year-round. "Not that anything will make you feel better, for a time."

Pain creased the lines around Warren's eyes. "Honey, I've no doubt that you thought you were doing the right thing, but number one, I am tired of being whipped into shape by Mim Sanburne. Number two, my family's diaries, maps, and genealogies stay right here at Eagle's Rest. Some are so old I keep them in the safe. Number three, I don't think anything of mine will interest Kimball Haynes, and number four, I'm exhausted. I don't want to argue with anyone. I don't even want to explain myself to anyone. No is no, and you'll have to tell Mim.''

Ansley, while not in love with Warren, liked him sometimes. This was one of those times. "You're right. I should have kept my mouth shut. I suppose I wanted to curry favor with Mim. She gives you business.''

Warren clasped his hands over the top rail of the fence. "Mim keeps a small army of lawyers busy. If I lose her business, I don't think it will hurt either one of us, and it won't hurt you socially either. All you have to do is tell Mim that I'm down and I can't have anything on my mind right now. I need to rest and repair—that's no lie.''

"Warren, don't take this the wrong way, but I never knew you loved your father this much.''

He sighed. "I didn't either.'' He studied his boot tips for a second. "It's not just Poppa. Now I'm the oldest living male of the line, a line that extends back to 1632. Until our sons are out of prep school and college, the burden of that falls entirely on me. Now I must manage the portfolio—''

"You have good help.''

"Yes, but Poppa always checked over the results of our investments. Truth be told, darling, my law degree benefitted Poppa, not me. I read over those transactions that needed a legal check, but I never really paid attention to the investments and the land holdings in an aggressive sense. Poppa liked to keep his cards close to his chest. Well, I'd better learn fast. We've been losing money on the market.''

"Who hasn't? Warren, don't worry so much.''

"Well, I might have to delay running for the state Senate.''

"Why?'' Ansley wanted Warren in Richmond as much as possible. She intended to work nonstop for his election.

"Might look bad.''

"No, it won't. You tell the voters you're dedicating this campaign to your father, a man who believed in self-determination.''

Admiring her shrewdness, he said, "Poppa would have liked

that. You know, it's occurred to me these last few days that I'm raising my sons the way Poppa raised me. I was packed off to St. Clement's, worked here for the summers, and then it was off to Vanderbilt. Maybe the boys should be different—maybe something wild for them like"—he thought—"Berkeley. Now that I'm the head of this family, I want to give my sons more freedom."

"If they want to attend another college, fine, but let's not push them into it. Vanderbilt has served this family well for a long time." Ansley loved her sons although she despised the music they blasted throughout the house. No amount of yelling convinced them they'd go deaf. She was sure she was half deaf already.

"Did you really like my father?"

"Why do you ask me that now, after eighteen years of marriage?" She was genuinely surprised.

"Because I don't know you. Not really." He gazed at the horses on the far side of the track, for he couldn't look at her.

"I thought that's the way your people did things. I didn't think you wanted to be close."

"Maybe I don't know how."

Too late now, she thought to herself. "Well, Warren, one step at a time. I got along with Wesley, but it was his way or no way."

"Yep."

"I did like what he printed on his checks." She recited verbatim: "These funds were generated under the free enterprise system despite government's flagrant abuse of the income tax, bureaucratic hostilities, and irresponsible controls."

Warren's eyes misted. "He was tough duty, but he was clear about what he thought."

"We'll know even more about that at the reading of the will."

25

The reading of the will hit Warren like a two-by-four. Wesley had prepared his will through the old prestigious firm of Maki, Kleiser, and Maki. Not that Warren minded. It would be indelicate to have your son prepare your will. Still, he wasn't prepared for this.

A clause in his father's will read that no money could ever be inherited by any Randolph of any succeeding generation who married a person who was even one-twentieth African.

Ansley laughed. How absurd. Her sons weren't going to marry women from Uganda. Her sons weren't even going to marry African Americans, quadroons, octoroons, no way. Those boys weren't sent to St. Clements to be liberals and certainly not to mix with the races—the calendar be damned.

Warren, ashen when he heard the clause, sputtered, "That's illegal. Under today's laws that's illegal."

Old George Kleiser neatly stacked his papers. "Maybe. Maybe not. This will could be contested, but who would do that? Let it stand. Those were your father's express wishes." Apparently George thought the proviso prudent, or perhaps he subscribed to the let-sleeping-dogs-lie theory.

"Warren, you aren't going to do anything about this? I mean, why would you?"

As if in a trance, Warren shook his head. "No—but, Ansley, if this gets out, there go my chances for the state Senate."

George's stentorian voice filled the room. "Word of this, uh, consideration will never leave this room."

"What about the person who physically prepared the will?" Warren put his foot in it.

George, irritated, glided over that remark as he made allowances for Warren's recent loss. He'd known Warren since infancy, so he knew the middle-aged man in front of him was unprepared to take the helm of the family's great, though dwindling, fortune. "Our staff is accustomed to sensitive issues, Warren. Issues of life and death."

"Of course, of course, George—I'm just flabbergasted. Poppa never once spoke of anything like this to me."

"He was a genteel racist instead of an overt one." Ansley wanted to put the subject out of her mind and couldn't see why Warren was so upset.

"And aren't you?" Warren fired back.

"Not as long as we don't intermarry. I don't believe in mixing the races. Other than that, people are people." Ansley shook off Warren's barb.

"Ansley, you must promise me never, never, no matter how angry you may become with me or the boys—after all, people do rub one another's nerves—but you must never repeat what you've heard in this room today. I don't want to lose my chance because Poppa had this thing about racial purity."

Ansley promised never to tell.

26

But she did. She told Samson.

The early afternoon sun slanted across Blair Bainbridge's large oak kitchen table. Tulips swayed outside the long windows, and the hyacinths would open in a few days if this welcome warmth continued.

"I'm not surprised," Samson told Ansley. "The old man made a lifetime study of bloodlines, and to him it would be like crossing a donkey with a Thoroughbred." Then he smirked. "Of course, who is the donkey and who is the Thoroughbred?"

She held his hand as she sipped her hot chocolate. "It seems so—extreme."

Samson shrugged. The contents of Wesley's will held scant interest for him. Another twenty minutes and he would have to hit the road. His stomach knotted up each time he left Ansley.

"Say, I've got people coming in from California to look at Midale. Think I'll show them some properties in Orange County too. Awful pretty up there and not so developed. If I can sell Midale, I'll have some good money." He pressed his other hand on top of hers. "Then you can leave Warren."

Ansley stiffened. "Not while he's in mourning for his father."

"After that. Six months is a reasonable period of time. I can set my house in order and you can do the same."

"Honey"—she petted his hand—"let's leave well enough alone—for now. Lulu will skin you alive and in public. There's got to be a way around her, but I haven't found it yet. I keep hoping she'll find someone, she'll make life easier—but she has too much invested in being the wronged woman. And that scene at Big Daddy's funeral. My God."

Samson coughed. The knot in his stomach grew tighter. "Just one of those things. She leaned over to whisper in my ear and said she smelled another woman's perfume. I don't know what got into her."

"She knows my perfume, Diva. Anyway, when we're together I don't wear any perfume."

"Natural perfume." He kissed her hand in his.

She kissed him on the cheek. "Samson, you are the sweetest man."

"Not to hear my wife tell it." He sighed and bowed his head. "I don't know how much longer I can stand it. I'm living such a lie. I don't love Lulu. I'm tired of keeping up with the Joneses, who can't keep up with themselves. I'm tired of being trapped in my car all day with strangers and no matter what they tell you they want to buy, they really want the opposite. I swear it. Buyers are liars, as my first broker used to say. I don't know how long I can hold out."

"Just a little longer, precious." She nibbled on his ear. "*Was* there another woman's perfume on your neck?"

He sputtered, "Absolutely not. I don't even know where she

came up with that. You know I don't even look at other women, Ansley." He kissed her passionately.

As she drew back from the kiss she murmured, "Well, she knows, she just doesn't know it's me. Funny, I like Lulu. I call her most every morning. I guess she's my best friend, but I don't like her as your wife and I never did. I couldn't get it, know what I mean? You can sometimes see a couple and know why they're together. Like Harry and Fair when they were together. Or Susan and Ned—that's a good pair—but I never felt the heat, I guess you'd say, between Lulu and you. I don't really feel like I'm betraying her. I feel like I'm liberating her. She deserves the heat. She needs the right man for her—you're the right man for me."

He kissed her again and wished the clock weren't ticking so loudly. "Ansley, I can't live without you. You know that. I'll never be as rich as Warren, but I'm not poor. I work hard."

Her voice low, she brushed his cheek with her lips as she said, "And I want to make sure you don't join the ranks of the nouveau pauvre. I don't want your wife to take you to the cleaners. Give me a little time. I'll think of something or someone." She leapt out of her chair. "Oh, no!"

"What?" He hurried to her side.

Ansley pointed out the kitchen window. Mrs. Murphy and Tucker merrily raced to the stable. "Harry can't be far behind, and she's no dummy."

"Damn!" Samson ran his hands through his thick hair.

"If you slip out the front door I'll go out to the stable and head her off. Hurry!" She kissed him quickly. She could hear the heels of his shoes as he strode across the hardwood floors to the front door. Ansley headed for the back screen door.

Harry, much slower than her four-footed companions, had just reached the family cemetery on the hill. Ansley made it to the stable before Harry saw her.

"What's she doing in Blair's house?" Tucker asked.

Mrs. Murphy paused to observe Ansley. *"High color. She's het up* about something and we know she's not stealing the silver. She's got too much of her own."

"What if she's a kleptomaniac?" Tucker cocked her head as Ansley walked toward them.

"Nah. But give her a sniff anyway."

"Hi there, Mrs. Murphy. You too, Tucker," Ansley called to the animals.

"Ansley, what are you up to?" Tucker asked as she poked her nose toward Ansley's ankles.

Ansley waved at Harry, who waved back. She reached down to scratch Tucker's big ears.

"Hi, how nice to find you here." Harry diplomatically smiled.

"Warren sent me over to look at Blair's spider-wheel tedder. Says he wants one and maybe Blair will sell it."

A spider-wheel tedder turns hay for drying and can row up two swathes into one for baling. Three or four small metal wheels that resemble spiderwebs are pulled by a tractor.

"Thought you all rolled up your hay."

"Warren says he's tired of looking at huge rolls of shredded wheat in the fields and the middle of them is always wasted. He wants to go back to baling."

"Be a while." Harry noted the season.

Ansley lowered her voice. "He's already planning Thanksgiving dinner for the family. I think it's how the grief is taking him. You know, if he plans everything, then nothing can go wrong, he can control reality—although you'd think he would have had enough of that with his father."

"It will take time." Harry knew. She had lost both her parents some years before.

Mrs. Murphy, on her haunches, got up and trotted off toward the house. "She's lying."

"Got that right." The dog followed, her ears sweeping back for a moment. "Let's nose around."

The two animals reached the back door. Tucker, nose straight to the ground, sniffed intently. Mrs. Murphy relied on her eyes as much as her nose.

Tucker picked up the scent easily. *"Samson Coles."*

"So that's it." Mrs. Murphy walked between the tulips. She loved feeling the stems brush against her fur. *"She must really be bored."*

27

The quiet at Eagle's Rest proved unnerving. Ansley regretted saying how much she loathed the loud music the boys played. Although cacophonous, it was preferable to silence.

Seven in the evening usually meant each son was in his room studying. How Breton and Stuart could study with that wall of reverberating sound fascinated her. They used to compete in decibel levels with the various bands. Finally she settled that by declaring that during the first hour of study time, from six to seven, Stuart could play his music. Breton's choice won out between seven and eight.

Both she and Warren policed what they called study hall. Breton and Stuart made good grades, but Ansley felt they needed to know how important their schoolwork was to their parents, hence the policing. She told them frequently, "We have our jobs to do, you have your schoolwork."

Unable, at last, to bear the silence, Ansley climbed the curving stairway to the upstairs hall. She peeked in Breton's room. She walked down to Stuart's. Her older son sat at his desk. Breton, cross-legged, perched on Stuart's bed. Breton's eyes were red. Ansley knew not to call attention to that.

"Hey, guys."

"Hi, Mom." They replied in unison.

"What's up?"

"Nothing." Again in unison.

"Oh." She paused. "Kind of funny not to have Big Daddy yelling about your music, huh?"

"Yeah," Stuart agreed.

"He's never coming back." Breton had a catch in his breath. "I can't believe he's never coming back. At first it was like he was on vacation, you know?"

"I know," Ansley commiserated.

Stuart sat upright, a change from his normal slouch. "Remember the times we used to recite our heritage?" He imitated his grandfather's voice. "The first Randolph to set foot in the New World was a crony of Sir Walter Raleigh's. He returned to the old country. His son, emboldened by stories of the New World, came over in 1632, and thus our line began on this side of the Atlantic. He brought his bride, Jemima Hessletine. Their firstborn, Nancy Randolph, died that winter of 1634, aged six months. The second born, Raleigh Randolph, survived. We descend from this son."

Ansley, amazed, gasped. "Word for word."

"Mom, we heard it, seems like every day." Stuart half smiled.

"Yeah. Wish I could hear him again and—and I hate all that genealogy stuff." Breton's eyes welled up again. "Who cares?"

Ansley sat next to Breton, putting her arm around his shoulders. He seemed bigger the last time she hugged him. "Honey, when you get older, you'll appreciate these things."

"Why is it so important to everyone?" Breton asked innocently.

"To be wellborn is an advantage in this life. It opens many
doors. Life's hard enough as it is, Breton, so be thankful for the
blessing."

"Go to Montana," Stuart advised. "No one cares there. Probably why Big Daddy never liked the West. He couldn't lord it over
everybody."

Ansley sighed. "Wesley liked to be the biggest frog in the
pond."

"Mom, do you care about that bloodline stuff?" Breton
turned to face his mother.

"Let's just say I'd rather have it and not need it than need it
and not have it."

They digested this, then Breton asked another question.
"Mom, is it always like this when someone dies?"

"When it's someone you love, it is."

28

Medley Orion left Monticello in the dispersal after Thomas Jefferson's death in 1826. Kimball burned up tank after tank of gas as he drove down the winding county roads in search of genealogies, slave records, anything that might give him a clue. A few references to Medley's dressmaking skills surfaced in the well-preserved diaries of Tinton Venable.

Obsessed with the murder and with Medley herself, Kimball even drove to the Library of Congress to read through the notations of Dr. William Thornton and his French-born wife. Thornton imagined himself a Renaissance man like Jefferson. He raced blooded horses, designed the Capitol and the Octagon House in Washington, D.C., was a staunch Federalist, and survived the burning of Washington in 1814. His efforts to save the city during that conflagration created a bitter enmity between himself and the mayor of Washington. Thornton's wife, Anna Maria, rang out his praises on the hour like a well-timed church bell. When she visited Monticello in 1802 she wrote: "There is something more grand and awful than convenient in the whole place. A situation you would rather look at now and then than inhabit."

Mrs. Thornton, French, snob that she was, possessed some humor. What was odd was that Jefferson prided himself on convenience and efficiency.

Kimball's hunch paid off. He found a reference to Medley. Mrs. Thornton commented on a mint-green summer dress belonging to Martha Jefferson—Patsy. The dress, Mrs. Thornton noted, was sewn by Patsy's genie, as she put it, Medley Orion. She also mentioned that Medley's daughter, not quite a woman, was "bright," meaning fair-skinned, and extraordinarily beautiful like her mother, but even lighter. She further noted that Medley and Martha Jefferson Randolph got along quite well, "a miracle considering," but Mrs. Thornton chose not to explain that pregnant phrase.

Mrs. Thornton then went on to discuss thoroughly her feelings about slavery—she didn't like it—and her feelings about mixing the races, which she didn't like either. She felt that slavery promoted laziness. Her argument for this, although convoluted, contained a kernel of logic: Why should people work if they couldn't retain the fruits of their labors? A roof over one's head, food in the stomach, and clothes on one's back weren't sufficient motivation for industriousness, especially when one saw another party benefitting from one's own labor.

Kimball drove so fast down Route 29 on his way home that he received a speeding ticket for his excitement and still made it from downtown Washington to Charlottesville more than fifteen minutes faster than the usual two hours. He couldn't wait to tell Heike what he had discovered. He would have to decide what to tell Oliver, who grew more tense each day.

┌─────────┐
│   29   │
└─────────┘

Kimball Haynes, Harry, Mrs. Hogendobber, Mim Sanburne, and Lucinda Coles crammed themselves into a booth at Metropolitain, a restaurant in Charlottesville's Downtown Mall. The Metropolitain combined lack of pretension with fantastic food. Lulu happened to be strolling in the mall when Kimball spotted her and asked her to lunch with the others.

Over salads he explained his findings about Medley Orion and Jefferson's oldest child, Martha.

"Well, Kimball, I can see that you're a born detective, but where is this leading?" Mim wanted to know. She was ready to get down to brass tacks.

"I wish I knew." Kimball cut into a grits patty.

"You all may be too young to have heard an old racist expression." Mim glanced at the ceiling, for she had learned to

despise these sayings. " 'There's a nigger in the woodpile somewhere.' Comes from the Underground Railway, of course, but
you get the drift."

Lulu Coles fidgeted. "No, I don't."

"Somebody's hiding something," Mim stated flatly.

"Of course somebody's hiding something. They've been
hiding it for two hundred years, and now Martha Jefferson Randolph is in on it." Lulu checked her anger. She knew Mim had
yanked properties away from Samson because of his outburst at
the funeral. Angry as she was at her husband, Lucinda was smart
enough not to wish for their net worth to drop. Actually, she was
angry, period. She'd peer in the mirror and see the corners of her
mouth turning down just as her mother's had—an embittered
woman she swore never to emulate. She was becoming her own
mother, to her horror.

Harry downed her Coke. "What Mim means is that somebody is hiding something today."

"Why?" Susan threw her hands in the air. The idea was
absurd. "So there's a murderer in the family tree. By this time we
have one of everything in all of our family trees. Really, who
cares?"

" 'Save me, Lord, from liars and deceivers.' Psalm 120:2."
Mrs. Hogendobber, as usual, recalled a pertinent scripture.

"Forgive me, Mrs. H., but there's a better one." Kimball
closed his eyes in order to remember. "Ah, yes, here it is, 'Every
one deceives his neighbor, and no one speaks the truth; they have
taught their tongue to speak lies; they commit iniquity and are
too weary to repent.' "

"Jeremiah 9:5. Yes, it is better," Mrs. Hogendobber agreed.
"I suppose letting the cat out of the bag these many years later
wouldn't seem upsetting, but if it's in the papers and on television, well—I can understand."

"Yeah, your great-great-great-great-grandfather was murdered. How do you feel about that?" Susan smirked.

"Or your great-great—how many greats?" Harry turned to

Susan, who held up two fingers. "Great-great-grandfather was a murderer. Should you pay the victim's descendants recompense? Obviously, our society has lost the concept of privacy, and you can't blame anyone for wanting to keep whatever they can away from prying eyes."

"Well, I for one would like a breath of fresh air. Kimball, you're welcome to go through the Coleses' papers. Maybe you'll find the murderer there." Lulu smiled.

"How generous of you. The Coleses' papers will be invaluable to me even if they don't yield the murderer." Kimball beamed.

Mim shifted on the hard bench. "I wonder that Samson has never donated his treasures to the Alderman Library. Or some other library he feels would do justice to the manuscripts and diaries. Naturally, I prefer the Alderman."

The olive branch was outstretched. Lulu grabbed it. "I'll work on him, Mim. Samson fears that his family's archives will be labeled, stuck in a carton, and never again see the light of day. Decades from now, someone will stumble upon them and they'll be decayed. He keeps all those materials in his temperature-controlled library. The Coleses lead the way when it comes to preservation," she breathed, "but perhaps this is the time to share."

"Yes." Mim appeared enlightened when her entrée, a lightly poached salmon in dill sauce, was placed in front of her. "What did you order, Lucinda? I've already forgotten."

"Sweetbreads."

"Me too." Harry's mouth watered as the dish's tempting aroma wafted under her nose.

"What a lunch." Kimball inclined his head toward the ladies. "Beautiful women, delicious food, and help with my research. What more is there to life?"

"A 16.1-hand Thoroughbred fox hunter that floats over a three-foot-six-inch coop." The rich sauce melted in Harry's mouth.

"Oh, Harry, you and your horses. You have Gin Fizz and Tomahawk." Susan elbowed her.

"Getting along in years," Mim informed Susan. Mim, an avid fox hunter, appreciated Harry's desire. She also appreciated Harry's emaciated budget and made a mental note to see if she could strong-arm someone into selling Harry a good horse at a low price.

Six months earlier the idea of helping the postmistress wouldn't have occurred to her. But Mim had turned over a new leaf. She wanted to be warmer, kinder, and more giving. It wasn't easy, overnight, to dump six decades of living a certain way. The cause of this volte-face Mim kept close to her chest, which was, indeed, where it began. She had visited Larry Johnson for a routine checkup. He found a lump. Larry, the soul of discretion, promised not to tell even Jim. Mim flew to New York City and checked into Columbia-Presbyterian. She told everyone she was on her semiannual shopping spree. Since she did repair to New York every spring and then again every fall, this explanation satisfied. The lump was removed and it was cancerous. However, they had caught the disease in time. Her body betrayed no other signs of the cancer. Procedures are so advanced that Mim returned home in a week, had indeed accomplished some shopping, and no one was the wiser. Until Jim walked in on her in the bathtub. She told him everything. He sobbed. That shocked her so badly that she sobbed. She still couldn't figure out how her husband could be chronically unfaithful and love her so deeply at the same time, but she knew now that he did. She decided to give up being angry at him. She even decided to stop pretending socially that he didn't have a weakness for women. He was what he was and she was what she was, but she could change and she was trying. If Jim wanted to change, that was his responsibility.

"Earth to Mrs. Sanburne," Harry called.

"What? I must have been roller-skating on Saturn's rings."

"We're going to help Kimball read through the correspondence and records of Jefferson's children and grandchildren," Harry told her.

"I can read with my eyes closed," Miranda said. "Oh, that doesn't sound right, does it?"

After lunch Lulu escorted Mim to her silver sand Bentley Turbo R, a new purchase and a sensational one. Lulu apologized profusely a second time for her outburst during Wesley's funeral. After Mim's luncheon she had smothered her hostess in "sorries." She had also confessed to Reverend Jones and he had told her it wasn't that bad. He forgave her and he was sure that the Randolphs would too, if she would apologize, which she did. Mim listened. Lulu continued. It was as though she'd pried the first olive out of the jar and the others tumbled out. She said she thought she'd smelled another woman's perfume on Samson's neck. She'd been on edge. Later she'd entered his bathroom and found a bottle, new, of Ralph Lauren's Safari.

"These days you can't tell the difference between men's colognes and women's perfumes," Mim said. "There is no difference. They put the unguents into different bottles, invent these manly names, and that's that. What would happen if a man used a woman's perfume? He'd grow breasts overnight, I guess." She laughed at her own joke.

Lulu laughed too. "It strikes me as odd that the worst thing you can call a man is a woman, yet they claim to love us."

Mim arched her right eyebrow. "I never thought of that."

"I think of a lot of things." Lulu sighed. "I'm a tangle of suspicions. I know he's cheating on me. I just don't know who."

Mim unlocked her car, paused, and then turned. "Lucinda, I don't know if that part matters. The whole town knows that Jim has enjoyed his little amours over the years."

"Mim, I didn't mean to open old wounds," Lulu stammered, genuinely distraught.

"Don't give it a second thought. I'm older than you. I don't care as much anymore, or I care in a new way. But heed my advice. Some men are swordsmen. That's the only word I can think of for it. They swash and they buckle. They need the chase and the conquest to feel alive. It's repetitive, but for some reason I can't fathom, the repetition doesn't bore them. Makes them feel young and powerful, I suppose. It doesn't mean Samson doesn't love you."

Tears glistened in Lucinda's green eyes. "Oh, Mim, if only that were true, but Samson isn't that kind of man. If he's having an affair, then he's in love with her."

Mim waited to reply. "My dear, the only thing you can do is to take care of yourself."

30

"If you light another cigarette, then I'll have to light one too," Deputy Cynthia Cooper joshed.

"Here." Sheriff Shaw tossed his pack of Chesterfields at her. She caught them left-handed. "Out at first," he said.

She tapped the pack with a long, graceful finger, and a slender white cigarette slid out. The deep tobacco fragrance made her eyelids flutter. That evil weed, that scourge of the lungs, that drug, nicotine, but oh, how it soothed the nerves and how it added to the coffers of the great state of Virginia. "Damn, I love these things."

"Think we'll die young?"

"Young?" Cynthia raised her eyebrows, which made Rick laugh, since he was already middle-aged.

"Hey, you want another promotion someday, don't you, Deputy?"

"Just a beardless boy, that Rick Shaw." She placed the cigarette in her mouth, lighting it with a match from a box of Redbuds.

They inhaled in sweet silence, the blue smoke swirling to the ceiling like a slow whirling dervish of delight.

"Coop, what do you think of Oliver Zeve?"

"He took the news as I expected. A nervous twitch."

Rick grunted. "His press statement was a model of restraint. But nothing, nothing, will beat Big Marilyn Sanburne advancing her stalker theory. She's good. She's really good." Rick appreciated Mim's skills even though he didn't like her. "I'd better call her."

"Good politics, boss."

Rick dialed the Sanburne residence. The butler fetched Mim. "Mrs. Sanburne, Rick Shaw here."

"Yes, Sheriff."

"I wanted to give you the report from Washington concerning the human remains found at Monticello." He heard a quick intake of breath. "The skeleton is that of a white male, aged between thirty-two and thirty-five. In good health. The left femur had been broken in childhood and healed. Possibly the victim suffered a slight limp. The victim was five ten in height, which although not nearly as tall as Jefferson's six foot four, would have been tall for the times, and given the density of bone, he was probably powerfully built. There were no signs of degenerative disease in the bones, and his teeth, also, were quite good. He was killed by one forceful blow to the back of the skull with an as yet undetermined weapon. Death, more than likely, was instantaneous."

Mim asked, "How do they know the man was white?"

"Well, Mrs. Sanburne, determining race from skeletal remains can actually be a little tricky sometimes. We're all much more alike than we are different. The races have more in common than they have dissimilarities. You could say that race has more to do with culture than physical attributes. However, forensics starts by considering the bone structure and skeletal proportions of a specimen. Specifically, the amount of projection of the cheekbones, the width of the nasal aperture, and the shape and distance between the eye sockets. Another factor is the amount of projection of the jaw. For instance, a white man's jaw is generally less prominent than a black man's is. Prognathism is the term for the way the jaw figures more prominently in the faces of those of African descent. There is also in many white skeletons the presence of an extra seam in the skull, which extends from the top of the nasal arch to the top of the head. Perhaps even more helpful is the amount of curvature in the long bones, especially the femur, of an individual. A white person's skeleton tends to have more twisting in the neck or head of the femur."

"Amazing."

"Yes, it is," the sheriff agreed.

"Thank you," Mim said politely, and hung up the phone.

"Well?" Cooper asked.

"She didn't succumb to the vapors." Rick referred to the Victorian ladies' habit of fainting upon hearing unwelcome news. "Let's run over to Kimball Haynes's. I want to see him away from Oliver Zeve. Oliver will shut him down if he can."

"Boss, the director of Monticello isn't going to obstruct justice. I know that Oliver walks a tightrope up there, but he's not a criminal."

"No, I don't think so either, but he's so supersensitive about this. He'll put the crimp on Kimball somehow, and I think Kimball is the one person who can lead us to the killer."

"I think it's Medley Orion."

"How often have I told you not to jump to conclusions?"

"Eleventy million times." She rolled her big blue eyes. "Still do it though."

"Still right most of the time too." He kicked at her as she

walked by to stub out her cigarette. "Well, I happen to agree. It was Medley or a boyfriend, father, somebody close to her. If we could just find the motive—Kimball knows the period inside and out and he's got a feel for the people."

"Got the bug."

"Huh?"

"Harry told me that Kimball eats and sleeps this case."

"Harry—next she'll have the cat and dog on it too."

31

The night air, cool and deep, carried stories to Tucker's nose. Deer followed the warm air currents, raccoons prowled around Monticello, a possum reposed on a branch of the Carolina silverbell near the terrace which Mrs. Murphy, like Kimball, thought of as a boardwalk. Overhead, bats flew in and out of the tulip poplar, the purple beech, and the eaves of the brick house.

"I'm glad Monticello has bats." Mrs. Murphy watched the small mammals dart at almost right angles when they wanted.

"Why?" Tucker sat down.

"Makes this place less august. After all, when Thomas Jefferson lived here, it probably didn't look like this. The trees couldn't have been this grand. The garbage had to go somewhere—know what I mean?—and it must have been filled with noises. Now there's a reverential silence except for the shuffling of human feet on the tours."

"It must have been fun, all the grandchildren, the slaves calling to one another, the clanging in the smithy, the neighing of the horses. I can imagine it, and I can envision a bright corgi accompanying Mr. Jefferson on his rides."

"Dream on. If he had dogs out with him, they would have been big dogs—coach dogs or hunting dogs."

"Like Dalmatians?" Tucker's ears dropped for a moment as she considered her spotted rival. "He wouldn't have owned Dalmatians. I think he had corgis. We're good herding dogs and we could have been useful."

"Then you would have been out with the cattle."

"Horses."

"Cattle."

"Oh, what do you know? Next you'll say a cat sat by Jefferson's elbow when he wrote the Declaration of Independence."

Mrs. Murphy's whiskers twitched. "No cat would ever have allowed the phrase 'All men are created equal' to pass. Not only are all men not created equal, cats aren't created equal. Some cats are more equal than others, if you know what I mean."

"He wrote it in Philadelphia. Maybe that affected his brain." Tucker giggled.

"Philadelphia was a beautiful city then. Parts of it are still beautiful, but it just got too big, you know. All of our cities got too big. Anyway, it's absurd to plunk an idea like that down on parchment. Men aren't equal. And we know for sure that women aren't equal. They weren't even considered at the time."

"Maybe he meant equal under the law."

"That's a farce. Ever see a rich man go to jail? I take that back. Every now and then a Mafia don gets marched to the slammer."

"Mrs. Murphy, how could Thomas Jefferson have dreamed of the Mafia? When he wrote the Declaration of Independence, only a million people lived in the thirteen colonies and they were mostly English, Irish, Scottish, and German, and, of course, African from the various tribes."

"Don't forget the French."

"Boy, were they stupid. Had the chance to grab the whole New World and blew it."

"Tucker, I didn't know you were a Francophobe."

"They don't like corgis. The Queen of England likes corgis, so I think the English are the best."

"Jefferson didn't." The cat's silken eyebrows bobbed up and down.

"Not fair. George III was mental. The whole history of the world might have been different if he'd been right in the head."

"Yeah, but you could pick out any moment in history and say that. What would have happened if Julius Caesar had listened to his wife, Calpurnia, on March fifteenth, when she begged him not to go to the Forum? Beware the Ides of March. What would have happened if Catherine the Great's attempt on her looney-tunes husband's life had failed and she was killed instead? Moments. Turning points. Every day there's a turning point somewhere with someone. I think the creation of the Society for the Prevention of Cruelty to Animals gets my vote as most important."

Tucker stood up and inhaled. "I pick the founding of the Westminster Dog Show. Say, do you smell that?"

Mrs. Murphy lifted her elegant head. "Skunk."

"Let's go back in the house. If I see her, then I'll chase her and you know what will happen. The odor of skunk in Monticello."

"I think it would be pretty funny myself. I wonder if Jefferson would like the idea of his home being a museum. I bet he'd rather have it filled with children and laughter, broken pottery and worn-out furniture."

"He would, but Americans need shrines. They need to see how their great people lived. They didn't have indoor plumbing. Fireplaces were the only source of heat in the winter. No washing machines, refrigerators, stoves, or televisions."

"The last would be a blessing." Mrs. Murphy's voice dripped disdain.

"No telephones, telegraphs, fax machines, automobiles, airplanes . . ."

"Sounds better and better." The cat brushed up against the dog. "Quiet except for natural sounds. Just think, people actually sat down and really talked to one another. They were under an obligation to entertain one another with their conversational abilities. You know what people do today? They sit in their living room or family room—isn't that a dumb word? Every room is a family room—they sit there with the television on and if they talk they talk over the sound of the boob tube."

"*Oh, Mrs. Murphy, they can't all be that crude.*"

"*Humph,*" the cat replied. She did not consider the human animal the crown of creation.

"*I'm surprised you know your history.*" Tucker scratched her ear.

"*I listen. I know human history and our history and no matter what, I am an Americat.*"

"*And there is an Ameriskunk.*" Tucker scurried to the front door, which was open just enough so she could squeeze in as a fat skunk at the edge of the lawn hastened in the opposite direction.

Mrs. Murphy followed. The two ran to the narrow staircase behind the North Square Room, turned left, and scampered up to Kimball's makeshift workroom.

Harry, Mrs. Hogendobber, and Kimball, now bleary-eyed, had sifted through as much correspondence as they could. Martha Jefferson, the future president's daughter, married Thomas Mann Randolph on February 23, 1790. Together they produced twelve children, eleven of whom gained maturity and most of whom lived to a ripe old age. The last died in 1882, and that was Virginia Jefferson Randolph, born in 1801. Martha's children in turn begat thirty-five children. Maria, her sister, had thirteen grandchildren through her son Francis Eppes, who married twice, which brings that generation's count to forty-eight. They, too, were fruitful and multiplied—not that everyone lived to breed. A few grew to adulthood and never married, but the descendants were plentiful even so.

Mrs. Hogendobber rubbed her nose. "This is like finding a needle in a haystack."

"But which needle?" Harry joined her chorus.

"Which haystack, Martha or Maria?" Kimball was also wearing down.

"You'd think someone would say something about Medley or her child." Harry noticed her friends enter the room. "What have you two been up to?"

"*Discussion of history,*" Mrs. Murphy answered.

"*Yeah, deep stuff.*" Tucker plopped at her mother's feet.

"The sad truth is that back then black lives weren't that important." Mrs. Hogendobber shook her head.

"There sure are enough references to Jupiter, Jefferson's body servant, and King and Sally and Betsey Hemings, and well, the list could go on and on. Medley gets a footnote." Kimball started pulling on his lower lip, an odd habit indicating intense thought.

"What about Madison Hemings? He sure caused a sensation. A dead ringer for Thomas Jefferson with a deep brown tan. He waited on the dinner guests. Bet he gave them a start." Harry wondered what the real effect must have been upon seeing a young mulatto man in livery who surely shared the president's blood.

"Born in 1805, and as an old man he said he was Jefferson's son. Said his mother, Sally, told him." Kimball abruptly leapt up. "But that could be a desire to be the center of attention. And Jefferson had a wealth of male relatives, each and every one capable of congress with Sally or her pretty sister, Betsey. And what about the other white employees of the plantation?"

"Well, Thomas Jefferson Randolph, Martha's oldest son, who was born in 1792 and lived to 1875, swore that Sally was Peter Carr's favorite mistress and Sally's sister, Betsey, was mistress to Sam Carr. Those were Jefferson's nephews, the sons of Dabney Carr and Martha Jefferson's younger sister. Wild as rats they were too." Kimball smiled, imagining the charms of a black purdah with one white sultan, or, in this case, two.

"Wonder if Sally and Betsey thought it was so great?" Harry couldn't resist.

"Huh"—he blinked—"well, maybe not, but Harry, you can't remove sexual fantasy from the life of the male. I mean, we all want to imagine ourselves in the arms of a beautiful woman."

"Yeah, yeah," Harry grumbled. "The imagining isn't so bad, it's the doing it when one is married. Oh, well, this is an ancient debate."

He softened. "I get your point."

"*And who slept with Medley?*" Mrs. Murphy flicked her tail. "*If she was as pretty as she is reputed to have been, she would have turned a white head or two.*"

"What a loud purr." Kimball admired Mrs. Murphy.

"*You should hear her burp.*" Tucker wagged her nontail, hoping to be noticed.

"Jealous." Mrs. Hogendobber said matter-of-factly.

"*She's got your number, stumpy.*" Mrs. Murphy teased her friend, who didn't reply because Kimball was petting her.

"Is it me or is there a conspiracy of silence surrounding Medley Orion and her child?" Harry, like a hound, struck a faint, very faint scent.

Both Kimball and Mrs. Hogendobber stared at her.

"Isn't that obvious?" Kimball said.

"The obvious is a deceitful temptation." Mrs. Hogendobber, by virtue of working with Harry, picked up the line now too. "We're overlooking something."

"The master of Monticello may not have known about whatever Medley was up to or whoever killed that man, but I bet you dollars to doughnuts that Martha did, and that's why she took Medley. She could easily have been sold off, you know. The family could have ditched this slave if she became an embarrassment."

"Harry, the Jeffersons did not sell their slaves." Kimball almost sounded like Mim. It wasn't true though. Jefferson did sell his slaves, but only if he knew they were going to a good home. Jefferson's policy demonstrated more concern than many slave owners evidenced, yet the disposal of other humans seemed both callous and mercenary to some of Jefferson's contemporaries.

"They could have given her away after Thomas died." Mrs. Hogendobber shifted in her seat, a surge of energy enlivening her thoughts. "One or both daughters protected Medley. Martha *and* Maria."

Kimball threw his hands in the air. "Why?"

"Well, why in the hell did not one family member suggest they pack off Sally and Betsey Hemings? My God, Jefferson was crucified over his alleged affair with Sally. Think about it, Kimball. It may have been two hundred years ago, but politics is still politics and people have changed remarkably little." Harry nearly shouted.

"A cover-up?" Kimball whispered.

"Ah"—Mrs. Hogendobber held up her forefinger like a schoolmarm—"not a cover-up but pride. If the Hemingses were 'dismissed,' shall we say, then it would have been an admission of guilt."

"But surely keeping them on this hill fed the gossipmongers too," Kimball exploded in frustration.

"Yes, but Jefferson didn't buy into it. So if he's mum, what can they do? They can make up stories. Any newspaper today is full of the same conjecture posing as fact. But if Jefferson levitated above them all in his serene way, then he stole some of their fire. He never sweated in front of the enemy is what I'm saying, and he made a conscious decision not to bag the Hemingses."

"Harry, those slaves came from his mother's estate."

"Kimball, so what?"

"He was a very loyal man. After all, when Dabney Carr, his best friend, died young, he created the family cemetery for him, and would lean on his grave and read to be close to him."

Harry held up her hands as if asking for a truce, "Okay. Okay, then try this. Sally and Betsey's mother, Betty Hemings, was half white. The skinny from the other slaves was that her father was an English sea captain. Thomas Jefferson freed Bob and James, Sally and Betsey's brothers, in 1790. Except for another daughter, Thenia, who was acquired by James Monroe, all the Hemingses stayed at Monticello. They had a reputation for being good workers and for being intelligent. Sally was never set free, but her daughter was, by Jefferson, in 1822. At least, that's what I'm getting out of all these papers."

"I know all that," Kimball fretted.

"I don't." Mrs. Hogendobber made a sign indicating for Harry to continue.

"Jefferson made provision for Sally's sons Madison and Eston to be freed upon reaching the age of twenty-one. Now, he wouldn't have done that if he didn't think these people could earn a living. It would be cruel to send them into the world otherwise. Right?"

"Right." Kimball paced.

"And the lovers of Sally and Betsey may not have been the Carr brothers. The slaves said that John Wayles took Sally as, what should I say, his common-law wife, after his third wife died, and that Sally had six children by him. John Wayles was Martha Jefferson's brother, T.J.'s brother-in-law. Jefferson took responsibility, always, for any member of his family. He loved Martha beyond reason. His solicitude makes sense in this light. Of course, others said that John Wayles was the lover of Betty Hemings, so that Sally and Betsey would have been Martha's cousins. Guess we'll never really know, but the point is, Sally and Betsey had some blood tie, or deep-heart tie, to T.J."

Kimball sat back down. He spoke slowly. "That does make sense. It would force him into silence, too, concerning the paternity slanders."

"John Wayles wasn't equipped to handle this kind of scrutiny. Jefferson was." Mrs. Hogendobber hit the nail on the head. "And even though they hurt Jefferson, the slandermongers, they couldn't really abridge his power."

"Why not?" Kimball was perplexed.

"And flush out all those white jackrabbits in the briar patch?" Mrs. Hogendobber laughed. "The question is not which southern gentlemen slept with slave women, the question is which ones did not."

"Oh, I do see." Kimball rubbed his chin. "The Yankees could fulminate properly, but the Southerners shut up and rolled right over, so to speak."

"Hell, yes, they wouldn't have nailed Jefferson to the cross for their own sins." Harry laughed. "The Northerners could do the nailing, but they never could quite catch him to do it. He was far too smart to talk and he always sheltered those weaker than himself."

"He had broad, broad wings." Mrs. Hogendobber smiled.

"And where does that leave Medley Orion?" Kimball stood up and paced again.

"She may or may not have been related to the Hemingses. Obviously, from the description of her as 'bright,' she was one quarter white if not half white. And her lover was white. The lover is the key. He was being protected," Harry said.

"I disagree. I think it's Medley who was being protected. I can't prove it, but my woman's intuition tells me the victim was Medley's white lover."

"What?" Kimball stopped in his tracks.

"The Jeffersons extended their grace to many people: to Wayles if he was the amour of Betty Hemings or her daughter, Sally; to the Carrs if they were involved. The corpse in Cabin Four wasn't a family member. His absence or death would have been noted somewhere. Someone had to make an explanation for that. Don't you see, whoever that man is—or was, I should say—once the Jeffersons found out, they didn't like him."

She paused for breath and Kimball butted in. "But to countenance murder?"

Mrs. Hogendobber dropped her head for a second and then looked up. "There may be worse sins than murder, Kimball Haynes."

32

Warren Randolph buttoned his shirt as Larry Johnson leaned against the small sink in the examining room. Larry was tempted to tell Warren it had taken his father's death to force him into this check-up, but he didn't.

"The blood work will be back within the week." Larry closed the file with the plastic color code on the outside. "You're in good health and I don't anticipate any problems, but"—he wagged his finger—"the last time you had blood drawn was when you left for college. You come in for a yearly check-up!"

Warren sheepishly said, "Lately I haven't felt well. I'm tired, but then I can't sleep. I drag around and forget things. I'd forget my head if it weren't pinned to my shoulders."

Larry put his hand on Warren's shoulder. "You've suffered a

major loss. Grief is exhausting and the things that pop into your mind—it'll surprise you."

Warren could let down his guard around the doctor. If you couldn't trust your lifelong physician, whom could you trust? "I don't remember feeling this bad when Mother died."

"You were twenty-four when Diana died. That's too young to understand what and whom you've lost, and don't be surprised if some of the grieving you've suppressed over your mother doesn't resurface now. Sooner or later, it comes out."

"I got worried, you know, about the listlessness. Thought it might be the beginning of leukemia. Runs in the family. Runs? Hell, it gallops."

"Like I said, the blood work will be back, but you don't have any other signs of the disease. You took a blow and it will take time to get back up."

"But what if I do have leukemia like Poppa?" Warren's brow furrowed, his voice grew taut. "It can take you down fast. . . ."

"Or you can live with it for years." Larry's voice soothed. "Don't yell 'ouch' until you're hurt. You know, memory and history are age-related. What you call up out of your mind at twenty may not be what you call up at forty. Even if what you remember is a very specific event in time, say, Christmas 1968, how you remember it will shift and deepen with age. Events are weighted emotionally. It's not the events we need to understand, it's the emotions they arouse. In some cases it takes twenty or thirty years to understand Christmas of 1968. You are now able to see your father's life as a whole: beginning, middle, and end. That changes your perception of Wesley, and I guarantee you will think a lot about your mother too. Just let it go through you. Don't block it. You'll be better off."

"You know everything about everybody, don't you, Doc?"

"No"—the old man smiled—"but I know people."

Warren glanced up at the ceiling, pushing back his tears. "Know what I thought about driving over here today? The damnedest thing. I remembered Poppa throwing the newspaper across the room when Reagan and his administration managed that Tax Reform Act of 1986. What a disaster. Anyway, Poppa was fussing and cussing and he said, 'The bedroom, Warren, the bedroom is the last place we're free until these sons of bitches figure out how to tax orgasms.' "

Larry laughed. "They broke the mold when they made Wesley."

33

The graceful three-sash windows, copied from Monticello, opened onto a formal garden in the manner of Inigo Jones. The library was paneled in a deep red mahogany and glowed as if with inner light. Kimball sat at a magnificent Louis XIV desk, black with polished ormolu, which Samson Coles's maternal great-great-great-grandmother was reputed to have had shipped over from France in 1700 when she lived in the Tidewater.

Handwritten diaries, the cursive script elegant and highly individualistic, strained the archaeologist's eyes. If he stepped away from the documents, the writing almost looked Arabic, another language of surpassing beauty in the written form.

Lucinda, the consummate hostess, placed a pot of hot tea, a true Brown Betty, on a silver tray along with scones and sinful jams and jellies. She pulled a chair alongside him and read too.

"The Coles family has a fascinating history. And the Randolphs, of course, Jefferson's mother's family. It's hard to remember how few people there were even at the beginning of the eighteenth century and how the families all knew one another. Married one another too."

"You know that America enjoyed a higher rate of literacy during the American Revolution than it does today? That's a dismal statistic. These early settlers, I mean, even going back to the early seventeenth century, were as a rule quite well educated. That common culture, high culture if you will, at least in the literary sense and the sense of the living arts"—he rubbed the desk to make his point—"must have given people remarkable stability."

"You could seize your quill and inkwell, scratch a letter to a friend in Charleston, South Carolina, and know that an entire subtext was understood." Lulu buttered a scone.

"Lulu, what was your major?"

"English. Wellesley."

"Ah." Kimball appreciated the rigors of Wellesley College.

"What was a girl to study in my day? Art history or English."

"Your day wasn't that long ago. Now, come on, you aren't even forty."

She shrugged and grinned. She certainly wasn't going to correct him.

Kimball, at thirty, hadn't begun to think about forty. "We're youth-obsessed. The people who wrote these diaries and letters and records valued experience."

"The people who wrote this stuff weren't assaulted on a daily basis with photographs and television shows parading beautiful young women, and men, for that matter. Your wife, hopefully the best woman you could find, did not necessarily have to be beautiful. Not that it hurt, mind you, Kimball, but I think our ancestors were much more concerned with sturdy health and strong character. The idea of a woman as ornament—that was off waiting to afflict us during Queen Victoria's reign."

"You're right. Women and men worked as a team regardless

of their level of society. They needed one another. I keep coming across that in my research, Lulu, the sheer need. A man without a woman was to be pitied and a woman without a man was on a dead-end street. Everyone pitched in. I mean, look at these accounts kept by Samson's great-grandmother—many greats, actually—Charlotte Graff. Nails, outrageously expensive, were counted, every one. Here, look at this account book from 1693.''

"Samson really should donate these to the Alderman's rare books collection. He won't part with them, and I guess in a way I can understand, but the public should have access to this information, or scholars at least, if not the public. Wesley Randolph was the same way. I ran into Warren coming out of Larry Johnson's office yesterday and asked him if he'd ever read the stuff. He said no, because his father kept a lot of it in the huge house safe in the basement. Wesley figured that if there were a fire, the papers would be protected in the safe.''

"Logical.''

Lulu read again. "Whenever I read letters to and from Jefferson women I get totally confused. There are so many Marthas, Janes, and Marys. It seems like every generation has those names in it.''

"Look at it this way. They didn't know they were going to be famous. Otherwise maybe they would have varied the first names to help us out later.''

Lulu laughed. "Think anyone will be reading about us one hundred years from now?''

"They won't even care about me twenty minutes after I'm gone—in an archival sense, I mean.''

"Who knows?'' She gingerly picked up Charlotte Graff's account book and read. "Her accounts make sense. I picked up Samson's ledger the other day because he had laid it out on the desk and forgot to put it away. Couldn't make head or tails of it. I think the gene pool has degenerated, at least in the bookkeeping department.'' She rose and pulled a massive black book with a red spine out of the lower shelf of a closed cabinet. "You tell me, who does the better job?"

Good-naturedly, Kimball opened the book, the bright white paper with the vertical blue lines such a contrast from the aged papers he'd been reading. He squinted. He read a bit, then he paled, closed the book, and handed it back to Lulu. Not an accounting genius, he knew enough about double-entry bookkeeping to know that Samson Coles was lifting money out of clients' escrow funds. No broker or real estate agent is ever, ever to transfer money out of an escrow account even if he or she pays it back within the hour. Discovery of this abuse results in instant loss of license, and no real estate board in any county would do otherwise, even if the borrower were the president of the United States.

"Kimball, what's wrong?"

He stuttered, "Uh, nothing."

"You look pale as a ghost."

"Too much scones and jam." He smiled weakly and gathered the papers together just as Samson tooted down the driveway, his jolly red Wagoneer announcing his presence. "Lulu, put this book away before he gets here."

"Kimball, what's wrong with you?"

"Put the book back!" He spoke more sharply than he had intended.

Lulu, not a woman given to taking orders, did the exact reverse, she opened the account book and slowly and deliberately read the entries. Not knowing too much about bookkeeping or the concept of escrow even though she was married to a realtor, she was a bit wide of the mark. No matter, because Samson strode into the library looking the picture of the country squire.

"Kimball, my wife has enticed you with scones."

"Hello, dear." He leaned over and perfunctorily kissed her on the cheek. His gaze froze on the account book.

"If you two will excuse me, I must be going. Thank you so much for access to these materials." Kimball disappeared.

Samson, crimson-faced, tried to hide his shock. If he reacted, it would be far worse than if he didn't. Instead, he merely removed his ledger from Lulu's hands and replaced it on the lower shelf of the built-in cabinet. "Lulu, I was unaware that my ledger qualified as an archive."

Blithely she remarked, "Well, it doesn't, but I was reading over your umpteenth great-grandmother's accounts from 1693, and they made sense. So I told Kimball to see how the accounting gene had degenerated over the centuries."

"Amusing," Samson uttered through gritted teeth. "Methods have changed."

"I'll say."

"Did Kimball say anything?"

Lucinda paused. "No, not exactly, but he was eager to go after that. Samson, is there a problem?"

"No, but I don't think my ledger is anybody's business but my own."

Stung, Lulu realized he was right. "I'm sorry. I'd seen it when you left it out the other day, and I do say whatever pops into my head. The difference between the two ledgers just struck me. It isn't anybody else's business but it was—funny."

Samson left her gathering up the scones and the tea. He repaired to the kitchen for a bracing kick of Dalwhinnie scotch. What to do?

34

Mrs. Murphy, with special determination, squeezed her hindquarters into Mim Sanburne's post office box. From the postmistress's point of view, the wall of boxes was divided in half horizontally, an eight-inch ledge of oak being the divider. This proved handy when Harry needed to set aside stacks of mail or continue her refined sorting, as she called it.

As a kitten, Mrs. Murphy used to sleep in a large brandy snifter. She never acquired a taste for brandy, but she did learn to like odd shapes. For instance, she couldn't resist a new box of tissues. When she was small she could claw out the Kleenex and secrete herself into the box. This never failed to elicit a howl and laughter from Harry. As she grew, Mrs. Murphy discovered that less and less of her managed to fit into the box. Finally, she was reduced to sticking her hind leg in there. Hell on the Kleenex.

Usually the cat contented herself with the canvas mail bin. If Harry, or on rare occasion, Mrs. Hogendobber, wheeled her around, that was kitty heaven. But today she felt like squishing herself into something small. The scudding, frowning putty-colored clouds might have had something to do with it. Or the fact that Market Shiflett had brought over Pewter and three T-bones for the animals. Pewter had caused an unwelcome sensation in Market's store when she jumped into Ellie Wood Baxter's shopping cart and sunk her considerable fangs into a scrumptious pork roast.

Harry adored Pewter, so keeping her for the day was fine. The two cats and Tucker gnawed at their bones until weary. Everyone was knocked out asleep. Even Harry and Mrs. H. wanted to go to sleep.

Harry stopped in the middle of another massive catalogue sort. "Would you look at that?"

"Looks like a silver curtain. George and I loved to walk in the rain. You wouldn't think it to look at him, but George Hogendobber was a romantic. He knew how to treat a lady."

"He knew how to pick a good lady."

"Aren't you sweet?" Mrs. Hogendobber noticed Mrs. Murphy, front end on the ledge, back end jammed into Mim's box. She pointed.

Harry smiled. "She's too much. Dreaming of white mice or pink elephants, I guess. I do love that cat. Where's the culprit?" She bent down to see Pewter asleep under the desk, her right paw draped over the remains of her T-bone. The flesh had been stripped clean. "Boy, I bet Ellie Wood pitched a holy fit."

"Market wasn't too happy either. Maybe you ought to give him a vacation and take Pewter home tonight. She certainly could use a little outdoor exercise."

"Good idea. I can't keep my eyes open. I'm as bad as these guys."

"Low pressure system. The pollen ought to be a factor soon

too. I dread those two weeks when my eyes are red, my nose runs, and my head pounds.''

"Get Larry Johnson to give you an allergy shot."

"The only person an allergy shot does any good for is Larry Johnson." She grumbled. "He'll come by soon to give us a lunch hour today. He's back working full-time again. Remember when he first retired and he'd come in so you could take time for lunch? That lasted about six months. Then he was back working at his practice Monday, Wednesday, and Friday mornings. Soon it was every morning, and now he's back to a full schedule."

"Do you think people should retire?"

"Absolutely not, I mean, unless they want to. I am convinced, convinced, Mary Minor, that retirement killed my George. His hobbies weren't the same as being responsible to people, being in the eye of the storm, as he used to say. He loved this job."

"I'm trying to find a business I can do on the side. That way, when I retire, I can keep working. These government jobs are rigid. I'll have to retire."

Miranda laughed. "You aren't even thirty-five."

"But it goes by so fast."

"That it does. That it does."

"Besides, I need money. I had to replace the carburetor in my tractor last week. Try finding a 1958 John Deere carburetor. What I've got in there is a hybrid of times. And I don't know how much longer the truck will hold up, she's a 1978. I need four-wheel drive—the inside of the house needs to be painted. Where am I going to get the money?"

"Things were easier when you were married. Anyone who doesn't think a man's salary helps isn't very realistic. Divorce and poverty seem to be the same word for most women."

"Well, I lived just fine on my own before I was married."

"You were younger then. You weren't maintaining a house. As you go along in life, creature comforts get mighty important. If

I didn't have my automatic coffee maker, my electric blanket, and my toaster oven, I'd be a crab and a half," she joked. "And what about my organ that George bought me for my fiftieth birthday? I couldn't live without that."

"I want a Toyota Land Cruiser. Never could afford it though."

"Does Mim have one of those?"

"Along with one of everything else. But yes, she's got the Land Cruiser and Jim's got the Range Rover. Little Marilyn has a Range Rover too. Speak of the devil."

Mim pulled up and sat in the car, trying to decide if the rain would let up. It didn't, so she made a dash for it. "Whoo," she said as she closed the door behind her. Neither Harry nor Mrs. Hogendobber informed her of Mrs. Murphy's slumber. She opened her post box. "A cat's tail. I have always wanted a cat's tail. And a cat's behind. Mrs. Murphy, what are you doing?" she asked as she gently squeezed the feline's tail.

Mrs. Murphy, tail tweaked, complained bitterly. *"Leave me alone. I don't pull your tail."*

Harry and Miranda laughed. Harry walked over to the cat, eyes now half open. "Come on, sweet pea, out of there."

"I'm comfortable."

Sensing deep resistance, Harry placed her hands under the cat's arms and gently removed her amid a torrent of abuse from the tiger. "I know you're comfy in there, but Mrs. Sanburne needs to retrieve her mail. You can get back in there later."

Tucker raised her head to observe the fuss, saw the situation, and put her head down on the floor again.

"You're a big goddamned help," the cat accused the dog.

Tucker closed her eyes. If she ignored Mrs. Murphy, the feline usually dropped it.

"Did she read my mail too?" Mim asked.

"Here it is." Miranda handed it over to Mim, whose engagement diamond, a marquise cut, caught the light and splashed a tiny rainbow on the wall.

"Bills, bills, bills. Oh, just what I always wanted, a catalogue from Victoria's Secret." She underhanded it into the trash, looked up, and beheld Harry and Miranda beholding her. "I love my cashmere robe. But this sexy stuff is for your age group, Harry."

"I sleep in the nude."

"True confessions." Mim leaned against the counter. "Heard you all have been helping Kimball Haynes. I guess he told you about the pathology report, or whatever they call those things."

"Yes, he did," Miranda said.

"All we have to do is find a thirty-two-year-old white male who may have walked with a slight limp in his left leg—in 1803."

"That, or find out more about Medley Orion."

"It is a puzzle." Mim crossed her arms over her chest. "I spoke to Lulu this morning and she said Kimball spent all of yesterday over there and Samson's mad at her."

"Why?" asked Harry innocently.

"Oh, she said he got out of sorts. And she admitted that maybe she should have waited until Samson was home. I don't know. Those two." She shook her head.

As if on cue, Samson stamped into the post office with customers from Los Angeles. "Hello there. What luck, finding you here, Mim. I'd like you to meet Jeremy and Tiffany Diamond. This is Marilyn Sanburne."

Mim extended her hand. "How do you do?"

"Fine, thank you." Jeremy's smile revealed a good cap job. His wife was on her second face-lift, and her smile no longer exactly corresponded to her lips.

"The Diamonds are looking at Midale."

"Ah," cooed Mim. "One of the most remarkable houses in central Virginia. The first to have a flying staircase, I believe."

Samson introduced the Diamonds to Harry and Miranda.

"Isn't this quaint?" Tiffany's voice hit the phony register. "And look, you have pets here too. How cozy."

"They sort the mail." Harry didn't have the knee-jerk response to these kinds of people that Mim did, but she marveled at big city people's assumption of superiority. If you lived in a small town or the country, they thought, then you must be unambitious or stupid or both.

"How cute."

Jeremy brushed a few raindrops off his pigskin blazer, teal yet. "Samson's been telling us about his ancestor, Thomas Jefferson's mother."

I bet he has, Harry thought to herself. "Samson and Mrs. Sanburne—Mrs. Sanburne is the chair, actually—have raised money for the current restorations at Monticello."

"Ah, and say, what about the body in the slave quarters? I know why you look familiar." He stared at Mim. "You were the lady on *Wake-up Call* with Kyle Kottner. Do you really think the victim was a stalker?"

"Whoever he was, he posed some danger," she replied.

"Wouldn't it be ironic, Samson, if he were one of your relatives." Tiffany sank a small fishhook into Samson's ego. Her unfortunate obsession with looking young and cute, and her faint hint of superiority, hadn't dimmed her mind. She'd endured enough of Samson's genealogical bragging.

Harry stifled a giggle. Mim relished Samson's discomfort, especially since she hadn't fully forgiven him for his behavior at Wesley's funeral.

"Well," he gulped, "who knows? Instead of living up to the past, I might have to live it down."

"I'd rather live in the present," Tiffany replied, although her penchant for attempting to keep her face in the twenty-year distant past stated otherwise.

After they vacated the premises, Mim walked back over and leaned against the counter. "Sharp lady."

"She's got Samson's number, that's for sure."

"Harry"—Mim turned to Miranda—"Miranda, have you found anything at all?"

"Just that Medley Orion lived with Martha Jefferson Randolph after 1826. She continued her trade. She had a daughter, but we don't know her name."

"What about searching for the victim? Surely the possibility of a limp could give him away. Someone somewhere knew a lame man visited Medley Orion. And he wasn't a tradesman."

"It's baffling." Miranda leaned on the opposite side of the counter. "But I've turned this over and over in my mind and I believe this has something to do with us now. Someone knows this story."

Mim tapped the counter with her mail. "And if we know, it will upset the applecart." She grabbed a letter opener off the counter and opened her personal mail. Her eyes widened as a letter fell out of a plain envelope postmarked Charlottesville. Letters were pasted on the paper: "Let the dead bury the dead." Mim blanched, then read it aloud.

"Already has," Harry said. "Yeah, the applecart's upset."

"I resent this cheap theatric!" Mim vehemently slapped the letter on the counter.

"Cheap or not, we'd better all be careful," Miranda quietly commented.

35

Ansley, in defiance of Warren, allowed Kimball Haynes to read the family papers. She even opened the safe. After she heard about Lulu's trouble with Samson, she figured the girls ought to stick together, especially since she didn't see anything particularly wrong with allowing it.

Reflecting on that later, she realized that she felt a kinship with Lulu since they shared Samson. Ansley knew she got the better part of him. Samson, a vain but handsome man, evidenced a streak of fun and true creativity in bed. As a young man, he was always in one scrape or another. The one told most often was how he got drunk and ran his motorcycle through a rail fence. Stumbling out of the wreckage, he cursed, "Damn mare refused the fence." Warren had been riding with him that day on his sleek Triumph 750cc.

They must have been wild young bucks, outrageous, still courteous, but capable of anything. Warren lost the wildness once out of law school. Samson retained vestiges of it but seemed subdued in the company of his wife.

Ansley wondered what would happen if and when Lucinda ever found out. She thought of Lucinda as a sister. Conventional emotion dictated that she should hate Lucinda as a rival. Why? She didn't want Samson permanently. Temporary use of his body was quite sufficient.

The more she thought about why she allowed Kimball access to the papers, the more she realized that Wesley's death had opened a Pandora's box. She had lived under that old man's thumb. So had Warren, and over the years she lost respect for her husband, watching him knuckle under to his father. Wesley had displayed virtues, to be sure, but he was harsh toward his son.

Worse, both men shut her out of the business. She wasn't an idiot. She could have learned about farming or Thoroughbred breeding, if nothing else. She might have even offered some new ideas, but no, she was trotted out to prospective customers, pretty bait. She served drinks. She kept the wives entertained. She stood on high heels for cocktail party after cocktail party. Her Achilles' tendon was permanently shortened. She bought a new gown for every black-tie fund-raiser on the East Coast and in Kentucky. She played her part and was never told she did a good job. The men took her for granted, and they had no idea how hard it was to be set aside, yet still be expected to behave graciously to people so hideously boring they should never have been born. Ansley was too young for that kind of life. The women in their sixties and seventies bowed to it. Perhaps some enjoyed being a working ornament, the unsung part of the proverbial marital team. She did not.

She wanted more. If she left Warren, he'd be hurt initially, then he'd hire the meanest divorce lawyer in the state of Virginia with the express purpose of starving her out. Rich men in divorce proceedings were rarely generous unless they were the ones caught with their pants down.

Ansley awoke to her fury. Wesley Randolph had crowed about his ancestors, notably Thomas Jefferson, one time too many. Warren, while not as bad, sang the refrain also. Was it because they couldn't accomplish much today? Did they need those ancestors? If Warren Randolph hadn't been born with a silver spoon in his mouth, he'd probably be on welfare. Her husband had no get-up-and-go. He couldn't think for himself. And now that Poppa wasn't there to tell him how and when to wipe his ass, Warren was in a panic. She'd never seen her husband so distressed.

It didn't occur to her that he might be distressed because she was cheating on him. She thought that she and Samson were too smart for him.

Nor did it occur to Ansley that a rich man's life was not necessarily better than a poor man's, except in creature comforts.

Warren, denied self-sufficiency, was like a baby learning to walk. He was going to fall down many times. But at least he was trying. He pored over the family papers, he studied the account books, he endured meetings with lawyers and accountants concerning his portfolio, estate taxes, death duties, and what have you. Ansley had waited so long for him to be his own man that she couldn't recognize that he was trying.

She took a sour delight from the look on his face when she told him that Kimball had read through the family papers from the years 1790 to 1820.

"Why would you do a thing like that when I asked you to keep him and everyone else out—at least until I could make a sound decision. I'm still—rocky." He was more shocked than angry.

"Because I think you and your father have been selfish. Anyway, it doesn't amount to a hill of beans."

He folded his hands as if in prayer and rested his chin on his fingertips. "I'm not as dumb as you think, Ansley."

"I never said you were dumb," came the hot retort.

"You didn't have to."

Since the boys were in their bedrooms, both parents kept their voices low. Warren turned on his heel and walked off to the stable. Ansley sat down and decided to read the family papers. Once she started, she couldn't stop.

36

The dim light filtering through the rain clouds slowly faded as the sun, invisible behind the mountains, set. The darkness gathered quickly and Kimball was glad he had driven straight home after leaving the Randolphs'. He wanted to put the finishing touches on his successful research before presenting it to Sheriff Shaw and Mim Sanburne. He was hopeful that he could present it on television too, for surely the media would return to Monticello. Oliver would not be pleased, of course, but this story was too good to suppress.

A knock on the door drew him away from his desk.

He opened the door, surprised. "Hello. Come on in and—"

He never finished his sentence. That fast, a snub-nosed .38 was pulled out of a deep coat pocket and Kimball was shot once in the chest and once in the head for good measure.

37

The much-awaited movie date with Fair turned into an evening
work date at Harry's barn. The rain pattered on the standing-seam
tin roof as Fair and Harry, on their knees, laid down the rubber-
ized bricks Warren had given her. She did as her benefactor suggested, putting the expensive flooring in the center of the wash
stall, checking the grade down to the drain as she did so. Fair
snagged the gut-busting task of cutting down old black rubber
trailer mats and placing them around the brick square. They
weighed a ton.

"*This is Mother's idea of a hot date.*" Mrs. Murphy laughed from
the hayloft. She was visiting Simon as well as irritating the owl,
but then, everyone and everything irritated the owl.

Tucker, ground-bound since she couldn't climb the ladder
and never happy about it, sat by the wash stall. Next to her was

Pewter, on her sleepover visit as suggested by Mrs. Hogendobber. Pewter could climb the ladder into the hayloft, but why exert herself?

"*Don't you think the horses get more attention than we do?*" Pewter asked.

"*They're bigger,*" Tucker replied.

"*What's that got to do with it?*" Mrs. Murphy called down.

"*They aren't as independent as we are and their hooves need constant attention,*" Tucker said.

"*Is it true that Mrs. Murphy rides the horses?*"

"*Of course it's true.*" Mrs. Murphy flashed her tail from side to side. "*You ought to try it.*"

Pewter craned her neck to observe the two horses munching away in their stalls. "*I'm not the athletic type.*"

"You're awfully good to help me." Harry thanked her ex-husband as he groaned, pulling a rubber mat closer to the wall. "Want a hand?"

"I've got it," he replied. "The only reason I'm doing this, Skeezits"—he used her high school nickname—"is that you'd do it yourself and strain something. For better or for worse, I'm stronger." He paused. "But you have more endurance."

"Same as mares, I guess."

"I wonder if the differences between human males and females are as profound as we think they are. Mares made me think of it. The equine spread is narrow, very narrow. But for whatever reason, humans have created this elaborate code of sexual differences."

"We'll never know the answer. You know, I'm so out of it, I don't even care. I'm going to do what I want to do and I don't much care if it's feminine or masculine."

"You always were that way, Harry. I think that's why I liked you so much."

"You liked me so much because we were in kindergarten together."

"I was in kindergarten with Susan, and I didn't marry her," he replied with humor.

"Touché."

"I happened to think you were special once I synchronized my testosterone level with my brain. For a time there, the gonads took over."

She laughed. "It's a miracle anyone survives adolescence. Everything is so magnified and so new. My poor parents." She smiled, thinking of her tolerant mother and father.

"You were lucky. Remember when I totaled my dad's new Saab? One of the first Saabs in Crozet too. I thought he was gonna kill me."

"You had help. Center Berryman is not my idea of a stable companion."

"Have you seen him since he got out of the treatment center?"

"Yeah. Seems okay."

"If I was ever tempted by cocaine, Center certainly cured me of that."

"He came to Mim's Mulberry Row ceremony at Monticello. One of his first appearances since he got back. He did okay. I mean, what must it have been like to have everyone staring at you and wondering if you're going to make it? There are those who wish you well, those who are too self-centered to care, those that are sweet but will blunder and say the wrong thing, and those—and these are my absolute faves—those who hope you'll fall flat on your face. That's the only way they can be superior—to have the next guy fail. Jerks." Harry grimaced.

"We became well acquainted with that variety of jerks during our divorce."

"Oh, Fair, come on. Every single woman between the ages of twenty and eighty fawned over you, invited you to dinner—the poor-man-alone routine. I got it both barrels. How could I toss out my errant husband? All boys stray. That's the way they're made. What a load of shit I heard from other women. The men, at least, had the sense to shut up."

He stopped cutting through the heavy rubber, sweat pouring off him despite the temperature in the low fifties. "That's what makes life interesting."

"What"—she was feeling angry just remembering—"dealing with jerks?"

"No—how we each see a slice of life, a degree or two of the circle but not the whole circle. What I was getting while you were getting that was older men like Herbie Jones or Larry Johnson on my case."

"Herbie and Larry?" Harry's interest shot into the stratosphere. "What did they say?"

"Basically that we all fall from grace and I should beg your forgiveness. Know who else invited me over for a powwow? Jim Sanburne."

"I don't believe it." She felt oddly warmed by this male solicitude.

"Harry, he's an unusual man. He said his life was no model but that infidelity was his fatal flaw and he knew it. He really blew me away because he's much more self-aware than I reckoned. He said he thought he started having affairs when he was young because he felt Mim lorded it over him, his being a poor boy, so to speak."

"He learned how to make money in a hurry." Harry always admired self-made people.

"Yeah, he did, and he didn't use a penny of her inheritance either. Fooling around was not just his way to get even but a way to restore his confidence." Fair sat down for a minute. Tucker immediately came over and sat in his lap.

"*Oh, Tucker, you're always sucking up to people,*" accused Pewter, who was the original brown-noser the minute the refrigerator door opened.

"*Pewter, you're jealous,*" Mrs. Murphy teased.

"No, I'm not," came the defensive reply. "But Tucker is so—so *obvious. Dogs have no subtlety.*"

"Pewter, you're just a chatty Cathy." Harry reached over and stroked her chin.

"*Gag me,*" Tucker said.

"Why do you think you fooled around?" Harry thought the question would shake her, but it didn't. She was glad it was finally out there even if it did take three years.

"Stupidity."

"That's a fulsome reply."

"Don't get testy. I was stupid. I was immature. I was afraid I was missing something. The rose not smelled, the road not taken. That kind of crap. I do know, though, that I still had a lot of growing-up to do even after we were married—I spent so much of my real youth with my nose in a textbook that I missed a lot of the life experiences from which a person grows. What I was missing was me."

Harry stopped putting in the brick and sat down, facing him.

He continued. "With a few exceptions like wrecking the Saab, I did what was expected of me. Most of us in Crozet do, I guess. I don't think I knew myself very well, or maybe I didn't want to know myself. I was afraid of what I'd find out."

"Like what? What could possibly be wrong with you? You're handsome, the best in your field, and you get along with people."

"I ought to come over here more often." He blushed. "Ah, Harry, haven't you ever caught yourself driving down Garth Road or waking up in the middle of the night, haven't you ever wondered what the hell you were doing and why you were doing it?"

"Yes."

"Scared me. I wondered if I was as smart as everyone tells me I am. I'm not. I'm good in my field, but I can sure be dumb as a sack of hammers about other things. I kept running into limitations, and since I was raised to believe I shouldn't have any, I ran away from them—you, me. That solved nothing. Boom Boom was an exercise in terrible judgment. And the one before her—''

Harry interrupted. "She was pretty."

"Pretty is as pretty does. Anyway, I woke up one morning and realized that I'd smashed my marriage, I'd hurt the one person I loved most, I'd disappointed my parents and myself, and I'd made a fool of myself to others. Thank God I'm in a business where my patients are animals. I don't think any people would have come to me. I was a mess. I even thought about killing myself."

"You?" Harry was stunned.

He nodded. "And I was too proud to ask for help. Hey, I'm Fair Haristeen and I'm in control. Six-foot-four men don't break down. We might kill ourselves working, but we don't break down."

"What did you do?"

"Found myself at the good reverend's house on Christmas Eve. Christmas with Mom and Dad, oh, boy. Grim, resentful." He shook his head. "I flew out of that house. I don't know. I showed up at Herb's and he sat down and talked to me. He told me that no one's a perfect person and I should go slow, take a day at a time. He didn't preach at me either. He told me to reach out to people and not to hide myself behind this exterior, behind a mask, you know?"

"I do." And she did.

"Then I did something so out of character for me." He played with the edge of the rubber matting. "I found a therapist."

"No way."

"Yeah, I really did, and you're the only person who knows. I've been working with this guy for two years now and I'm making progress. I'm becoming, uh, human."

The phone cut into whatever Fair would have said next. Harry jumped up and walked into the tack room. She heard Mrs. Hogendobber almost before she picked up the phone. Mrs. H. told her that Kimball Haynes had just been found by Heike Holtz.

Shot twice. When he didn't show up for a date or answer his phone, she became worried and drove out to his place.

Harry, ashen-faced, paused for a moment. "Fair, Kimball Haynes has been murdered." She returned to Mrs. H. "We'll be right over."

38

A tea table filled with tarts and a crisp apple pie aroused the interest of Tucker, Mrs. Murphy, and Pewter. The humans at that moment were too upset to eat. Mrs. Hogendobber, a first-rate baker, liked to experiment with recipes before taking them to the Church of the Holy Light for suppers and benefits. The major benefit was to Harry, who was used as the guinea pig. If Harry ever stopped doing her high-calorie-burning farm chores, she'd be fat as a tick. Mrs. H. had planned to bring the treats to work tomorrow, but everything was up in the air.

"That bright young man. He had everything to live for." Miranda wiped her eyes. "Why would anyone kill Kimball?"

Fair sat next to her on one side of the sofa, Harry on the other.

Harry patted her hand. An awkward gesture, but it suited Mrs. Hogendobber, who was not a woman given to hugs or much public display of affection. "I don't know, but I think he stuck his nose too far in somebody's business."

Mrs. Hogendobber lifted her head. "You mean over this Monticello murder?"

"Not exactly. I don't know what I mean." Harry sighed.

Fair's baritone filled the room. "Crozet is a town filled with secrets, generations deep."

"Isn't every town full of secrets? The precepts for living don't seem to take into account true human nature." Harry smelled the apple pie. Pewter crouched, making ready to spring onto the teacart. "Pewter, no."

"*Nobody else is going to eat it,*" the cat sassed her. "*Why waste good food?*"

Her anger rising because Pewter not only refused to budge but wiggled her haunches again for the leap, Harry rose and chased the cat away from the cart. Pewter ran a few steps away and then sat down defiantly.

"*You're pushing it,*" Mrs. Murphy warned her.

"*What's she going to do? Smack pie in my face?*" Pewter wickedly crept closer to the sweet-laden cart.

"Listen, let's eat some of this before Pewter wears me out." Harry sliced three portions of pie, the rich apple aroma deliciously filling the room as the knife opened up the heart of the pie.

"Oh, Miranda, this is beautiful." Harry handed out three plates. She sat down to eat, but Pewter's creeping along toward the cart disturbed the peacefulness, which had been disturbed enough. Giving up, she cut a small slice for the two cats and a separate one for Tucker.

"You spoil those animals," said Mrs. Hogendobber.

"They're great testers. If they won't eat something, you know it's bad—not that your pastries could ever fall into that category."

"Many times I wished I weren't such a baker." She patted her stomach.

They enjoyed the pie until their thoughts returned to Kimball. As they talked, Harry got up and poured coffee for everyone. She often felt better if she could move around. Harry's mother used to say she had ants in her pants, which wasn't true, but she thought better if she walked about.

"Super. The best, Mrs. H.," Fair congratulated her.

"Thank you," she replied listlessly, then a tear fell again. "I hate crying. I keep thinking that he never had the chance to be married or to have children." She placed her cup on the coffee table. "I'm calling Mim. Surely she's heard."

Harry, Fair, and the animals watched as she dialed and Mim came on the line. A long conversation followed, but as Mim did most of the talking, Miranda's audience could only guess.

"She's right here. Let me ask her." Mrs. Hogendobber put her hand over the mouthpiece. "Mim wants us to meet with the sheriff tomorrow. Oliver Zeve has already been questioned. Noon?"

Harry nodded in the affirmative.

Miranda continued. "That's fine. We'll see you at your place, then. Can we bring anything? All right. Bye."

"Take her some of this pie," Fair suggested.

"I think I will." She remained by the phone. "Sheriff Shaw is doing a what-do-you-call-it, ballistics check? They're hoping to trace the gun."

"Fat chance." Harry put her face in her hands.

"Maybe not." Fair thought out loud. "What if the killer acted in haste?"

"Even if he acted in haste, I bet he's not that stupid—or she," Harry countered. "And to make matters worse, the rains washed out any chance of making a mold from tire tracks."

"*And washed out the scent too,*" Tucker mourned.

"This is so peculiar." Mrs. Hogendobber joined them on the davenport.

"We need to go through the papers that Kimball read. I'm sure that Rick Shaw has already thought of that, but since we're somewhat familiar with the period and the players of that day, maybe we could help."

"And expose yourselves to risk? I won't have it," Fair said flatly.

"Fair, you didn't give me orders when we were married. Don't start now."

"When we were married, Mary Minor, your life was not in danger. If you don't have the sense to see where this is leading, I do! There's a man dead because he uprooted something. If he found it, chances are you'll find it, especially given your disposition toward investigation."

"Unless the killer removes the evidence."

"If that's possible," Mrs. Hogendobber said to Harry. "This may be a matter of going over those records and diaries and putting two and two together. It may not be one document—then again, it may."

"And I am telling you two nitwits"—Fair's voice rose, making Tucker prick up her ears—"what Kimball Haynes found may be something of current interest. In his research he might have stumbled over something that's dangerous to someone right now. It's very hard to believe that Kimball would have been killed over a murder in 1803."

"You've got a point there," Mrs. Hogendobber agreed, but she felt uneasy, deeply uneasy.

"I'm going through those papers." Harry was as defiant as Pewter had been. The gray cat watched in astonishment. Mrs. Murphy, privy to a few Mr.-and-Mrs. scenes, was less astonished.

"Harry, I forbid it!" He slammed his hand on the coffee table.

"*Don't do that,*" Tucker barked, but she didn't want her mother in danger either.

"Settle down, you two, just settle down." Mrs. Hogendobber leaned back on the sofa. "We know for certain that Kimball read

through Mim's family histories, and the Coleses'. Don't know if
he got the Randolphs' yet. Anyone else?"

"He kept a list. We'd better get that list or get Rick to let us
photocopy it." Harry, mad at Fair, was still glad he cared, although she was confused as to why that should make her so
happy. Harry was slow that way.

Fair crossed his arms over his chest. "You aren't listening to a
word I'm saying. Let the police handle it."

"I am listening, but I liked Kimball. We were also helping
him piece together the facts on this thing. If I can help catch
whoever did him in, I will."

"I liked him too, but not enough to die for him, and that
won't bring him back." Fair spoke the truth.

"You can't stop me." Harry's chin jutted out.

"No, but I can go along and help."

Mrs. Hogendobber clapped. "Bully for you!"

"*What do you think, Tucker?*" Mrs. Murphy picked up her tail
with a front paw.

"*He's still in love with her.*"

"*That's obvious.*" Pewter lay down, far more interested in the
pastries than human emotions.

"*Yeah, but will he win her back?*" the tiger asked.

39

"No." Sheriff Shaw shook his balding head for emphasis.

"Rick, they have a sound argument." Mim defended Harry and Mrs. Hogendobber. "You and your staff aren't familiar with the descendants of Thomas Jefferson or the personal histories of certain of his slaves. They are."

"The department will hire an expert."

"The expert is dead." Mim's lips pressed tightly together.

"I'll hire Oliver Zeve," the frustrated sheriff stated.

"Oh, and how long do you think that will last? Furthermore, he wasn't exactly interested in pursuing this case, nor was he as interested in the genealogies as Kimball. Harry and Mrs. Hogendobber were working with Kimball already."

"Fair Haristeen called me this morning and said you both ought to be locked up. I'll make that three." He cast his eyes at

Mim, who didn't budge. "He also said that whatever Kimball discovered must be threatening to somebody right now. And you all are obsessed with this Monticello thing."

"And you aren't?" Harry fired back.

"Well—well—" Rick Shaw stuck his hands in his Sam Browne belt. "Focused but not obsessed. Anyway, this is my job and I am mindful of the danger to you ladies."

"I'll work with them," Cynthia Cooper gleefully volunteered.

"You women sure stick together." He slapped his hat against his thigh.

"And men don't?" Mim laughed.

"Yeah, I bet Fair chewed your ears off because he thinks we're in danger. He's being a worrywart."

"He's being sensible and responsible." Rick fought the urge to enjoy another piece of Mrs. Hogendobber's pie. The urge won out. "Miranda, you ought to go into business."

"Why, thank you."

"Does anyone know if there will be a service for Kimball?" Harry inquired.

"His parents removed the body to Hartford, Connecticut, where they live. They'll bury him there. But that reminds me, Mrs. Sanburne, Oliver wants you to help him plan a memorial service for Kimball here. I doubt anyone will journey to Hartford, and he said he'd like some kind of remembrance."

"Of course. I'm sure Reverend Jones will assist in this matter also."

"Well?" Harry had her mind on business.

"Well, what?"

"Sheriff. Please." She sounded like a clever, pleading child at that moment.

Rick quietly looked at Harry and Mrs. Hogendobber, then at Cynthia, who was grinning in high hopes. "Women." They'd won. "The Coleses have agreed to allow us access to their libraries. The Berrymans, Foglemans, and Venables too, and I've got a list here of names that Kimball drew up. Mim, you're first on the list."

"When would you like to start?"

"How about after work today? Oh, and Mim, I need to bring Mrs. Murphy and Tucker along, otherwise I'd have to run them home. Churchill won't mind, will he?"

Churchill was Mim's superb English setter, a champion many times over. "No."

"Pewter too." Miranda reminded Harry of her visitor.

"Ellie Wood still hasn't recovered from the pork roast incident. Which reminds me, I think she is distantly related to one of the Eppes of Poplar Forest. Francis, Polly's son."

Polly was the family nickname for Maria, Thomas Jefferson's youngest daughter, who died April 17, 1804, an event which caused her father dreadful grief. Fortunately her son Francis, born in 1801, survived until 1881, but he, along with Jefferson's other grandchildren, bore the consequences of the president's posthumous financial disaster.

"We'll leave not a stone unturned," Mrs. Hogendobber vowed.

40

That evening, as Harry, Mrs. Hogendobber, and Deputy Cooper worked in Mim's breathtaking cherrywood library, Fair worked out in the stables. Book work soured him. He'd do it diligently if he had to, but he wondered how he'd gotten through Auburn Veterinary College with high honors. Maybe it was easier to read then, but he sure hated it now.

He was floating the teeth of Mim's six Thoroughbreds, filing down the sharp edges. Because a horse's upper jaw is slightly wider than the lower one, its teeth wear unevenly, requiring regular maintenance, or at least inspection. If the teeth are allowed to become sharp and jagged, they can cause discomfort to the animal when it has a bit in its mouth, sometimes making it more difficult to ride, and often this situation can cause digestive or nutrition problems because of the animal's restricted ability to chew and break down its food.

Mim's stable manager held the horses as Mim sat in a camp chair and chatted. "You made a believer out of me, Fair. I don't know how I lived without Strongid C. The horses eat less and get more nutrition from their food." Strongid C was a new wormer that came in pellet form and was added to a horse's daily ration. This saved the owner those monthly paste-worming tasks that more often than not proved disagreeable to both parties.

"Good. Took me a while to convince some of my clients, but I'm getting good results with it."

"Horse people are remarkably resistant to change. I don't know why, but we are." She pulled a pretty leather crop out of an umbrella stand. "How are the Wheelers doing?"

"Winning at the hunter shows and the Saddlebred shows, as always. You ought to get over there to Cismont Manor, Mim, and see the latest crop. Good. Really good." He finished with her bright bay. "Now, I happen to think you've got one of the best fox hunters in the country."

She beamed. "I do too. So much for modesty. Warren's cornered the market on racing Thoroughbreds."

"What market?" Fair shook his head. The depression, laughingly called a recession, coupled with changes in the tax laws, was in the process of devastating the Thoroughbred business, along with many other aspects of the equine industry. As most congressmen were no longer landowners, they hadn't a clue as to what they had done to livestock breeders and farmers with their stupid "reforms."

Mim spun the whip handle around in her hands. "I tell Jim he ought to run for Congress. At least then there'd be one logical voice in the bedlam. Won't do it. Won't even hear of it. Says he'd rather bleed from the throat. Fair, have you seen a reasonably priced fox hunter in your travels?"

"Mim, what's reasonable to you may not be reasonable to me."

"Quite so." She appreciated that insight. "I'll come directly to the point. Gin Fizz and Tomahawk are long in the tooth and you know Harry doesn't have two nickels to rub together—now."

He sighed. "I know. She absolutely refused alimony. My lawyer said I was crazy to want to pay. I do her vet work for free and it's a struggle to get her to go along with that."

"The Hepworths as well as the Minors have always been prickly proud about money. I don't know who was worse, Harry's mother or her father."

"Mim, I'm—touched that you'd be thinking of Harry."

"Touched, or amazed?"

He smiled. "Both. You've changed."

"For the better?"

He held up his hands for mercy. "Now, that's a loaded question. You seem happier and you seem to want to be friendlier. How's that sound?"

"I wearied of being a bitch. But what's funny, or not so funny, about Crozet is that once people get an idea about you in their heads, they're loath to surrender it. Not that I won't step on toes, I'll always do that, but I figured out, thanks to a little scare in my life, that life is indeed short. My being so superior made me feel in charge, I guess, but I wasn't happy, I wasn't making my husband happy, and the truth is, my daughter detests me underneath all her politeness. I wasn't a good mother."

"Good horsewoman though."

"Thank you. What is there about a stable that pulls the truth out of us?"

"It's real. Society isn't real." He studied Mim, her perfectly coiffed hair, her long fingernails, her beautiful clothes perfect even in the stable. The human animal could grow at any time in its life that it chooses to grow. On the outside she looked the same, but on the inside she was transforming. He felt the same way about himself. "You know, there's a solid 16.1$\frac{1}{2}$-hand Percheron cross that Evelyn Kerr has. The mare is green and only six, but Harry can bring her along. Good bone, Mim. Good hooves too. Of course, it's got a biggish, draft-type head, but not roman-nosed, and no feathers on the fetlocks. Smooth gaits."

"Why is Evelyn selling the horse?"

"She's got Handyman, and when she retired she thought she'd have more time, so she bought this young horse. But Evelyn's like Larry Johnson. She's working harder in retirement than before."

"Why don't you talk to her? Sound her out for me? I'd like to buy the mare if she suits and then let Harry pay me off over time."

"Uh—let me buy the mare. In fact, I wish I'd thought of this myself."

"We can share the expense. Who's to know?" Mim swung her legs under the chair.

41

The night turned unseasonably cool. The Reverend Jones built a fire in his study, his favorite room. The dark green leather chairs bore testimony to years of use; knitted afghans were tossed over the arms to hide the wear. Herb Jones usually wrapped one around his legs as he sat reading a book accompanied by Lucy Fur, the young Maine coon cat he'd brought home to enliven Elocution, or Ella, his older first cat.

Tonight Ansley and Warren Randolph and Mim Sanburne joined him. They were finishing up planning Kimball's memorial service.

"Miranda's taking care of the music." Mim checked that off her list. "Little Marilyn's hired the caterer. You've got the flowers under control."

"Right." Ansley nodded.

"And I'm getting a program printed up." Warren scratched his chin. "What do you call it? It's not really a program."

"In Memoriam," Ansley volunteered. "Actually, whatever you call it, you've done a beautiful job. I had no idea you knew so much about Kimball."

"Didn't. Asked Oliver Zeve for Kimball's résumé."

Mim, without looking up from her list, continued checking off jobs. "Parking."

"Monticello, or should I say Oliver, is taking care of that?"

"Well, that's it, then." Mim put down her pencil. She could have afforded any kind of expensive pencil, but she preferred a wooden one, an Eagle Mirado Number 1. She carried a dozen in a cardboard container, the sale carton, wherever she journeyed. Carried a pencil trimmer too.

The little group stared into the fire.

Herb roused himself from its hypnotic powers. "Can I fetch anyone another drink? Coffee?"

"No thanks," everyone replied.

"Herb, you know people's secrets. You and Larry Johnson." Ansley folded her hands together. "Do you have any idea, any hunch, no matter how wild?"

Herb glanced up at the ceiling, then back at the group. "No. I've gone over the facts, or what we know as the facts, in my mind so many times I make myself dizzy. Nothing jumps out at me. But even if Kimball or the sheriff uncover the secret of the corpse at Monticello, I don't know if that will have anything to do with Kimball's murder. It's tempting to connect the two, but I can't find any link."

Mim stood up. "Well, I'd better be going. We've pulled a lot together on very short notice. I thank you all." She hesitated. "I'm sorry about the circumstances, much as I like working with everyone."

•   •   •

Warren and Ansley left about ten minutes later. Driving the dark, winding roads kept Warren alert.

"Honey . . ." Ansley watched for deer along the sides of the road—the light would bounce off their eyes. "Did you tell anyone that Kimball read the Randolph papers?"

"No, did you?"

"Of course not—make you look like a suspect."

"Why me?"

"Because women rarely kill." She squinted into the inky night. "Slow down."

"Do you think I killed Kimball?"

"Well, I know you sent that letter with the cut-out message to Mim."

He decelerated for a nasty curve. "What makes you think that, Ansley?"

"Saw The New Yorker in the trash in the library. I hadn't read it yet, so I plucked it out and discovered where your scissors had done their work."

He glowered the rest of the way home, which was only two miles. As they pulled into the garage he shut off the motor, reached over, and grabbed her wrist. "You're not as smart as you think you are. Leave it alone."

"I'd like to know if I'm living with a killer." She baited him. "What if I get in your way?"

He raised his voice. "Goddammit, I played a joke on Marilyn Sanburne. It wasn't the most mature thing to do, but it was fun considering how she's cracked the whip over my head and everyone else's since year one. Just keep your mouth shut."

"I will." Her lips clamped tight, making them thinner than they already were.

Without letting go of her wrist he asked, "Did you read the papers? The blue diary?"

"Yes."

He released her wrist. "Ansley, every old Virginia family has its fair share of horse thieves, mental cases, and just plain bad eggs. What's the difference if they were crooked or crazy in 1776 or today? One doesn't air one's dirty laundry in public."

"Agreed." She opened the door to get out, and he did the same on the driver's side.

"Ansley."

"What?" She turned from her path to the door.

"Did you really think, for one minute, that I killed Kimball Haynes?"

"I don't know what to think anymore." Wearily she reached the door, opened it, and without checking behind her, let it slam, practically crunching Warren's nose in the process.

42

Harry, Mrs. Hogendobber, and Deputy Cooper exhausted themselves reading. Mim's connection to Thomas Jefferson was through the Wayles/Coolidge line. Ellen Wayles Randolph, his granddaughter, married Joseph Coolidge, Jr., on May 27, 1825. They had six children, and Mim's mother was related to a cousin of one of those offspring.

Slender though it was, it was a connection to the Sage of Monticello. Ellen maintained a lively correspondence with her husband's family. Ellen, the spark plug of Maria's—or Polly's—children, inherited her grandfather's way with words just as her older brother, called Jeff, inherited his great-grandfather's, Peter Jefferson's, enormous frame and incredible strength.

One of the letters casually mentioned that Ellen's younger

brother, James Madison Randolph, had fallen violently in love with a great beauty and seemed intent upon a hasty marriage.

Harry read and reread the letter, instantly conceiving an affection for the effervescent author. "Miranda, I don't remember James Madison Randolph marrying."

"I'm not sure. Died young though. Just twenty-eight, I think."

"These people had such big families." Deputy Cooper wailed as the task had begun to overwhelm her. "Thomas Jefferson's mother and father had ten children. Seven made it to adulthood."

Miranda pushed back her half-spectacles. When they slid down her nose again she took them off and laid them on the diary before her. "Jane, his favorite sister, died at twenty-five. Elizabeth, the one with the disordered mind, also died without marrying. The remainder of Thomas's brothers and sisters bequeathed to Virginia and points beyond quite a lot of nieces and nephews for Mr. Jefferson. And he was devoted to them. He really raised his sister Martha's children, Peter and Sam Carr. Dabney Carr, who married Martha, was his best friend, as you know."

"*Another* Martha?" Cynthia groaned. "His wife, sister, and daughter were all named Martha?"

"Well, Dabney died young, before thirty, and Thomas saw to the upbringing of the boys," Miranda went on, absorbed. "I am convinced it was Peter who sired four children on Sally Hemings. A stir was caused when Mr. Jefferson freed, or manumitted, one of Sally's daughters, Harriet, quite the smashing beauty. That was in 1822. You can understand why the Jefferson family closed ranks."

Officer Cooper rubbed her temples. "Genealogies drive me bats."

"Our answer rests somewhere with Jefferson's sisters and brother Randolph, or with one of his grandchildren," Harry posited. "Do you believe Randolph was simple-minded? Maybe not as bad as Elizabeth."

"Well, now, she wasn't simple-minded. Her mind would wander and then she'd physically ramble about aimlessly. She wandered off in February and probably died of the cold. Poor thing. No, Randolph probably wasn't terribly bright, but he seems to have enjoyed his faculties. Lived in Buckingham County and liked to play the fiddle. That's about all I know."

"Miranda, how would you like to be Thomas Jefferson's younger brother?" Harry laughed.

"Probably not much. Not much. I think we're done in. Samson's tomorrow night?"

43

Pewter grumbled incessantly as she walked with Harry, Mrs. Murphy, and Tucker to work. The fat cat's idea of exercise was walking from Market's back door to the back door of the post office.

"*Are we there yet?*"

"*Will you shut up!*" Mrs. Murphy advised.

"*Hey, look,*" Tucker told everyone as she caught sight of Paddy running top-speed toward them. His ears were flat back, his tail was straight out, and his paws barely touched the ground. He was scorching toward them from town.

"Murph," Paddy called, "*follow me!*"

"*You're not going to, are you?*" Pewter swept her whiskers forward in anticipation of trouble.

"*What's wrong?*" Mrs. Murphy called out.

"*I've found something—something important.*" He skidded to a stop at Harry's feet.

Harry reached down to scratch Paddy's ears. Not wanting to be rude, he rubbed against her leg. "*Come on, Murph. You too, Tucker.*"

"*Will you tell me what this is all about?*" the little dog prudently asked.

"*Well spoken.*" Pewter sniffed.

"*Larry Johnson and Hayden McIntire's office.*" Paddy caught his breath. "*I've found something.*"

"*What were you doing over there?*" Tucker needed to be convinced it really was important.

"*Passing by. Look, I'll explain on the way. We need to get there before the workmen do.*"

"*Let's go.*" Mrs. Murphy hiked up her tail and dug into the turf.

"*Hey—hey,*" Tucker called, then added after a second's reflection, "*Wait for me!*"

Pewter, furious, sat down and bawled. "*I will not run. I will not take another step. My paws are sore and I hate everybody. You can't leave me here!*"

Perplexed at the animals' wild dash toward downtown Crozet, Harry called after them once but then remembered that most people were just waking up. She cursed under her breath. Harry wasn't surprised, though, by Pewter's staunch resistance to walk another step, having been quickly deserted by her fitter friends. She knelt down and scooped up the rotund kitty. "I'll carry you, you lazy sod."

"*You're the only person I like in this whole wide world,*" Pewter cooed. "*Mrs. Murphy is a selfish shit. Really. You should spend more time with me. She's running off with her no-account ex-husband, and that silly dog is going along like a fifth wheel.*" The cat laughed. "*Why, I wouldn't even give that two-timing tom the time of day.*"

"Pewter, you have a lot on your mind." Harry marveled that the smallish cat could weigh so much.

•   •   •

As the three animals raced across the neat square town plots, Paddy filled them in.

"*Larry and Hayden McIntire are expanding the office wing of the house. I like to go hunting there. Lots of shrews.*"

"*You've got to catch them just right because they can really bite,*" Mrs. Murphy interrupted.

"*It's easy to get in and out of the addition,*" he continued.

The tidy house appeared up ahead, with its curved brick entranceway splitting to the front door and the office door. The sign, DR. LAWRENCE JOHNSON & DR. HAYDEN MCINTIRE, swung, creaking, in the slight breeze. "*No workmen yet,*" Paddy triumphantly meowed. He ducked under the heavy plastic covering on the outside wall and leapt into the widened window placement. The window had not yet been installed. The newest addition utilized the fireplace as its center point of construction. A balancing, new fireplace was built on the other end of the new room. It matched the old one.

"*Hey! What about me?*"

"*We'll open the door, Tucker.*" Mrs. Murphy gracefully sailed through the window after Paddy and landed on a sawdust-covered floor. She hurried to the door of the addition, which as yet had no lock, although the fancy brass Baldwin apparatus, still boxed, rested on the floor next to it. Mrs. Murphy pushed against the two-by-four propped up against the door. It clattered to the floor and the door easily swung open. The corgi hurried inside.

"*Where are you?*" Mrs. Murphy couldn't see Paddy.

"*In here,*" came the muffled reply.

"*He's crazier than hell.*" Tucker reacted to the sound emanating from the large stone fireplace.

"*Crazy or not, I'm going in.*" Mrs. Murphy trotted to the cavernous opening, the firebrick a cascade of silky and satiny blacks and browns from decades of use. The house was originally constructed in 1824; the addition had been built in 1852.

Tucker stood in the hearth. *"The last time we stood in a fireplace there was a body in it."*

"Up here," Paddy called, his deep voice ricocheting off the flue.

Mrs. Murphy's pupils enlarged, and she saw a narrow opening to the left of the large flue. In the process of remodeling, a few loose bricks had become dislodged—just enough room for an athletic cat to squeeze through. *"Here I come."* She sprang off her powerful haunches but miscalculated the depth of the landing. *"Damn."* The tiger hung on to the opening, her rear end dangling over the side. She scratched with her hind claws and clambered up the rest of the way.

"Tricky." Paddy laughed.

"You could have warned me," she complained.

"And miss the fun?"

"What's so important up here?" she challenged him, then, as her eyes became accustomed to the diminished light, she saw he was sitting on it. A heavy waxed oilskin much like the covering of an expensive foul-weather coat, like a Barbour or Dri-as-a-Bone, covered what appeared to be books or boxes. *"Can we open this up?"*

"Tried. Needs human hands," Paddy casually remarked although he was ecstatic that his find had produced the desired thrill in Mrs. Murphy.

"What's going on up there?" Tucker yelped.

Mrs. Murphy stuck her head out of the opening. *"Some kind of stash, Tucker. Might be books or boxes of jewelry. We can't open it up."*

"Think the humans will find it?"

"Maybe yes and maybe no." Paddy's fine features now came alongside Mrs. Murphy's.

"If workmen repoint the fireplace, which they're sure to do, it's anyone's guess whether they'll look inside here or just pop bricks in and mortar them up." Mrs. Murphy thought out loud. *"This is too good a find to be lost again."*

"Maybe it's treasure." Tucker grinned. *"Claudius Crozet's lost treasure!"*

"That's in the tunnel; one of the tunnels," Paddy said, knowing that

Crozet had cut four tunnels through the Blue Ridge Mountains in what was one of the engineering feats of the nineteenth century —or any century. He accomplished his feat without the help of dynamite, which hadn't yet been invented.

"*How long do you think this has been in here?*" Paddy asked.

Mrs. Murphy turned to pat the oilskin. "*Well, if someone hid this, say, in the last ten or twenty years, they'd probably have used heavy plastic. Oilskin is expensive and hard to come by. Mom wanted one of those Australian raincoats to ride in and the thing was priced about $225, I think.*"

"*Too bad humans don't have fur. Think of the money they'd save,*" Paddy said.

"*Yeah, and they'd get over worrying about what color they were because with fur you can be all colors. Look at me,*" Tucker remarked. "*Or Mrs. Murphy. Can you imagine a striped human?*"

"*It would greatly improve their appearance,*" Paddy purred.

Mrs. Murphy, mind spinning as the fur discussion flew on, said, "*We've got to get Larry over here.*"

"*Fat chance.*" Paddy harbored little hope for human intelligence.

"*You stay here with your head sticking out of the hole. Tucker and I will get him over here. If we can't budge him, then we'll be back, but don't you leave. Okay?*"

"*You were always good at giving orders.*" He smiled devilishly.

Mrs. Murphy landed in the hearth and took off for the door, Tucker close behind. They crossed the lawn, stopping under the kitchen window, where a light glowed. Larry was fixing his cup of morning coffee.

"*You bark, I'll jump up on the windowsill.*"

"*Not much of a windowsill,*" Tucker observed.

"*I can bank off it, if nothing else.*" And Mrs. Murphy did just that as Tucker yapped furiously. The sight of this striped animal, four feet planted on a windowpane and then pushing off, jolted Larry wide awake. The second thud from Mrs. Murphy positively sent him into orbit. He opened his back door and, seeing the culprits, thought they wanted to join him.

"Mrs. Murphy, Tucker, come on in."

"*You come out,*" Tucker barked.

"*I'll run in and right out.*" Mrs. Murphy flew past Larry, brushing his legs in the process, turned on a dime, and ran back out through his legs.

"What's the matter with you two?" The old man enjoyed the spectacle but was perplexed.

Again Mrs. Murphy raced in and raced out as Tucker ran forward, barked, and then ran a few steps away. "*Come on, Doc. We need you!*"

Larry, an intelligent man as humans go, deduced that the two animals, whom he knew and valued, were highly agitated. He grabbed his old jacket, slapped his porkpie hat on his head, and followed them, fearing that some harm had come to another animal or even a person. He'd heard about animals leading people to the site of an injured loved one, and a flash of fear ran through him. What if Harry'd been hurt on her way in to work?

He followed them into the addition. He stopped after walking through the door as Mrs. Murphy and Tucker dashed to the fireplace.

"*Howl, Paddy. He'll think you're trapped or something.*"

Paddy sang at his loudest, " '*Roll me over in the clover/Roll me over/ Lay me down and do it again.*' "

Tucker giggled as Mrs. Murphy leapt up to join Paddy, although she refrained from singing the song. Larry walked into the fireplace and beheld Paddy, his head thrown back and warbling for all he was worth.

"Got stuck up in there?" Larry looked around for a ladder. Not finding one, he did spy a large spackling compound bucket. He lifted it by the handle, discovering how heavy it was. He lugged it over to the hearth, positioned it under the opening, where both cats now meowed piteously, and carefully stood on it. He could just see inside.

He reached for Paddy, who shrank back. "Now, now, Paddy, I won't hurt you."

"I know that, you silly twit. Look."

"His eyes aren't good in the dark, plus he's old. They're worse than most," Mrs. Murphy told her ex. *"Scratch on the oilskin."*

Paddy furiously scratched away, his claws making tiny popping noises as he pulled at the sturdy cloth.

"Squint, Larry, and look real hard," Mrs. Murphy instructed.

As if he understood, Larry shielded his eyes and peered inside. "What the Sam Hill?"

"Reach in." Mrs. Murphy encouraged him by back-stepping toward the treasure.

Larry braced against the fireplace with his left hand, now besmirched with soot, and reached in with his right. Mrs. Murphy licked his fingers for good measure. He touched the oilskin. Paddy jumped off and came to the opening. Mrs. Murphy tried to nudge the package, but it was too heavy. Larry tugged and pulled, succeeding in inching the weighty burden forward until it wedged into the opening. Forgetting the cats for a moment, he tried to pull out the oilskin-covered bundle, but it wouldn't fit. He poked at the bricks around the hole and they gave a bit. Cautiously he removed one, then two and three. These bricks had been left that way on purpose. The two kitty heads popped out of the new opening. Larry squeezed the package through and almost fell off the bucket because it was so heavy. He tottered and jumped off backward.

"Not bad for an old man," Tucker commented.

"Let's see what he's got." Mrs. Murphy sailed down. Paddy came after her.

Larry, on his knees, worked at the knot on the back side of the package. The three animals sat silent, watching with intent interest. Finally, victorious, Larry opened the oilskin covering. Inside lay three huge, heavy volumes, leather-bound. With a trembling hand Larry opened the first volume.

The bold, black cursive writing hit Larry like a medicine ball to the chest. He recognized the handwriting and in that instant the man he had admired and worked with came alive again. He was reminded of the fragrance of Jim's pipe tobacco, his habit of running his thumbs up and down under his braces, and his fervent belief that if he could cure human baldness, he'd be the richest doctor on the face of the earth. Larry whispered aloud, " 'The Secret Diaries of a Country Doctor, Volume I, 1912, by James C. Craig, M.D., Crozet, Virginia.' "

Seeing his distress, Mrs. Murphy and Tucker sat next to him, pressing their small bodies against his own. There are moments in every human life when the harpoon of fate rips into the mind and a person has the opportunity to perceive the world afresh through his own pain. This was such a moment for Larry, and through his tears he saw the two furry heads and reached out to pet them, wondering just how many times in this life we are surrounded by love and understanding and are too self-centered, too human-centered to know what the gods have given us.

44

A warm southerly breeze filled breasts with the hope that spring had truly arrived. Snowstorms could hit central Virginia in April, and once a snowstorm had blanketed the fields in May, but that was rare. The last frost generally disappeared mid-April, although days warmed before that. Then the wisteria would bloom, drenching the sides of buildings, barns, and pergolas with lavender and white. This was Mrs. Murphy's favorite time of the year.

She basked in the sun by the back door of the post office along with Pewter and Tucker. She was also basking in the delicious satisfaction of delivering to Pewter the news about the books in the hiding place. Pewter was livid, but one good thing was that her brief absence had allowed Market to overcome his temper and to make peace with Ellie Wood Baxter. The gray cat was now back

in his good graces, but if she had to hear the words "pork roast" one more time, she would scratch and bite.

The alleyway behind the buildings filled up with cars since the parking spaces in the front were taken. On one of the first really balmy days of spring, people always seem motivated to buy bulbs, bouquets, and sweaters in pastel colors.

Driving down the east end of the alleyway was Samson Coles. Turning in on the west end was Warren Randolph. They parked next to each other behind Market Shiflett's store.

Tucker lifted her head, then dropped it back on her paws. Mrs. Murphy watched through eyes that were slits. Pewter could not have cared less.

"How are you doing with the Diamonds?" Warren asked as he shut his car door.

"Hanging between Midale and Fox Haven."

Warren whistled, "Some kind of commission, buddy."

"How you been doing?"

Warren shrugged. "Okay. It's hard sometimes. And Ansley— I asked her for some peace and quiet, and what does she do but let Kimball Haynes go through the family papers. 'Course he was a nice guy, but that's not the point."

"I didn't like him," Samson said. "Lucinda pulled the same stunt on me that Ansley pulled on you. He should have come to me, not my wife. Smarmy—not that I wished him dead."

"Somebody did."

"Made your mind up about the campaign yet?" Samson abruptly changed the subject.

"I'm still debating, although I'm feeling stronger. I just might do it."

Samson slapped him on the back. "Don't let the press get hold of Poppa's will. Well, you let me know. I'll be your ardent supporter, your campaign manager, you name it."

"Sure. I'll let you know as soon as I do." Warren headed for the post office as Samson entered Market's by the back door. With remarkable self-control Warren acted as though not a thing was wrong, but he knew in that instant that Ansley had betrayed his trust and was betraying him in other respects too.

It never crossed Samson's mind that he had spilled the beans, but then, he was already spending the commission money from the Diamond deal in his mind before he'd even closed the sale. Then again, perhaps the trysting and hiding were wearing thin. Maybe subconsciously he wanted Warren to know. Then they could get the pretense over with and Ansley would be his.

45

Since Kimball had kept most of his private papers in his study room on the second floor of Monticello, the sheriff insisted that nothing be disturbed. But Harry and Mrs. Hogendobber knew the material and had been there recently with Kimball, so he allowed them, along with Deputy Cooper, to make certain nothing had been moved or removed.

Oliver Zeve, agitated, complained to Sheriff Shaw that lovely though the three ladies might be, they were not scholars and really had no place being there.

Shaw, patience ebbing, told Oliver to be grateful that Harry and Mrs. Hogendobber knew Kimball's papers and could decipher his odd shorthand. With a curt inclination of the head Oliver indicated that he was trumped, although he asked that Mrs. Murphy and Tucker stay home. He got his way on that one.

Shaw also had to pacify Fair, who wanted to accompany "the girls," as he called them. The sheriff figured that would put Oliver over the edge, and since Cynthia Cooper attended them, they were safe, he assured Fair.

Oliver's frazzled state could be explained by the fact that for the last two days he had endured network television interviews, local television interviews, and encampment by members of the press. He was not a happy man. In his discomfort he almost lost sight of the death of a valued colleague.

"Nothing appears to have been disturbed." Mrs. Hogendobber swept her eyes over the room.

Standing over his yellow legal pad, Harry noticed some new notes jotted in Kimball's tight scribble. She picked up the pad. "He wrote down a quote from Martha Randolph to her fourth child, Ellen Wayles Coolidge." Harry mused. "It's curious that Martha and her husband named their fourth child Ellen Wayles even though their third child was also Ellen Wayles—she died at eleven months. You'd think it'd be bad luck."

Mrs. Hogendobber interjected, "Wasn't. Ellen Coolidge lived a good life. Now, poor Anne Cary, that child suffered."

"You talk as though you know these people." Cynthia smiled.

"In a way we do. All the while we worked with Kimball, he filled us in, saving us years of reading, literally. Lacking telephones, people wrote to one another religiously when they were apart. Kind of wish we did that today. They left behind invaluable records, observations, opinions in their letters. They also cherished accurate judgments of one another—I think they knew one another better than we know each other today."

"The answer to that is simple, Harry." Mrs. H. peeked over her shoulder to examine the legal pad. "They missed the deforming experience of psychology."

"Why don't you read what he copied down?" Cooper whipped out her notebook and pencil.

"This is what Martha Randolph said: 'The discomfort of slavery I have borne all my life, but its sorrows in all their bitterness I never before perceived.' He wrote below that this was a letter dated August 2, 1825, from the Coolidge papers at U.V.A.''

"Who is Coolidge?" Cooper wrote on her pad.

"Sorry, Ellen Wayles married a Coolidge—''

Cooper interrupted. "That's right, you told me that. I'll get the names straight eventually. Does Kimball make any notation about why that was significant?''

"Here he wrote, 'After sale of Colonel Randolph's slaves to pay debts. Sale included one Susan, who was Virginia's maid,' '' Harry informed Cynthia. "Virginia was the sixth child of Thomas Mann Randolph and Martha Jefferson Randolph, the one we call Patsy because that's what she was called within the family.''

"Can you give me an abbreviated history course here? Why did the colonel sell slaves, obviously against other family members' wishes?''

"We forgot to tell you that Colonel Randolph was Patsy's husband.''

"Oh.'' She wrote that down. "Didn't Patsy have any say in the matter?''

"Coop, until a few decades ago, as in our lifetime, women were still chattel in the state of Virginia.'' Harry jammed her right hand in her pocket. "Thomas Mann Randolph could do as he damn well pleased. He started out with advantages in this life but proved a poor businessman. He became so estranged from his family toward the end that he would leave Monticello at dawn and return only at night.''

"He was the victim of his own generosity.'' Mrs. Hogendobber put in a good word for the man. "Always standing notes for friends and then, pfft.'' She flipped her hand upside down like a fish that bellied up. "Wound up in legal proceedings against his own son, Jeff, who had become the anchor of the family and upon whom even his grandfather relied.''

"Know the old horse expression 'He broke bad'?" Harry asked Cooper. "That was Thomas Mann Randolph."

"He wasn't the only one now. Look what happened to Jefferson's two nephews Lilburne and Isham Lewis." Mrs. Hogendobber adored the news, or gossip, no matter the vintage. "They killed a slave named George on December 15, 1811. Fortunately their mother, Lucy, Thomas Jefferson's sister, had already passed away, on May 26, 1810, or she would have perished of the shame. Anyway, they killed this unfortunate dependent and Lilburne was indicted on March 18, 1812. He killed himself on April tenth and his brother Isham ran away. Oh, it was awful."

"Did that happen here?" Cooper's pencil flew across the page.

"Frontier. Kentucky." Mrs. Hogendobber took the tablet from Harry. "May I?" She read. "Here's another quote from Patsy, still about the slave sale. 'Nothing can prosper under such a system of injustice.' Don't you wonder what the history of this nation would be like if the women had been included in the government from the beginning?—Women like Abigail Adams and Dolley Madison and Martha Jefferson Randolph."

"We got the vote in 1920 and we still aren't fifty percent of the government," Harry bitterly said. "Actually, our government is such a tangled mess of contradictions, maybe a person is smart to stay out of it."

"Oh, Harry, it was a mess when Jefferson waded in too. Politics is like a fight between banty roosters," Mrs. Hogendobber noted.

"Could you two summarize Jefferson's attitude about slavery? His daughter surely seems to have hated it." Cooper started to chew on her eraser, caught herself, and stopped.

"The best place to start is to read his *Notes on Virginia*. Now, that was first printed in 1785 in Paris, but he started writing before that."

"Mrs. Hogendobber, with all due respect, I haven't the time

to read that stuff. I've got a killer to find with a secret to hide and we're still working on the stiff from 1803, excuse me, the remains.''

"The corpse of love," Harry blurted out.

"That's how we think of him," Miranda added.

"You mean because he was Medley's lover, or you think he was?" Cooper questioned her.

"Yes, but if she loved him, she had stopped."

"Because she loved someone else?" Cynthia, accustomed to grilling, fell into it naturally.

"It was some form of love. It may not have been romantic."

Cynthia sighed. Another dead end for now. "Okay. Someone tell me about Jefferson and slavery. Mrs. Hogendobber, you have a head for dates and stuff."

"Bookkeeping gives one a head for figures. All right, Thomas Jefferson was born April 13, 1743, new style calendar. Remember, everyone but the Russians moved up to the Gregorian calendar from the Julian. By the old style he was born on April 2. Must have been fun for all those people all over Europe and the New World to get two birthdays, so to speak. Well, Cynthia, he was born into a world of slavery. If you read history at all, you realize that every great civilization undergoes a protracted period of slavery. It's the only way the work can get done and capital can be accumulated. Imagine if the pharaohs had had to pay labor for the construction of the pyramids."

"I never thought of it that way." Cynthia raised her eyebrows.

"Slaves have typically been those who were conquered in battle. In the case of the Romans, many of their slaves were Greeks, most of whom were far better educated than their captors, and the Romans expected their Greek slaves to tutor them. And the Greeks themselves often had Greek slaves, those captured from battles with other poleis, or city-states. Well, our slaves were no different in that they were the losers in war, but the twist for America came in this fashion: The slaves that came to America were the losers in tribal wars in Africa and were sold to the Portuguese by the leaders of the victorious tribes. See, by that time the world had shrunk, so to speak. Lower Africa had contact with Europe, and the products of Europe enticed people every- where. After a while other Europeans elbowed in on the trade and sailed to South America, the Caribbean, and North America with their human cargo. They even began to bag some trophies them- selves—you know, if the wars slowed down. Demand for labor was heavy in the New World."

"Mrs. Hogendobber, what does this have to do with Thomas Jefferson?"

"Two things. He grew up in a society where most people considered slavery normal. And two—and this still plagues us today—the conquered, the slaves, were not Europeans, they were Africans. They couldn't pass. You see?"

Cynthia bit her pencil eraser again. "I'm beginning to get the picture."

"Even if a slave bought his or her way to freedom or was granted freedom, or even if the African started as a free person, he or she never looked like a Caucasian. Unlike the Romans and the Greeks, whose slaves were other European tribes or usually other indigenous Caucasian peoples, a stigma attached to slavery in America because it was automatically attached to the color of the skin—with terrible consequences."

Harry jumped in. "But he believed in liberty. He thought slavery cruel, yet he couldn't live without his own slaves. Oh, sure, he treated them handsomely and they were loyal to him because he looked after them so well compared to many other slave owners of the period. So he was trapped. He couldn't imag- ine scaling down. Virginians then and today still conceive of themselves as English lords and ladies. That translates into a high, high standard of living."

"One that bankrupted him." Mrs. Hogendobber nodded her head in sadness. "And saddled his heirs."

"Yeah, but what was most interesting about Jefferson, to me anyway, was his insight into what slavery does to people. He said it destroyed the industry of the masters while degrading the victim. It sapped the foundation of liberty. He absolutely believed that freedom was a gift from God and the right of all men. So he favored a plan of gradual emancipation. Nobody listened, of course."

"Did other people have to bankrupt themselves?"

"You have to remember that the generation that fought the Revolutionary War, for all practical purposes, saw their currency devalued and finally destroyed. The only real security was land, I guess." Mrs. Hogendobber thought out loud. "Jefferson lost a lot. James Madison struggled with heavy debt as well as with the contradictions of slavery his whole life, and Dolley was forced to sell Montpelier, his mother's and later their home, after his death. Speaking of slavery, one of James's slaves, who loved Dolley like a mother, gave her his life savings and continued to live with her and work for her. As you can see, the emotions between the master or the mistress and the slave were highly complex. People loved one another across a chasm of injustice. I fear we've lost that."

"We'll have to learn to love one another as equals," Harry solemnly said. " 'We hold these truths to be self-evident, that all men are created equal, that they are endowed by their Creator with inherent and unalienable rights, that among these are Life, Liberty, and the Pursuit of Happiness.' "

"History. I hated history when I was in college. You two bring it to life." Cynthia praised them and their short course on Jefferson.

"It is alive. These walls breathe. Everything that everyone did or did not do throughout the course of human life on earth impacts us. Everything!" Mrs. Hogendobber was impassioned.

Harry, spellbound by Mrs. Hogendobber, heard an owl hoot outside, the low, mournful sound breaking the spell and reminding her of Athena, goddess of wisdom, to whom the owl was sacred. Wisdom was born of the night, of solitary and deep thought. It was so obvious, so clearly obvious to the Greeks and those who used mythological metaphors for thousands of years. She just got it. She started to share her revelation when she spied a copy of Dumas Malone's magisterial series on the life of Thomas Jefferson. It was the final volume, the sixth, *The Sage of Monticello.*

"I don't remember this book being here."

Mrs. Hogendobber noticed the book on the chair. The other five volumes rested in the milk crates that served as bookcases. "It wasn't."

"Here." Harry opened to a page which Kimball had marked by using the little heavy gray paper divider found in boxes of teabags. "Look at this."

Cynthia and Mrs. Hogendobber crowded around the book, where on page 513 Kimball had underlined with a pink highlighter, "All five of the slaves freed under Jefferson's will were members of this family; others of them previously had been freed or, if able to pass as white, allowed to run away."

" 'Allowed to run away'!" Mrs. Hogendobber read aloud.

"It's complicated, Cynthia, but this refers to the Hemings family. Thomas Jefferson had been accused by his political enemies, the Federalists, of having an affair of many years' duration with Sally Hemings. We don't think he did, but the slaves declared that Sally was the mistress of Peter Carr, Thomas's favorite nephew, whom he raised as a son."

"But the key here is that Sally's mother, also a beautiful woman, was half white to begin with. Her name was Betty, and her lover, again according to oral slave tradition as well as what Thomas Jefferson Randolph said, was John Wayles, Jefferson's wife's brother. You see the bind Jefferson was in. For fifty years that man lived with this abuse heaped on his head."

"Allowed to run away," Harry whispered. "Miranda, we're on second base."

"Yeah, but who's going to come to bat?" Cooper scratched her head.

46

The Coleses' library yielded little that they didn't already know. Mrs. Hogendobber came across a puzzling reference to Edward Coles, secretary to James Madison and then the first governor of the Illinois Territory. Edward, called Ned, never married or sired children. Other Coleses carried on that task. But a letter dated 1823 made reference to a great kindness he performed for Patsy. Jefferson's daughter? The kindness was not clarified.

When the little band of researchers left, Samson merrily waved them off after offering them generous liquid excitements. Lucinda, too, waved.

After the squad car disappeared, Lucinda walked back into the library. She noticed the account book was not on the bottom shelf. She had not helped Harry, Miranda, and Cynthia go over the records because she had an appointment in Charlottesville,

and Samson had seemed almost overeager to perform the nice-
ties.

She scanned the library for the ledger.

Samson, carrying a glass with four ice cubes and his favorite
Dalwhinnie, wandered in, opened a cabinet door, and sat down in
a leather chair. He clicked on the television, which was concealed
in the cabinet. Neither he nor Lulu could stand to see a television
sitting out. Too middle class.

"Samson, where's your ledger?"

"Has nothing to do with Jefferson or his descendants, my
dear."

"No, but it has a lot to do with Kimball Haynes."

He turned up the sound, and she grabbed the remote out of
his hand and shut off the television.

"What the hell's the matter with you?" His face reddened.

"I might ask the same of you. I hardly ever reach you on
your mobile phone anymore. When I call places where you tell
me you're going to be, you aren't there. I may not be the brightest woman in the world, Samson, but I'm not the dumbest either."

"Oh, don't start the perfume accusation again. We settled
that."

"What is in that ledger?"

"Nothing that concerns you. You've never been interested in
my business before, why now?"

"I entertain your customers often enough."

"That's not the same as being interested in my business. You
don't care how I make the money so long as you can spend it."

"You're clever, Samson, much more clever than I am, but
I'm not fooled. You aren't going to sidetrack me about money.
What is in that ledger?"

"Nothing."

"Then why didn't you let those women go through it? Kimball read it. That makes it part of the evidence."

He shot out of his chair and in an instant towered over her, his bulk an assault against her frailty without his even lifting a hand. He shouted. "You keep your mouth shut about that ledger, or so help me God, I'll—"

For the first time in their marriage Lucinda did not back down. "Kill me?" she screamed in his face. "You're in some kind of trouble, Samson, or you're doing something illegal."

"Keep out of my life!"

"You mean get out of your life," she snarled. "Wouldn't that make it easier for you to carry on with your mistress, whoever she is?"

Menace oozed from his every pore. "Lucinda, if you ever mention that ledger to anyone, you will regret it far more than you can possibly understand. Now leave me alone."

Lucinda replied with an icy calm, frightening in itself. "You killed Kimball Haynes."

47

The squad car, Deputy Cooper at the wheel, picked up an urgent dispatch. She swerved hard right, slammed the car into reverse, and shot toward Whitehall Road. "Hang on, Mrs. H."

Mrs. Hogendobber, eyes open wide, could only suck in her breath as the car picked up speed, siren wailing and lights flashing.

"Yehaw!" Harry braced herself against the dash.

Vehicles in front of them pulled quickly to the side of the road. One ancient Plymouth puttered along. Its driver also had a lot of miles on him. Coop sucked up right behind him and blasted the horn as well. She so astonished the man that he jumped up in his seat and cut hard right. His Plymouth rocked from side to side but remained upright.

"That was Loomis McReady." Mrs. Hogendobber pressed

her nose against the car window, only to be sent toward the other side of the car when Cynthia tore around a curve. "Thank God for seat belts."

"Old Loomis ought not to be on the road." Harry thought elderly people ought to take a yearly driver's test.

"Up ahead," Deputy Cooper said.

Mrs. Hogendobber grasped the back of the front seat to steady herself while she looked between Harry's and Cynthia's heads. "It's Samson Coles."

"Going like a bat out of hell, and in his Wagoneer too. Those things can't corner and hold the road." Harry felt her shoulders tense.

"Look!" Mrs. Hogendobber could now see, once they were out of another snaky turn, that a car in front of Samson's sped even faster than his own.

"Holy shit, it's Lucinda! Excuse me, Miranda, I didn't mean to swear."

"Under the circumstances—" Miranda never finished that sentence because a second set of sirens screeched from the opposite end of the road.

"You've got them now," Harry gloated.

As soon as Lucinda saw Sheriff Rick Shaw's car coming toward her, she flashed her lights and stopped. Cooper, hot on Samson's tail, slowed since she thought he'd brake, but he didn't. He swerved around Lulu's big brown Wagoneer on the right-hand side, one set of wheels grinding into a runoff ditch. Beaver Dam Road lay just ahead, and he meant to hang a hard right.

Sheriff Shaw stopped for Lucinda, who was crying, sobbing, screaming, "He'll kill me! He'll kill me!"

"Ladies, this is dicey," Cooper warned as she, too, plowed into the runoff ditch to the right of Lucinda. The squad car tore out huge hunks of earth and bluestone before reaching the road again.

Samson gunned the red Wagoneer toward Beaver Dam, which wasn't a ninety-degree right but a sharp, sharp reverse thirty-degree angle heading northeast off Whitehall Road. It was a punishing turn under the best of circumstances. Just as Samson reached the turn, Carolyn Maki, in her black Ford dually, braked for the stop sign. Samson hit the brakes and sent his rear end skidding out from underneath him. He overcorrected by turning hard right. The Wagoneer flipped over twice, finally coming to rest on its side. Miraculously, the dually remained untouched.

Carolyn Maki opened her door to assist Samson.

Cooper screeched to a stop next to the truck and leapt out of the squad car, gun in hand. "Get back in the truck," she yelled at Carolyn.

Harry started to open her door, but the strong hand of Mrs. Hogendobber grasped her neck from behind. "Stay put."

This did not prevent either one of them from hitting the automatic buttons to open the windows so they could hear. They stuck their heads out.

Cooper sprinted to the car where Samson clawed at the driver's door, pointing skyward as the car rested on its right side. Oblivious of the minor cuts on his face and hands, he thrust open the door and crawled out head first, only to stare into the barrel of Cynthia Cooper's pistol.

"Samson, put your hands behind your head."

"I can explain everything."

"Behind your head!"

He did as he was told. A third squad car pulled in from Beaver Dam Road, and Deputy Cooper was glad for the assistance. "Carolyn, are you okay?"

"Yes," a wide-eyed Carolyn Maki called from her truck.

"We'll need a statement from you, and one of us will try to get it in a few minutes so you can go home."

"Fine. Can I get out of the truck now?"

Cooper nodded yes as the third officer frisked Samson Coles. The wheels of his Jeep were still spinning.

Carolyn walked over to Mrs. Hogendobber and Harry, now waiting outside the squad car.

Harry heard Sheriff Shaw's voice on the special radio. She picked up the receiver, the coiled cord swinging underneath. "Sheriff, it's Harry."

"Where's Cooper?" came his gruff response.

"She's holding Samson Coles with his hands behind his head."

"Any injuries?"

"No—unless you count the Wagoneer."

"I'll be right there."

The sheriff left Lucinda Coles with one of his deputies. He was less than half a mile away, so he arrived in an instant. He strode purposefully over to Samson. "Read him his rights."

"Yes, sir," Cooper said.

"All right, handcuff him."

"Is that necessary?" Samson complained.

The sheriff didn't bother to respond. He sauntered over to the Wagoneer and stood on his tiptoes to look inside. Lying on the passenger side window next to the earth was a snub-nosed .38.

48

"Copious in his indignation, he was." Miranda held the attention of her rapt audience. She had reached the point in her story where Samson Coles, being led away to the sheriff's car, hands cuffed behind his back, started shouting. He didn't want to go to jail. He hadn't done anything wrong other than chase his wife down the road with his car, and hasn't every man wanted to bash his wife's head in once in a while? "Wasn't it Noel Coward who wrote, 'Women are like gongs, they should be struck regularly'?"

"He said that?" Susan Tucker asked.

"*Private Lives*," Mim filled in. Mim was sitting on the school chair that Miranda had brought around for her from the back of the post office. Larry Johnson, who hadn't told anyone about the diaries, Fair Haristeen, and Ned Tucker stood while Market Shiflett, Pewter next to him, sat on the counter. Mrs. Hogendobber paced the room, enacting the details to give emphasis to her story. Tucker paced with her as Mrs. Murphy sat on the postage scale. When Miranda wanted verification she would turn to Harry, also sitting on the counter, and Harry would nod or say a sentence or two to add color.

The Reverend Jones pushed open the door, come to collect his mail. "How much did I miss?"

"Almost the whole thing, Herbie, but I'll give you a private audience."

Herb was followed by Ansley and Warren Randolph. Mrs. Hogendobber was radiant because this meant she could repeat the adventure anew with theatrics. Three was better than one.

"*Oscar performance,*" Mrs. Murphy laconically commented to her two pals.

"*Wish we'd been there.*" Tucker hated to miss excitement.

"*I'd have thrown up. Did I tell you about the time I threw up when Market was taking me to the vet?*" Pewter remarked.

"*Not now,*" Mrs. Murphy implored the gray cat.

When Mrs. Hogendobber finished her tale for the second time, everyone began talking at once.

"Did they ever find the murder weapon? The gun that killed Kimball Haynes?" Warren asked.

"Coop says the ballistics proved it was a snub-nosed .38-caliber pistol. It was unregistered. Frightening how easy it is to purchase a gun illegally. The bullets matched the bore of the .38 they found in Samson's car. It had smashed the passenger window to bits. Must have had it on the seat next to him. Looks like he really was going to do in Lulu. Looks like he's the one that did in Kimball Haynes." Miranda shook her head at such violence.

"I hope not." Dr. Johnson's calm voice rang out. "Everyone has marital problems, and Samson's may be larger than most, but we still don't know what happened to set this off. And we don't know if he killed Kimball. Innocent until proven guilty. Remember, we're talking about one of Crozet's own here. We'd better wait and see before stringing him up."

"I didn't say anything about stringing him up," Miranda huffed. "But it's mighty peculiar."

"This spring has been mighty peculiar." Fair edged his toes together and then apart, a nervous habit.

"Much as I like Samson, I hope this settles the case. Why would he kill Kimball Haynes? I don't know." Ned Tucker put his arm around his wife's shoulders. "But we would sleep better at night if we knew the case was closed."

"Let the dead bury the dead." The little group murmured their assent to Ned's hopes.

No one noticed that Ansley had turned ghostly white.

49

Samson Coles denied ever having seen the snub-nosed .38. His lawyer, John Lowe, having argued many cases for the defense in his career, could spot a liar a mile away. He knew Samson was lying. Samson refused to give the sheriff any information other than his name and address and, in a funny reversion to his youth, his army ID number. By the time John Lowe reached his client, Samson was the picture of sullen hostility.

"Now, Samson, one more time. Why did you threaten to kill your wife?"

"And for the last time, we'd been having problems, real problems."

"That doesn't mean you kill your wife or threaten her. You're paying me lots of money, Samson. Right now it looks pretty bad for you. The report came back on the gun. It was the gun that killed Kimball Haynes.'' John, not averse to theatrics himself, used this last stunner, which was totally untrue—the ballistics results hadn't come back yet—in hopes of blasting his client into some kind of cooperation. It worked.

"No!" Samson shook. "I never saw that gun before in my life. I swear it, John, I swear it on the Holy Bible! When I said I was going to kill her, I didn't mean I really would, I wouldn't shoot her. She just pushed all my buttons.''

"Buddy, you could get the chair. This is a capital-punishment state, and I wasn't born yesterday. You'd better tell me what happened.''

Tears welled up in Samson's eyes. His voice wavered. "John, I'm in love with Ansley Randolph. I spent money trying to impress her, and to make a long story short, I've been dipping into escrow funds which I hold as the principal broker. Lucinda saw the ledger—'' He stopped because his whole body was shaking. "Actually, she showed it to Kimball Haynes when he was over to read the family histories and diaries, you know, to see if there was anything that could fit into the murder at Monticello. There wasn't, of course, but I have accounts beginning in the last decades of the seventeenth century, kept by my maternal grandmother of many greats, Charlotte Graff. Kimball read those accounts, meticulously detailed, and Lucinda laughed that she couldn't make sense out of my books but how crystal clear Granny Graff's were. So Lucinda gave Kimball my ledger to prove her point. He immediately saw what I'd been doing. I kept two columns, you know how it's done. That's the truth.''

"Samson, you have a high standing in Crozet. To many people's minds that would be more than sufficient motive to kill Kimball—to protect that standing as well as your livelihood. Answer me. Did you kill Kimball Haynes?''

Tears gushing down his ruddy cheeks, Samson implored John, "I'd rather lose my license than my life.''

John believed him.

50

Obsessed by his former partner's diaries, Dr. Larry Johnson read at breakfast, between patients, at dinner, and late into the night. He finished volume one, which was surprisingly well written, especially considering he'd never thought Jim a literary man.

References to the grandparents and great-grandparents of many Albemarle County citizens enlivened the documents. Much of volume one centered on the effects of World War I on the returning servicemen and their wives. Jim Craig was then fairly new to the practice of medicine.

Z. Calvin Coles, grandfather to Samson Coles, returned from the war carrying a wicked dose of syphilis. Mim's paternal line, the Urquharts, flourished during the war, as they invested heavily in armaments, and Mim's father's brother, Douglas Urquhart, lost his arm in a threshing accident.

All the patients treated, from measles to bone cancer, were meticulously mentioned as well as their character, background, and the history of specific diseases.

The Minors, Harry's paternal ancestors, were prone to sinus infections, while on her mother's side, the Hepworths, they either died very young or made it into their seventies and beyond— good long innings then. Wesley Randolph's family often suffered a wasting disease of the blood which killed them slowly. The Hogendobbers leaned toward coronary disorders, and the Sanburnes to gout.

Jim's keen powers of observation again won Larry's admiration. Being young when he joined Jim Craig's practice, Larry had looked up to his partner, but now, as an old man, he could measure Jim in the fullness of his own experience. Jim was a fine doctor and his death at sixty-one was a loss for the town and for other doctors.

With eager hands Larry opened volume two, dated February 22, 1928.

51

Jails are not decorated in designer colors. Nor is the privacy of one's person much honored. Poor Samson Coles listened to stinking men with the DTs hollering and screaming, bottom-rung drug sellers protesting their innocence, and one child molester declaring that an eight-year-old had led him on. If Samson ever doubted his sanity, this "vacation" in the cooler reaffirmed that he was sane—stupid perhaps, but sane.

He wasn't so sure about the men in the other cells. Their delusions both fascinated and repelled him.

His only delusion was that Ansley Randolph loved him when in fact she did not. He knew that now. Not one attempt to contact him, not that he expected her to show her face at the correctional institute, as it was euphemistically called. She could have smuggled him a note though—something.

Like most men, Samson had been used by women, especially when he was younger. One of the good things about Lucinda was that she didn't use him. She had loved him once. He felt the searing pain of guilt each time he thought of his wife, the wife he'd betrayed, his once good name which he had destroyed, and the fact that he would lose his real estate license in the bargain. He'd wrecked everything: home, career, community standing. For what?

And now he stood accused of murder. Fleeting thoughts of suicide, accomplished with a bedsheet, occurred to him. He fought them back. Somehow he would have to learn to live with what he'd done. Maybe he'd been stupid, but he wasn't a coward.

As for Ansley, he knew she'd fall right back into her routine. She didn't love Warren a bit, but she'd never risk losing the wealth and prestige of being a Randolph. Not that being a Coles was shabby, but megamillions versus comfort and a good name—no contest. Then, too, she had her boys to consider, and life would be far more advantageous for them if she stayed put.

In retrospect he could see that Ansley's ambitions centered more on the boys than on herself, although she had the sense to be low-key about them. If she was going to endure the Randolph clan, then, by God, she would have successful and loving sons. Blood, money, and power—what a combination.

He swung his legs over the side of his bunk. He'd turn to pure fat in this place if he didn't do leg raises and push-ups. One good thing about being in the slammer, no social drinking. He wanted to cry sometimes, but he didn't know how. Just as well. Wimps get buggered in places like this.

How long he sat there, dangling his legs just to feel some circulation, he didn't know. He jerked his legs up with a start when he realized he was aptly named.

52

The buds on the trees swelled, changing in color from dark red to light green. Spring, in triumph, had arrived.

Harry endured a spring-cleaning fit each year when the first blush of green swept over the meadows and the mountains. The creeks and rivers soared near their banks from the high melting snow and ice, and the air carried the scent of earth again.

Piles of newspapers and magazines, waiting to be read, were stacked on the back porch. Harry succumbed to the knowledge that she would never read them, so out they went. Clothes, neatly folded, rested near the periodicals. Harry hadn't much in the way of clothing, but she finally broke down and threw out those articles too often patched and repatched.

She decided, too, to toss out the end table with three legs instead of four. She'd find one of those unfinished-furniture stores and paint a new end table. As she carried it out she stubbed her toe on the old cast-iron doorstop. This had been her great-grandmother's iron, heated on top of the stove.

"Goddammit!"

"*If you'd look where you were going, you wouldn't run into things.*" Tucker sounded like a schoolteacher.

Harry rubbed her toe, took off her shoe, and rubbed some more. Then she picked up the offending iron, ready to hurl it outside. "That's it!" She joyously called to Mrs. Murphy and Tucker. "The murder weapon. Medley Orion was a seamstress!"

53

Holding the iron aloft, Harry demonstrated to Mim Sanburne, Fair, Larry Thompson, Susan, and Deputy Cooper how the blow would have been struck.

"It certainly could account for the triangular indentation." Larry examined the iron.

Mrs. Murphy and Pewter sat tight against each other on the kitchen table. Although Mrs. Murphy would rather lose fur than admit it—she liked having a feline companion. Pewter did, too, but then, Pewter camped out on the kitchen table, since that's where the food was placed.

Tucker circled the table. "*Smart of Mom to call Big Marilyn.*"

"*Mim is head of the restoration project.*" Mrs. Murphy glanced down at her little friend. "*This way, too, Mim can tell Oliver Zeve and Coop can tell Sheriff Shaw. It's a pretty good theory.*"

"I believe you've got it." Larry handed the iron to Mim, who felt its weight.

"One solid blow pushing straight out or slightly upward. People performed so much physical labor back then, she was no doubt strong enough to inflict a fatal blow. We know she was young." Mim gave the iron to Miranda.

"The shape of this iron would help when pressing lace or all the fripperies and fancies those folks wore."

"May I borrow the iron to show Rick? If he doesn't see it with his own eyes, he'll be skeptical." Cynthia Cooper held out her hands for the iron.

"Sure."

"We hear that Samson categorically denies killing Kimball even though that gun was in his car." Mim hated that Sheriff Shaw didn't tell her everything. But then, Mim wanted to know everything about everybody, as did Miranda, though for different reasons.

"He's sticking to his story."

"Has anyone visited Lulu?" Susan Tucker asked. "I thought about going there this evening."

"I've paid a call." Mim spoke first, as the first citizen of Crozet, which in essence she was. "She's terribly shaken. Her sister has flown up from Mobile to attend to her. She wonders how people will treat her now, and I've assured her that no blame attaches itself to her. Why don't you give her a day or two, Susan, and then go over."

"She loves shortbread," Mrs. Hogendobber remembered. "I'll bake some."

The rest of the group raised their hands and Miranda laughed. "I'll be in the kitchen till Easter!"

"I'm still not giving up on finding out the real story behind the corpse in Cabin Four." Harry walked over to the counter to make coffee.

"And I was thinking that I'd read through Dr. Thomas Walker's papers. He attended Peter Jefferson on his deathbed.

Quite a man of many parts, Thomas Walker of Castle Hill. Maybe, just maybe, I can find a reference to treating a broken leg. There was another physician also, but I can't think of his name off the top of my head," Larry said.

"We owe it to Kimball." Harry ground the beans, releasing the intoxicating scent.

"Harry, you never give up." Fair joined her, setting out cups and saucers. "I hope you all do get to the bottom of the story just so it's over, but more than anything, I'm glad Kimball's murderer is behind bars. That had me worried."

"Does it seem possible that Samson Coles could kill a man in cold blood?" Mim poured half-and-half into her cup.

"Mrs. Sanburne, the most normal-looking persons can commit the most heinous crimes," stated Deputy Cooper, who ought to know.

"I guess." Mim sighed.

"*Do you think Samson did it?*" Pewter asked.

Mrs. Murphy flicked her tail. "*No. But someone wants us to think he did.*"

"*The gun was in his car.*" Tucker wanted to believe the mess was over.

The tiger cat's pink tongue hung out of her mouth for a second. "*It's not over—feline intuition.*"

Miranda asked, "Did Kimball ever get to the Randolph papers?"

"Gee, I don't know." Harry paused, then walked over to the phone and dialed.

"Hello, Ansley. Excuse me for bothering you. Did Kimball ever get to read your family papers?" She listened. "Well, thanks again. I'm sorry to bother you." She hung up the phone receiver. "No."

"We still have a few more stops in duplicating Kimball's research. Something will turn up." Mrs. H. tried to sound helpful.

54

"What a wuss," Mrs. Murphy groaned about Pewter. "It's too far. It's too cold. I'll be so tired tomorrow."

Tucker's dog trot ate up the miles. "Be glad she stayed home. She would have sat down and cried before we'd gone two miles. This way we can get our work done."

Mrs. Murphy, following feline instincts, felt the whole story was not out, not by a long shot. She convinced Tucker to head out to Samson Coles's estate late at night. The game little dog needed no convincing. Besides, the thrill of finding the books in the fireplace hadn't worn off. Right now they thought they could do anything.

They cut across fields, jumped creeks, ducked under fences. They passed herds of deer, the does with newborn fawns by their sides. And once, Mrs. Murphy growled when she smelled a dog fox. Cats and foxes are natural enemies because they compete for the same food.

As Lucinda and Samson's place was four miles by the path they took, they arrived around eleven o'clock. Lights were on upstairs as well as in the living room.

Massive walnut trees guarded the house. Mrs. Murphy climbed up one and walked out a branch. She saw Lucinda Coles and Warren Randolph through the living room window. She backed down the tree and jumped onto the broad windowsill so she could hear their conversation, since the window was open to allow the cool spring air through the house, a welcome change from the stuffy winter air trapped inside. The cat scarcely breathed as she listened.

Tucker, knowing Mrs. Murphy to be impeccable in these matters, decided to pick up whatever she could by scent.

Lucinda, handkerchief dabbing her eyes, nodded more than she spoke.

"You had no idea?"

"I knew he was fooling around, but I didn't know it was Ansley. My best friend, God, it's so typical." She groaned.

"Look, I know you've got enough troubles, and I don't want you to worry about money. If you'll allow me, I can organize the estate and do what must be done, along with your regular lawyers, of course. Just don't act precipitously. Even if Samson is convicted, it doesn't mean you have to lose everything."

"Oh, Warren, I don't know how to thank you."

He sighed deeply. "I still can't believe it myself. You think you know someone and then—I guess if the truth be told, I'm more upset about the, uh, affair than the murder."

"When did you know?"

"Behind the post office. Tuesday. He slipped, made a comment about something only my wife could have known." He hesitated. "I drove over here one night and cut the lights off. I was going to come in and tell you, and then I chickened out in the middle of it. Well, I saw his car in the driveway. So, like I said, I backed out. I don't know if it would have made any difference if you'd known a few days ago instead of today."

"It wouldn't have saved the marriage." She cried anew.

"Did he really threaten to kill you?"

She nodded and sobbed.

Warren wrung his hands. "That should make the divorce go faster." He glanced to the window. "Your cat wants in."

Mrs. Murphy froze. Lucinda looked up. "That's not my cat." That fast Mrs. Murphy shot off the windowsill. "Funny, that looked like Mrs. Murphy."

"Tucker, vamoose!"

Mrs. Murphy streaked across the front lawn as Tucker, who could run like blazes, caught up with her. The front door opened and Lucinda, curious as well as wanting to forget the pain for a moment, saw the pair. "Those are Harry's animals. What in the world are they doing all the way over here?"

Warren stood beside her and watched the two figures silhouetted against silver moonlight. "Hunting. You'd be amazed at how large hunting territories are. Bears prowl a hundred-mile radius."

"You'd think there'd be enough mice at Harry's."

55

The crowd had gathered along the garden level at Monticello. Kimball Haynes's memorial service was held in the land he loved and understood. Monticello, shorn as she is of home life, makes up for it by casting an emotional net over all who work there.

At first Oliver Zeve balked at holding a memorial at Monticello. Enough negative attention, in his mind, had been drawn to the shrine. He brought it before the board of directors, each of whom had ample opportunity to know and care for Kimball. He was an easy man to like. The board decided without much argument to allow the ceremony to take place after public hours. Somehow it was fitting that Kimball should be remembered

where he was happiest and where he served to further understanding of one of the greatest men this nation or any other has
ever produced.

The Reverend Jones, Montalto looming behind him, cleared
his throat. Mim and Jim Sanburne sat in the front row along with
Warren and Ansley Randolph, as those two couples had made the
financial arrangements for the service. Mrs. Hogendobber, in her
pale gold robes with the garnet satin inside the sleeves and around
the collar, stood beside the reverend with the choir of the Church
of the Holy Light. Although an Evangelical Lutheran, Reverend
Jones had a gift for bringing together the various Christian groups
in Crozet.

Harry, Susan and Ned Tucker, Fair Haristeen, and Heike
Holtz sat in the second row along with Leah and Nick Nichols,
social friends of Kimball's. Lucinda Coles, after much self-torture,
joined them. Mim, in a long, agonizing phone conversation, told
Lulu that no one blamed her for Kimball's death and her presence
would be a tribute to the departed.

Members of the history and architecture departments from
the University of Virginia were in attendance, along with all of the
Monticello staff including the wonderful docents who conduct
the tours for the public.

The Reverend Jones opened his well-worn Bible and in his
resonant, hypnotic voice read the Twenty-seventh Psalm:

        The Lord is my light and my salvation;
          whom shall I fear?
        The Lord is the stronghold of my life;
          of whom shall I be afraid?

        When evildoers assail me,
          uttering slanders against me,
        My adversaries and foes,
          they shall stumble and fall.

Though a host encamp against me,
　my heart shall not fear;
Though war rise up against me,
　yet I will be confident.

One thing have I asked of the Lord,
　that will I seek after;
That I may dwell in the house of the Lord
　all the days of my life—

The service continued and the reverend spoke directly of sufferings needlessly afflicted, of promising life untimely cut down, of the evils that men do to one another, and of the workings of faith. Reverend Jones reminded them of how one life, Kimball Haynes's, had touched so many others and how Kimball sought to help us touch those lives lived long ago. By the time the good man finished, there wasn't a dry eye left.

As the people filed out to leave, Fair considerately placed his hand under Lulu's elbow, for she was much affected. After all, apart from her liking for Kimball and her feelings of responsibility, it was her husband who stood accused of his murder. And Samson sure had a motive. Kimball could have blown the whistle on his escrow theft. Worse, Samson had bellowed that he would kill her.

Ansley stumbled up ahead. High-heeled shoes implanted her in the grass like spikes. Lucinda pulled Fair along with her and hissed at Ansley. "I thought you were my best friend."

"I am," Ansley stoutly insisted.

Warren, high color in his cheeks, watched as if waiting for another car wreck to happen.

"What a novel definition of a best friend: one who sleeps with your husband." Lucinda raised her voice.

"Not here," Ansley begged through clenched teeth.

"Why not? Sooner or later everyone here will know the

story. Crozet is the only town where sound travels faster than light."

Before a rip-roaring shouting match could erupt, Harry slid alongside Lucinda on the right. Susan ran interference.

"Lulu, you are making a career of disrupting funerals," Harry chided her.

It was enough.

56

Dr. Larry Johnson, carrying his black Gladstone bag of medical gear, buoyantly swung into the post office. Tucker rushed up to greet him. Mrs. Murphy, splayed on the counter on her right side, tail slowly flicking back and forth, raised her head, then put it back down again.

"I think I know who the Monticello victim is."

Mrs. Murphy sat up, alert. Harry and Miranda hurried around the counter.

Larry straightened his hand-tied bow tie before addressing his small but eager audience. "Now, ladies, I apologize for not telling you first, but that honor belonged to Sheriff Shaw, and you will, of course, understand why I had to place the next call to Mim Sanburne. She in turn called Warren and Ansley and the other major contributors. I also called Oliver Zeve, but the minute the political calls were accounted for, I zoomed over here."

"We can't stand it. Tell!" Harry clapped her hands together.

"Thomas Walker, like any good medical man, kept a record of his patients. All I did was start at the beginning and read. In 1778 he set the leg of a five-year-old child, Braxton Fleming, the eighth child of Rebecca and Isaiah Fleming, who owned a large tract along the Rivanna River. The boy broke his leg wrestling with his older brother in a tree." He laughed. "Don't kids do the damnedest things? In a tree! Well, anyway, Dr. Walker noted that it was a compound fracture and he doubted that it would heal in such a manner as to afford the patient full facility with the limb, as he put it. He duly noted the break was in the left femur. He also noted that the boy was the most beautiful child he had ever seen. That aroused my curiosity, and I called down to the Albemarle County Historical Society and asked for help. Those folks down there are just terrific—volunteer labor. I asked them if they'd comb their sources for any information about Braxton Fleming. Seems he trod the course a wellborn young fellow typically trod in those days. He was tutored in Richmond, but then instead of going to the College of William and Mary he enrolled in the College of New Jersey, as did Aaron Burr and James Madison. We know it as Princeton. The Flemings were intelligent. All the surviving sons completed their studies and entered the professions, but Braxton was the only one to go north of the Mason-Dixon line to study. He spent some time in Philadelphia after graduating and apparently evidenced some gift for painting. Well, it was as hard then as now to make a living in the arts, so finally Braxton slunk home. He tried his hand at farming and did enough to survive, but his heart wasn't in it. He married well but not happily and he turned to drink. He was reputed to have been the handsomest man in central Virginia."

"What a story!" Mrs. Hogendobber exclaimed.

Larry held up his hands as if to squelch applause. "But we

don't know why he was killed. We only know how, and we have a strong suspect.''

"Dr. J., does anyone know what happened to him? You know, some kind of mention about him not coming home or something?''

"Yes." He tilted his head and stared at the ceiling. "His wife declared that he took a gallon of whiskey and set out for Kentucky to make his fortune. May 1803. No more was ever heard from Braxton Fleming.''

Harry whistled. "He's our man.''

Larry stroked Mrs. Murphy under her chin. She rewarded him with important purrs. "You know, Fair and I were talking the other day, and he was telling me about retroviruses in cats and horses. He also mentioned a feline respiratory infection that can pass from mother to child and may erupt ten years later. Feline leukemia is rampant too. Well, Mrs. Murphy, you look healthy enough and I'm glad of it. I hadn't realized life was so precarious for cats.''

"*Thank you*," the cat responded.

"Larry, you must let us know if you find out anything else. What a detective you are." Praise from Mrs. Hogendobber was high praise indeed.

"Oh, heck, the folks down at the historical society did most of the work.''

He picked up his mail, blew them a kiss, and left, eager to return to Jim Craig's diaries.

57

Diseases, like rivers, course through human history. What might have happened if Pericles had survived the plague in fifth-century B.C. Athens, or if the Europeans nearly two thousand years later had discovered that the bubonic plague was transmitted to humans by rat fleas?

Mrs. Murphy's ancestors saved medieval Europe, only to be condemned in a later century as accessories to witchcraft, then hunted and killed.

And what might have been Russia's fate had Alexei, the heir to the throne, not been born with hemophilia, a blood disease passed on by Queen Victoria's offspring?

One never realizes the blessings of health until they are snatched away.

Medical science, since opening up a cadaver to prove there

was such a thing as a circulatory system, became better at identifying diseases. The various forms of cancer no longer were lumped together as a wasting disease but categorized and named as cancer of the colon, leukemia, skin cancer, and so forth.

The great breakthrough came in 1796, when Sir William Jenner created the vaccine for smallpox.

After that, human hygiene improved, preventative medicine improved, and many could look forward to reaching their fourscore and ten years. Yet some diseases resisted human efforts, cancer being the outstanding example.

As Larry read his deceased partner's diagnoses and prognoses late into each night, he felt like a young man again.

He was pleased to read that Dr. Craig gruffly wrote down, "Young pup's damned good," and he was excited as he delved again into the 1940s cases he'd seen himself.

Vividly he recalled the autopsy they performed on Z. Calvin Coles, Samson's grandfather, in which the old man's liver was grotesquely enlarged and fragile as tissue paper.

When he prepared to write alcoholism on the death certificate as the cause of death, Jim stayed his hand.

"Larry, put down heart failure."

"But that's not what killed him."

"In the end we all die because our hearts stop beating. Write down alcoholism and you break his wife's heart and his children's too.

Through his mentor, Larry had learned how to diplomatically handle unsavory problems such as venereal disease. A physician had to report this to the state health department. This both Dr. Craig and Dr. Johnson did. The individual was to warn former sexual partners of his or her infectious state. Many people couldn't do it, so Dr. Craig performed the service. Larry specialized in scaring the hell out of the victims in the hope that they would repair their ways.

From Dr. Craig Larry learned how to tell a patient he was dying, a chore that tore him to pieces. But Dr. Craig always said,

"Larry, people die as they live. You must speak to each one in his or her own language." Over the years he marveled at the courage and dignity of seemingly ordinary people as they faced death.

Dr. Craig never aspired to being other than what he was, a small-town practitioner. He was much like a parish priest who loves his flock and harbors no ambition to become a bishop or cardinal.

As Larry read on, he was surprised to learn of the termination of a pregnancy for a young Sweet Briar College junior, Marilyn Urquhart. Dr. Craig wrote: "Given the nervous excitability of the patient, I fear having a child out of wedlock would unhinge this young woman."

There were secrets Dr. Craig kept even from his young partner. It was part of the old man's character to protect a lady, no matter what.

The clock read two thirty-five A.M. Larry's head had begun to nod. He forced his eyes open to read just a bit more, and then they popped wide open.

March 3, 1948. Wesley Randolph came in today with his father. Colonel Randolph seems to be suffering from the habitual ailment of his clan. He hates needles. The son does also, but the old man shamed Wesley into getting blood pulled.

My suspicion, quite strong, is that the colonel has developed leukemia. I sent the blood to U.V.A. for analysis, requesting that they use the new electron microscope.

March 5, 1948. Dr. Harvey Fenton asked me to meet him at the U.V.A. Hospital. When I arrived he asked me of my relation to Colonel Randolph and his son. I replied that relations were cordial.

Dr. Fenton didn't say anything to my reply. He merely

pointed to the electron microscope. A blood sample, underneath, showed an avalanche of white cells.

"Leukemia," I said. "Colonel Randolph or Wesley?"

"No," Fenton replied. He slid another sample under
the microscope. "Look here."

I did, and a peculiar shape of cell was prominent. "I'm
not familiar with this cell deformation," I said.

"We're learning to identify this. It's a hereditary blood
disease called sickle cell anemia. The red blood cells lack
normal hemoglobin. Instead, they contain hemoglobin S and
the cells become deformed—they look like a sickle. Because
of the awkward shape, the hemoglobin S blood cells can't
flow like normal cells and they clog up capillaries and blood
vessels. Those traffic jams are extremely painful to the suf-
ferer.

"But there's a less serious condition in which red blood
cells have half normal hemoglobin and half hemoglobin S.
Someone with this condition has the sickle cell trait, but he
won't develop the disease.

"However, if he marries someone else with the trait,
their children stand a twenty-five percent chance of inherit-
ing the disease. The risk is very high.

"We don't know why, but sickle cells occur among
blacks. Occasionally, but rarely, someone of Greek, Arab, or
Indian descent will display the trait. The whole thing is baffling.

"You know all those jokes about Negroes being either
lazy or having hookworm?—well, in many cases we're real-
izing they had sickle cell anemia."

I didn't know what to say, as I have observed since
childhood that the white race delights in casting harsh judgments on the black race. So, I looked at the blood sample
again.

"Did the Negro from whom you obtained this blood
die?"

"The man this blood was drawn from is alive but failing from cancer. He has the trait but not the disease." Dr. Fenton paused. "This is Colonel Randolph's blood sample."

Stunned, I blurted out, "What about Wesley?"

"He's safe, but he carries the trait."

As I drove back home I knew I'd have to tell Colonel Randolph and Wesley the truth. The happy portion of the news was that the colonel was in no immediate danger. The unhappy portion of the news is obvious. I wonder what Larry will make of this? I want to take him down to Dr. Fenton to see for himself.

Larry pushed the book away.

Jim Craig was murdered March 6, 1948. He never got to tell Larry anything.

Legs wobbly and eyes bleary from so much reading, Larry Johnson stood up from his desk. He put on his hat and his Sherlock Holmes coat, as he called it. He hadn't paced the streets of Crozet like this since he tried to walk off a broken heart when Mim Urquhart spurned him for Big Jim Sanburne back in 1950.

As the sun rose, Larry felt his first obligation was to Warren Randolph. He called. Ansley answered, then put Warren on the phone. All the Randolphs were early risers. Larry offered to drive over to see Warren, but Warren said he'd come over to Larry's later that morning. It was no inconvenience.

What was inconvenient was that Larry Johnson was shot at 7:44 Saturday morning.

58

Harry, Miranda, Mim, Fair, Susan, Ned, Mrs. Murphy, and Tucker watched with mounting grief as their dear friend's body was rolled away under a sheet on a gurney. Deputy Cooper said Larry's maid, Charmalene, had found him at nine, when she came to work. He was lying in the front hall. He must have opened the door to let in the killer and taken a few steps toward the kitchen, when he was shot in the back. Probably the man never knew what hit him, but this was cold comfort to his friends. The maid said the coffee he'd made was fresh. He'd made more than usual, so maybe he expected company. He was probably awaiting the arrival of his killer, who then ransacked his office. Sheriff Shaw climbed in the back of the ambulance and they sped away.

Tucker, nose to the ground, picked up the scent easily enough, but the killer wore crepe-soled shoes which left such a distinct rubber smell that the dog couldn't catch a clear human signature. Unfortunately, the ambulance workers trudged over the footprints, for the killer, no fool, tiptoed on the sidewalk and put a foot down hard only in the driveway, probably when disembarking from the car.

"What have you got, Tucker?" Mrs. Murphy, worried, asked.

"Not enough. Not enough."

"A trace of cologne?"

"No, just this damned crepe-sole smell. And a wet smell—sand."

The tiger bent her own nose to the task. "Is anyone else doing construction work? There's always sand involved in construction."

"Sand on a lot of driveways too."

"Tucker, we've got to stick close to Mom. She's done enough research to get her in trouble. Whoever the killer is, he's losing it. Humans don't kill one another in broad daylight unless it's passion or war. This was cold-blooded."

"And hasty," Tucker added, still straining to place the rubber smell. She decided then and there to hate crepe-soled shoes.

Fair Haristeen read Larry's notes on a piece of blue-lined white paper as Cynthia Cooper held the paper with tweezers.

"Can you make some sense of this, Fair? You're a medical man."

"Yes, it's a kind of medical shorthand for sickle cell anemia."

"Don't only African Americans get that?"

"Mostly blacks are affected, but I don't think there's a hundred percent correspondence. It passes from generation to generation."

Cooper asked, "How many generations back?"

Fair shrugged, "That I can't tell you, Coop. I'm just a vet, remember."

"Thanks, Fair."

"Is there a nut case on the loose in Crozet?"

"That depends on how you define nut case, but it's safe to say that if the killer feels anyone is closing in on the truth, he's going to strike."

59

Diana Robb swept aside the ambulance curtains as Rick Shaw pulled the sheet off Larry Johnson.

The bullet had narrowly missed the right side of the good doctor's heart. It passed clearly through his body. The force of the blow, the shock, temporarily knocked him unconscious. When Charmalene discovered him, he was awakening.

Rick Shaw, the instant he knew Larry would live, bent over the older man who, just like a doctor, was giving orders as to how to handle him. "I need your help."

"Yes." Larry assented through a tight jaw.

"Who shot you?"

"That's just it. I left the front door open. I was expecting Warren Randolph sometime late morning. I walked out of the living room into the front hall. Whoever shot me—maybe Warren

—must have tiptoed in, but I never saw him." These five sentences took Larry a long time to utter, and his brow was drenched in sweat.

"Help me, Larry." The doctor nodded yes as Rick fervently whispered, "I need you to pretend you're dead for twenty-four hours."

"I nearly was."

Rick swore Charmalene to secrecy as well as the ambulance staff. When he crawled into the back of the vehicle he had but one thought, how to bait and trap Warren Randolph.

60

Back in the office Rick Shaw banged his fists against the wall. The staff outside his office jumped. No one moved. Rarely did the man they obeyed and had learned to admire show this much emotion.

Deputy Cooper, in the office with him, said nothing, but she did open a fresh pack of cigarettes and made a drinking sign when a fresh-faced patrolman snuck by. That meant a cold Coca-Cola.

"I let my guard down! I know better. How many years have I been an officer of the law? How many?"

"Twenty-two, Sheriff."

"Well, you'd think I would have goddamned learned something in twenty-two years. I relaxed. I allowed myself to think because of circumstantial evidence, because the bullet matched the thirty-eight that killed Kimball, that we had an open-and-shut

case. Sure, Samson protested his innocence. My God, ninety percent of the worst criminals in America whine and lie and say
they're innocent. I didn't listen to my gut."

"Don't be so hard on yourself. The case against Samson
looked airtight. I was sure a confession would be a matter of time,
once he figured out he couldn't outsmart us. It takes time for
reality to set in."

"Oh, Coop." Rick slumped heavily into his chair. "I blame
myself for Larry Johnson's shooting."

The patrolman held up the cold Coke at the glass window.
Cynthia rose, opened the door, took the Coke, and thanked the
young officer. She winked at him too, then gave the can to Rick,
whose outburst had parched him.

"You couldn't have known."

The sheriff's voice dropped. "When Larry called me about
Braxton Fleming, I should have known the other shoe hadn't
dropped. Kimball Haynes wasn't killed over Samson's stealing escrow money. I know that now."

"Hey, the state Samson Coles was in when we arrested him, I
would have believed he could have killed anybody."

"Oh, yeah, he was hot." Rick gulped down some more soda,
the carbonation fizzing down his throat. "He had a lot to lose, to
say nothing of his affair with Ansley blowing out the window."

"Lucinda Coles took care of that at Kimball's memorial service."

"Can't blame her. Imagine how she felt, being put in a social
situation with the woman who's playing around with her husband."

They sat and stared at each other.

"We've got twenty-four hours. If an obit notice doesn't appear in the papers after that, it's going to look awfully peculiar."

"And we've got to hold off the reporters without actually
lying." He rubbed his chin. Larry Johnson's wife had died some
years before, and his only son was killed in Vietnam. "Coop, who
would place the obituary notice?"

"Probably Mrs. Hogendobber, with Harry's help."

"You go over there and enlist their cooperation. See if they can stall a little."

"Oh, brother. They'll want to know why."

"Don't—don't even think about it." He twiddled the can. "I'm going to the hospital. I'm pretty sure we can trust Dr. Ylvisaker and the nurses. I'll set up a twenty-four-hour vigil, just in case." He stood up. "I've got to go get the rest of the story."

"I thought he never saw his attacker."

"He didn't. Before he passed out he told me this had to do with his partner, Dr. Jim Craig."

Cooper inhaled sharply. "Dr. Craig was found shot in the cemetery one icy March morning. I remember, when I first came on the force, reading through the files on the unsolved crimes. I wonder how it all fits?"

"We aren't home yet, but we're rounding second toward third."

61

Sunday morning at six-thirty, the air carried little tiny teeth of rain, not a whopping big rain, but a steady one that might lead to harder rain later.

Harry usually greeted the day with a bounce in her step, but this morning she dragged out to the barn. Larry's murder weighed heavily upon her heart.

She mixed up a warm bran mash which was Sunday's treat for the horses, plus a bit of insurance against colic, she believed. She took a scoop of sweet feed per horse, a half-scoop of bran, and mushed it up with hot water and a big handful of molasses. She stirred her porridge together and for an extra treat threw in two quartered apples. That along with as much timothy hay as Gin and Tommy would eat made them happy, and her too. Except for today.

She finished with the horses, climbed the loft ladder, and put out a bag of marshmallows for Simon, the possum. Then she clambered down and decided she might as well oil some tack since she'd fallen behind in her barn chores over these last few crazy weeks. She threw a bridle up on the tack hook, ran a small bucket full of hot water, grabbed a small natural sponge and her Murphy's Oil Soap, and started cleaning.

Tucker and Mrs. Murphy, feeling her sorrow, quietly sat beside her. Tucker finally laid down, her head between her paws.

She jerked her head up. *"That's the smell."*

"What?" Mrs. Murphy's eyes widened to eight balls.

"Yes! It's not a crepe sole, it's this stuff. I swear it."

"Eagle's Rest." The cat's long white whiskers swept forward then back as her ears flattened. *"But why?"*

"Warren must be in on the escrow theft," Tucker said.

"Or connected to the murder at Monticello." Mrs. Murphy blinked her eyes. *"But how?"*

"What are we going to do?"

"I don't know." The tiger's voice trembled with fear, not for herself, but for Harry.

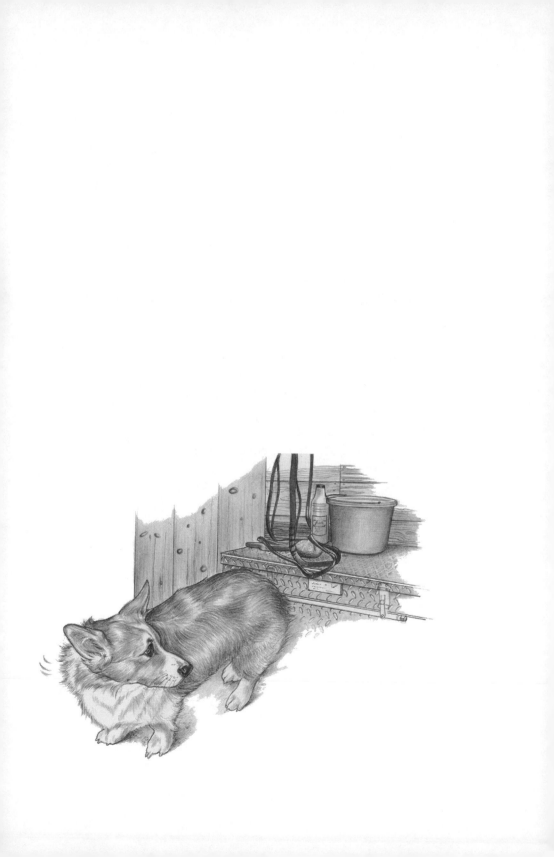

62

" 'No laborious person was ever yet hysterical,' " Harry read aloud. Thomas Jefferson wrote this to his teenage daughter, Patsy, while she studied at the Abbaye Royale de Panthemont in the France of Louis XVI and Marie Antoinette.

"Sensible but not really what a young girl is inclined to wish to hear." Mrs. Hogendobber, fussy today and low over the loss of her old friend, reset the stakes for her sweet peas one more time as the Sunday sunshine bathed over her. The early morning rains had given way to clear skies.

Mrs. Murphy, Pewter, who had escaped Market one more time, and Tucker watched as the squarely built woman walked first to one side of the garden outline, then to the other. She performed this march every spring, and she turned her corners with all the precision of a Virginia Military Institute cadet on drill.

"*The garden will be like last year's and the year's before that. The sweet peas go along the alleyway side of her yard.*" Pewter licked her paws and washed her pretty face.

"*Don't deny her the pleasure of worrying about it,*" Mrs. Murphy advised the gray cat.

"*We know who the killer is.*" Tucker shadowed Mrs. Hogendobber's every move, but from the other side of the garden.

"*Why didn't you tell me the instant you got here? You're hateful.*" Pewter pouted.

Mrs. Murphy relished Pewter's distress for a moment. After all, Pewter lorded it over everybody if she knew something first. "*I thought you weren't interested in human affairs unless food was involved.*"

"*That's not true,*" the cat yowled.

"Harsh words are being spoken, and on the Sabbath." Mrs. Hogendobber chastized the two cats. "Harry, what is the matter with your dog? If I walk, she walks. If I stop, she stops. If I stand, she stands and watches me."

"Tucker, what are you doing?" Harry inquired of her corgi.

"*Being vigilant,*" the dog responded.

"*Against Mrs. Hogendobber?*" Mrs. Murphy laughed.

"*Practice makes perfect.*" The dog turned her back on the cats. Tucker believed that the good Lord made cats first, as an experiment. Then He created the dog, having learned from His mistake.

"*Who?*" Pewter cuffed Mrs. Murphy, who sat on her haunches and cuffed the gray cat right back. Within seconds a fierce boxing match exploded, causing both humans to focus their attention on the contenders.

"My money's on Pewter." Mrs. Hogendobber reached into her voluminous skirt pocket and pulled out a wrinkled dollar bill.

"Mrs. Murphy." Harry fished an equally wrinkled bill out of her Levi's.

"Pewter's bigger. She'll have more pow to her punch."

"Murphy's faster."

The two cats circled, boxed, then Pewter leapt on the tiger cat, threw her to the ground, and they wrestled. Mrs. Murphy wriggled free of the lard case on top of her and tore across the middle of the garden plot then up a black gum tree. Pewter, close behind, raced to the bottom of the trunk and decided to wait her out as opposed to climbing in pursuit.

"*She'll back down the tree and then shove off over your head,*" Tucker told Pewter.

"*Whose side are you on?*" Mrs. Murphy spat out.

"*Entertainment's.*"

Mrs. Murphy backed down just as Tucker had predicted, but then she dropped right on top of the chubby gray and rolled her over. A fulsome hissing and huffing emanated from the competitors. This time it was Pewter who broke and ran straight to Mrs. Hogendobber. Mrs. Murphy chased up to the lady's legs and then reached around Mrs. H.'s heavy English brogues to swat Pewter. Pewter replied in kind.

"They're going to scratch me and I've got on a new pair of nylons."

"*Shut up, Mrs. Hogendobber, we aren't going to touch your nylons,*" Pewter crabbed at her, though relishing the attention too.

" '*Fraidy-cat,*" Mrs. Murphy taunted.

"*Of what, a skinny alley cat? Dream on.*" Another left jab.

"*Fatty, fatty, two by four, can't get through the bathroom door!*" Mrs. Murphy cat-called.

"*That is so childish and gross.*" Pewter twirled on her rear end and stalked off.

"*Hey, you started it, bungbutt,*" Mrs. Murphy yelled at her.

"*Only because you had to get high and mighty about who the killer is. Why should I care? It's human versus human. I'm not a candidate for the graveyard.*"

"*You don't know,*" Mrs. Murphy sang out. "*It's Warren Randolph.*"

"*No!*" The gray cat spun around and ran right up to Mrs. Murphy.

"*We're pretty sure.*" She nodded toward Tucker.

As Tucker padded over to fully inform Pewter, Mrs. Hogendobber and Harry laughed at the animals.

"Spring, wondrous spring—not a season associated with

sorrows, but we've had plenty of them." Miranda blinked hard, then consulted her garden blueprint. "Now, Harry, what were you telling me about Patsy Jefferson Randolph before these little scamps put on such an adorable show?"

"Oh, just that her father might not have known how to talk to young women. But she was said to be a lot like him, so I guess it wasn't so bad. The younger sister never was as close, although she loved him, of course."

"Must have been quite an education for Patsy, being in an expensive French school. When was that now? Refresh my memory."

"You've been studying Patsy's and Polly's children. I've been studying Thomas Jefferson's brothers and sister and his own children. Otherwise you'd have these dates cold. Let's see. I think she enrolled at Panthemont in 1784. Apparently there were three princesses there also and they wore royal blue sashes. Called the American among them 'Jeffy.' "

"How fortunate Patsy was."

"She didn't feel that way when she had to read Livy. Of course, I didn't either. Livy and Tacitus just put me into vapor lock." Harry made a twisting motion at her temple, as though locking something.

"I stopped at Virgil. I didn't go to college or I would have continued. What else about Patsy?"

"Mrs. Hogendobber, you know I'd help you. I feel silly sitting here while you figure out your garden."

"I'm the only one who can figure it out. I'd like to stop those Japanese beetles before they start."

"Don't plant roses, then."

"Don't be absurd, Harry, one simply cannot have a garden without roses. The beetles be damned. If you'll pardon my French." She smiled a sly smile.

Harry nodded. "Okay, back to Panthemont. Patsy conceived a desire to be a nun. It was a Catholic school. That put her father's knickers in a twist and he paid the bill for both Patsy and her sister in full on April 20, 1789, and yanked those kids out of there. Pretty funny. Oh, yeah, something I forgot. Sally Hemings, who was about Patsy's age, traveled to France with her as her batman, you might say. What do you call a batman for a lady?"

"A lady's maid."

"Oh, that's easy enough. Anyway, I've been thinking that the experience of freedom, the culture of France, and being close to Patsy like that in a foreign country must have drawn the two together. Kind of like how Jefferson loved Jupiter, his man, who was also his age. They'd been together since they were boys."

"The self on the other side of the mirror," Miranda said with a dreamy look in her eye.

"Huh?"

"Their slaves who were their ladies' maids and batmen. They must have been alter egos. I never realized how complex, how deep and tangled the emotions on both sides of that mirror must have been. And now the races have drifted apart."

"Ripped apart is more like it."

"Whatever it is, it isn't right. We're all Americans."

"Tell that to the Ku Klux Klan."

"I'd be more inclined to tell them to buy a better brand of bedsheet." Miranda was in fine fettle today. "You know, if you listen to the arguments of these extremist groups or the militant right wing, there's a kernel of truth in what they say. They have correctly pinpointed many of our society's ills, and I must give them credit for that. At least they're thinking about the society in which they live, Harry, they aren't indulging in mindless pleasures, but their solutions—fanatical and absurd."

"But simple. That's why their propaganda is so effective and then I think, too, that it's always easier to be against something than to be for something new. I mean, we never have lived in a community of true racial equality. That's new and it's hard to sell something new."

"I never thought of that." Mrs. H. cupped her chin in her

hand and decided at that instant to shift the sweet peas to the other side of the garden.

"That's what makes Jefferson and Washington and Franklin and Adams and all those people so remarkable. They were willing to try something brand new. They were willing to risk their lives for it. What courage. We've lost it, I think. Americans have lost their vision and their appetite for struggle."

"I don't know. I remember World War Two clearly. We didn't lack courage then."

"Miranda, that was fifty years ago. Look at us now."

"Maybe we're storing up energy for the next push toward the future."

"I'm glad one of us is an optimist." Harry, by virtue of her age, had never lived through an American epoch in which people pulled together for the common good. "There's another thing, by the way. Sally and Betsey Hemings were like sisters to Medley Orion, although she was younger than they were. Apparently they were three beautiful women. It must have been fun to sit outside in the twilight, crickets chirping, and listen to Sally's tales of France before the Revolution."

Pewter meanwhile disagreed with Mrs. Murphy and Tucker over Warren Randolph as murderer. She countered that a man with that much money doesn't have to kill anyone. He can hire someone to do it for him.

Mrs. Murphy rejoined that Warren must have slipped a stitch somewhere along the line.

Pewter's only response was *"Gross."*

"Regardless of what you think, I don't want Mother to get in trouble."

"She's not going to do anything. She doesn't know that Warren's the killer," Pewter said.

The sweet purr of the Bentley Turbo R caught their attention. Mim got out of the car. "Miranda, have you spoken to Sheriff Shaw about Larry's obituary notice and funeral?"

Miranda, stake in hand poised midair, looked as though she

were ready to dispatch a vampire. "Yes, and I find it mighty peculiar."

Mim's crocodile loafers fascinated Mrs. Murphy as she crossed the lawn to join Harry and Mrs. Hogendobber.

"*Those are beautiful,*" the tiger cat admired.

"*Piddle. It's a big skink, that's all.*" Pewter compared the exotic crocodile skin to that of a sleek lizard indigenous to Virginia.

As the three women consulted, worried, and wondered about Rick Shaw's request, Harry noticed that Mrs. Murphy was stalking Mim's shoes. She bent down to scoop up her cat, but Mrs. Murphy scooted just out of reach.

"*Slowpoke,*" the cat taunted.

Harry did not answer but gave the cat a stern look.

"*Don't get her in a bad mood, Murph,*" Tucker pleaded.

In reply, Mrs. Murphy flattened her ears and turned her back on Tucker as Mim strode over to her Bentley to retrieve her portable phone. Miranda walked into her house. After ten minutes of phone calls, which left Harry reduced to putting in the garden stakes, Miranda reappeared.

"No, no, and no."

Mim's head jerked up. "Impossible."

Miranda's rich alto boomed. "Hill and Woods does not have the body. Thacker Funeral Home, ditto, and I even called places in western Orange County. Not a trace of Larry Johnson, and I don't mind telling you that I think this is awful. How can the rescue squad lose a body?"

Harry reached for Mim's mobile phone. "May I?"

"Be my guest." Mim handed over the small, heavy phone.

"Diana"—Harry reached Diana Robb—"do you know what funeral parlor has Larry Johnson's body?"

"No—we just dropped him off at the hospital." Diana's evasive tone alerted Harry, who'd known the nurse since their schooldays.

"Do you know the name of the hospital admissions clerk?"

"Harry, Rick Shaw will take care of everything. Don't worry."

Acidly Harry replied, "Since when do sheriffs arrange funerals? Diana, I need your help. We've got a lot of work to do here."

"Look, you talk to Rick." Diana hung up.

"She hung up on me!" Harry's face turned beet red. "Something is as queer as a three-dollar bill. I'm going down to the hospital."

"Don't do that—just yet." Mim smiled. She reached out for the phone, her frosted mauve fingernails complementing her plum-colored sweater. She dialed. "Is Sheriff Shaw there? All right, then. What about Deputy Cooper? I see." Mim paused. "Try and get her out of her meeting, if only for an instant."

A long pause ensued, during which Mim tapped her foot in the grass and Mrs. Murphy resumed stalking those crocodile loafers. "Ah, Deputy Cooper. I need your assistance. Neither Mrs. Hogendobber, Mrs. Haristeen, nor I can locate Larry Johnson's body at any of the funeral parlors in either Albemarle or Orange County. There are many arrangements to be made. I'm sure you appreciate that and—"

"Mrs. Sanburne, the body is still at the hospital. Sheriff Shaw wanted more tests run, and until he's satisfied that Pathology has everything they need, the body won't be released. You'll have to wait until tomorrow, I'm afraid."

"I see. Thank you." Mim pushed down the aerial and clicked the power to off. She related Cynthia's explanation.

"I don't buy it." Harry crossed her arms over her chest.

"I suppose once the blood is drained out of the body, the samples won't be as, uh, fresh." Mim grimaced.

Now Miranda grabbed the phone. She winked. "Hello, this is Mrs. Johnson and I'd like an update on my husband, Dr. Larry Johnson."

"Larry Johnson, Room 504?"

"That's right."

"He's resting comfortably."

Mrs. Hogendobber repeated the answer. "He's resting comfortably—he ought to be, he's dead."

A sputter and confusion on the other end of the phone convinced Miranda that something was really amiss. The line was disconnected. Miranda's eyebrows shot into her coiffure. "Come on, girls."

As Mrs. Hogendobber climbed into the front seat of the Bentley, Harry unlocked the back door of the post office, shushing the two cats and crestfallen dog inside.

"No fair!" was the animal chorus.

Harry hopped in the back seat as Mim floored it.

"By God, we'll get to the bottom of this!"

63

The front desk clerk at the Martha Jefferson Hospital tried to way-lay Mim, but Harry and Miranda outflanked her. Then Mim, taking advantage of the young woman's distress, slipped away too.

The three women dashed to the elevator. They reached the fifth floor and were met, as the doors opened, by a red-haired officer from the sheriff's department.

"I'm sorry, ladies, you aren't permitted up here."

"Oh, you've taken over the whole floor?" Mim imperiously criticized the young officer, who cringed because he knew more was coming. "I pay taxes, which means I pay your salary and . . ."

Harry used the opportunity to blast down the corridor. She reached Room 504 and opened the door. She screamed so loud, she scared herself.

64

"What a dirty, rotten trick." Mim lit into the sheriff, who was standing at Larry's bedside. This was after Harry, Miranda, and Mim cried tears of joy upon seeing their beloved friend again. They even made Larry cry. He had no idea how much he was loved.

"Mrs. Sanburne, it had to be done and I'm running out of time as it is."

Mim sat on the uncomfortable chair as Harry and Miranda stood on the other side of Larry's bed. Miranda would not release the older gentleman's hand until a sharp glance from Mim made her do so. She then remembered that Larry and Mim were once an item.

"Still jealous," Miranda thought to herself.

Larry, propped up on pillows, reached for a sip of juice.

Mim instantly supplied it to him. "Now, Larry, if we fatigue you, we can leave and the sheriff can fill us in. However, if you can talk . . ."

He slurped and handed the drink back to Mim, as unlikely a nurse as ever was born. "Thank you, dear. I can talk if Sheriff Shaw allows me."

A defeated Rick rubbed his receding hairline. "It's fine with me, because I think if these girls"—he came down heavy on "girls"—"hear from your own lips what happened, then maybe they'll behave."

"We will," came the unconvincing chorus.

"Harry, I have Mrs. Murphy, Tucker, and that funny Paddy to thank for this."

"Mrs. Murphy again?" Rick shook his head.

"They led me to where Jim Craig, who was killed before you were born, had hidden his diaries. He was my partner, as you may know. Actually, he took me into his practice and I would have purchased part of it in time—with a considerable discount, as Jim was a generous, generous man—but he died and, in effect, I inherited the practice, which afforded me the opportunity to become somewhat comfortable." He looked at Mim.

Mim couldn't meet his gaze, so she fiddled with the juice glass and the fat, bendable straw.

He continued. "Jim's diaries commenced in 1912 and went through to the day he died, March 5, 1948. I believe that either Colonel Randolph killed him, or Wesley, who was right out of the Army Air Corps at the time."

"But why?" Miranda exclaimed.

Larry leaned his white head back on the pillows and took a deep breath. "Ah, for reasons both sad and interesting. As detection advanced with the electron microscope, it was Jim who discovered that Wesley and his father carried the sickle cell trait. Now, that didn't give them leukemia—you can develop that disease quite apart from carrying the sickle cells—but what it meant was that no descendant of the colonel or Wesley could, uh, marry someone of color—not without fear of passing on the trait. You see, if the spouse also carried the trait, the children could very well contract the full-blown disease, which has painful episodes, and there's no cure. The accumulated damage of those episodes can kill you."

"Oh, God." Mim's jaw dropped. "Wesley was, well, you know . . ."

"A racist." Harry said it for her.

"That's a harsh way of putting it." Mim smoothed out the bed sheet. "He was raised a certain way and couldn't cope with the changes. But if he knew about the sickle cell anemia, you'd think he would soften."

"Or become worse. Who is more anti-Semitic than another Jew? Who is more antigay than another homosexual? More antifeminist than another woman? The oppressed contain reservoirs of viciousness reserved entirely for their own kind."

"Harry, you surprise me," Mim primly stated.

"She's right though." The sheriff spoke up. "Tell people they're"—he paused because he was going to say "shit"—"worthless, and strange behaviors occur. Let's face it. Nobody wants to ape the poor. They want to ape the rich, and how many rich black folks do you know?"

"Not in Albemarle County." Miranda began to walk around the small room. "But the Randolphs don't appear to be black in any fashion."

"No, but it's in the blood. With rare exceptions, sickle cell anemia affects only people with African blood. It must be inherited. It can't be caught as a contagion, so to speak. This disease seems to be the only remaining vestige of Wesley Randolph's black heritage," Larry informed them.

"And Kimball Haynes found this out somehow." Harry's mind was spinning.

"But how?" Larry wondered.

"Ansley said Kimball never read the Randolph papers," Harry chipped in.

"Absurd! It's absurd to kill over something like this!" Miranda exploded.

"Mrs. Hogendobber, I've seen a fourteen-year-old boy knifed for the five-dollar-bill in his pocket. I've seen rednecks blow each other away because one got drunk and accused the other of sleeping with his wife or called him a faggot. Absurd?" Rick shrugged.

"Did you know?" Harry, ever direct, asked Larry.

"No. Wesley came in for his physical occasionally through the years but always refused to have his blood taken. Being rich, he would fly out to one of those expensive drying-out or treatment clinics, they would take a blood test, and he'd have them read me the white cell count. I accepted that he had leukemia. He wouldn't let me treat him for it and I assumed it was because I am, after all, a country doctor. Oh, he'd come in for a flu shot, stuff like that, and we'd discuss his condition. I'd push and he'd retreat and then he'd check into the Mayo Clinic. He was out of reach, but Warren wasn't. He hated needles and I could do a complete physical on him only about once every fifteen years."

"Who do you think killed Jim Craig?" Mim spoke.

"Wesley, most likely. The colonel would have hated it, but I don't think he would have killed over the news. Jim wouldn't have made it public, after all. I could be wrong, but I just don't think Colonel Randolph would have murdered Jim. Wesley was a hothead when he was young."

"Do you think the Randolphs have always known?" Harry pointed to Mrs. Hogendobber, busily pacing back and forth, indicating that she sit down. She was making Harry dizzy.

"No, because it wouldn't have been picked up in blood tests until the last fifty years or so," said Larry. "All I'm saying is that in medical terms earlier generations would not have known about the sickle cell trait. What else they knew is anybody's guess."

"Never thought of that," Sheriff Shaw said.

"I don't care who knew what. You don't kill over something like that." Miranda couldn't accept the horror of it.

"Warren lived under the shadow of his father. His only out-let has been Ansley. Let's face it, she's the only person who re-garded Warren as a man. When he found out she was carrying on with another man, right after his father's death, I think it was too much. Warren's not very strong, you know," Harry said.

"I thought Samson Coles was the one carrying on. Not Ans-ley too?" Miranda put her foot in it.

"Look no further." Mim pursed her lips.

"No." Harry, like Miranda, found the scandal, well, odd.

"Why don't you arrest Warren?" Mim drilled the sheriff.

"First off, Dr. Johnson didn't see his would-be killer, al-though we both believe it was Warren. Second, if I can trap War-ren into giving himself away, it will make the prosecution's task much easier. Warren is so rich that if I don't nail him down, he'll get off. He'll shell out one or two million for the best defense lawyers in America and he'll find a way out, I can guarantee it. I had hoped that keeping Larry's survival under wraps for twenty-four hours might give me just the edge I need, but I can't go much further than that. The reporters will bribe someone, and it's cruel to have everyone mourning Larry's death. I mean, look at your response."

"Most gratified, ladies." Tears again welled up in Larry's eyes.

"Why can't you just go up to Warren and say Larry's alive and watch his response?" Mim wanted to know.

"I could, but he'd be on guard."

"He won't be on guard with me. He likes me," Harry said.

"No." Rick's voice rose.

"Well, do you have a better idea?" Mim stuck it to the sher-iff.

65

As the Superman-blue Ford toodled down the long, winding, tree-lined road, Mrs. Murphy and Tucker plotted. Harry had been talking out loud, going back and forth over the plan, so they knew what she'd found out at the hospital. She was wired, and Sheriff Shaw and Deputy Cooper were positioned on a back road near the entrance to Eagle's Rest. They would hear every word she and Warren said.

"*We could bite Warren's leg and put him out of commission from the get-go.*"

"*Tucker, all that will happen is you'll be accused of having rabies.*" The cat batted the dog's upright ears with her paw.

"*I've had my rabies shots.*" Tucker sighed. "*Well, do you have any better ideas?*"

"I could pretend I'm choking to death."

"Try it."

Mrs. Murphy coughed and wheezed. Her eyes watered. She flopped on her side and coughed some more. Harry pulled the truck to the side of the driveway. She picked up the cat and put her fingers down her throat to remove the offending obstacle. Finding no obstacle, she placed Mrs. Murphy over her left shoulder, patting her with her right hand as though burping a baby. "There, there, pussywillow. You're all right."

"I know I'm all right. It's you I'm worried about."

Harry put Mrs. Murphy back on the seat and continued up to the house. Ansley, sitting on the side veranda under the towering Corinthian columns, waved desultorily as Harry, unannounced, came in sight.

Harry hopped out of the truck along with her critters. "Hey, Ansley, I apologize for not calling first, but I have some wonderful news. Where's Warren?"

"Down at the stable. Mare's ready to foal," Ansley laconically informed her. "You're flushed. Must be something big."

"Well, yes. Uh, come on down with me. That way I don't have to tell the story twice."

As they sauntered to the imposing stables, Ansley breathed deeply. "Isn't this the best weather? The spring of springs."

"I always get spring fever," Harry confessed. "Can't keep my mind on anything, and everyone has a glow—especially handsome men."

"Heck, don't need spring for that." Ansley laughed as they walked into the stable.

Fair, Warren, and the Randolphs' stable manager, Vanderhoef, crouched in the foaling stall. The mare was doing just fine.

"Hi." Fair greeted them, then returned to his task.

"I have the best news of the year." Harry beamed.

"I wish she wouldn't do this." Mrs. Murphy shook her head.

"*Me too,*" Tucker, heartsick, agreed.

"Well, out with it." Warren stood up and walked out of the stall.

"Larry Johnson's alive!"

"Thank God!" Fair exploded, then caught himself and lowered his voice. "I can't believe it." Luckily his crescendo hadn't startled the mare.

"Me neither." Warren appeared dazed for a moment. "Why anyone would want to kill him in the first place mystifies me. What a great guy. This is good news."

"Is he conscious?" Ansley inquired.

"Yeah, he's sitting up in bed and Miranda's with him. That's why I tore over here without calling. I knew you'd be happy to hear it."

"Did he see who shot him?" Warren asked, edging farther away from the stall door.

"Yes, he did."

"*Watch out!*" Tucker barked as Ansley knocked over Harry while running for her car.

"What in the hell?" Warren bolted down the aisle after her. "Ansley, Ansley, what's going on?"

She hopped into Warren's 911, parked in the courtyard of the barn, cranked it over, and spun out of the driveway. Warren ran after her. In a malicious curve she spun around—and baby, that car could handle—to bear down on her husband.

"Warren, zigzag!" Harry shouted from the end of the barn aisle.

"Get him back in here," Fair commanded just as the foal arrived.

Warren did zig and zag. The car was so nimble, Ansley almost caught him, but he darted behind a tree and she whirled around again and gunned down the driveway.

"Warren, Warren, get in here!" Harry called out. "In case she comes back."

Warren, sickly white, ran back into the stable. He sagged against the stall door. "My God, she did it."

Fair came out of the stall and put his arm around Warren's shoulder. "I'm gonna call the sheriff, Warren, for your own safety if nothing else."

"No, no, please. I can handle her. I'll take care of it and see she's put in a good home. Please, please," Warren pleaded.

"*Poor sucker.*" Mrs. Murphy brushed against Harry's legs.

"It's too late. Rick Shaw and Coop are at the end of the driveway," Harry told him.

Just then they heard the roar of the Porsche's engine, the peal of the siren and squealing tires. Ansley, a good driver, had easily eluded the sheriff and his deputy, who hadn't set up a roadblock but instead were prepared to roar into Eagle's Rest to assist Harry. They thought Harry could pull it off—and she did. The sirens faded away.

"She'll give them a good run for their money." Warren grinned even as the tears rolled down his cheeks.

"Yep." Harry felt like crying too.

Warren rubbed his eyes, then turned to admire the new baby.

"Boss, he's something special." Warren's stable manager hoped this foal would be something good for a man he had learned to like.

"Yes." Warren put his forehead on his hands, resting on the lower dutch door of the foaling stall, and sobbed. "How did you know?"

Harry, choking up, said, "We didn't—actually."

"*We had our wires crossed,*" Mrs. Murphy meowed.

"Suspicion was that it was you." Fair coughed. He was hugely embarrassed to admit this.

"Why?" Warren was dumbfounded. He turned and walked to the aisle doors. He stood looking out over the front fields.

"Uh, well," Harry stammered, then got it out. "Your daddy and well, uh, all the Randolphs put such a store by blood, pedigree, well, you know, that I thought because—I can't speak for anyone but me—I thought you'd be undone, just go ballistic about the African American blood. I mean about people knowing."

"Did you always know?" Fair joined them in front of the barn and handed Warren his handkerchief.

"No. Not until last year. Before Poppa's cancer went into remission he got scared he was going to die, so he told me. He insisted Ansley should never know—he'd never told Mother. I'm not making that mistake with my boys. All this secretiveness eats people alive."

The sirens were heading back toward Eagle's Rest.

"*Damn. We'd better get someplace safe—just in case,*" Tucker wisely noted.

"*Come on, Mom. Let's move it.*" Mrs. Murphy, no time to be subtle, sank her claws into Harry's leg, then ran away.

"Damn you, Murphy!" Harry cursed.

"*Run!*" Tucker barked.

Too late, the whine of the Porsche drowned out the animals' worries.

"Jesus H. Christ!" Harry beheld the Porsche heading straight for them.

Warren started to wave his wife off, but Fair, much stronger, picked Warren up and threw him back so she couldn't see him. Ansley swerved, nearly clipping the end of the barn, and headed down a farm road. Seconds behind her, Rick and Cooper, in their squad cars, threw gravel everywhere. In the distance more sirens could be heard.

"Can she get out that way?" Harry asked as she peered around the door.

"If she can corner the tight turn and take the tractor road around the lake, she can." Warren was shaking.

Harry stared at the dust, the noise. "Warren, Warren." She called his name louder. "How did she find out?"

"She read the diaries after Kimball did. She opened up the

safe and gave him the papers to defy me, and then sat down and read them herself.''

"You didn't hide them?''

"I kept them in the safe, but Ansley didn't have much interest in the family tree. I knew she'd never read them, but I never figured on—''

He didn't finish his sentence as the support cars drowned out his words.

Harry started to run down the farm road.

"*Don't, Mom, she might come back again,*" the cat sensibly warned.

The sirens stopped. The cat and dog, much faster than their human counterparts, flew down the lane and rounded the curve.

"*Oh—*" Tucker's voice trailed off.

Mrs. Murphy shuddered as she watched Ansley drowning in the Porsche which had skidded into the lake. Rick Shaw and Cooper had yanked off their bulletproof vests, their shoes, and dived in, but it was too late. By the time the others reached the lake, only the rear end of the expensive 911 was in view.

66

The grand library of Eagle's Rest smelled like old fires and fresh tobacco. Harry, Mrs. Hogendobber, Mim, Fair, Deputy Cooper, and a composed but subdued Warren had gathered around the fireplace.

"I have already read this to my boys. I've tried to explain to them that their mother's desire to protect them from this—news" —he blinked hard—"was a mistake. Times are different now, but no matter how wrong she was about race, no matter how wrong we all were and are, she acted out of love. It's important for them to have their mother's love." He couldn't continue, but slid the dark blue book over to Harry.

She opened the pages to where a ribbon, spotted and foxed with age, marked the place. Mrs. Murphy and Tucker, curled up at her feet, were as still as the humans.

Warren waved her on and excused himself. At the doorway he stopped. "People talk. I know some folks will be glad to see the Randolphs humbled. Some will even call my boys niggers just to be hateful. I want you all to know the real story, especially since you've worked with Kimball. And—and I thank you for your help." He put his hand over his eyes and walked down the hall.

A long, long moment of silence followed. Harry looked down at the bold, clear handwriting with the cursive flourishes of another age, an age when one's handwriting was a skill to be cultivated and shared.

The diary and papers wedged into it, other people's letters, belonged to Septimia Anne, the eleventh child of Patsy Jefferson and Thomas Randolph. Septimia's letter to her mother was either lost or in someone else's possession, but Patsy's response, written in 1834, was interesting so Harry started there. In the letter she recalled a terrific scandal in 1793, three years after she married Thomas Mann Randolph, the same year in which they acquired Edgehill for $2,000. At the time the farm was 1500 acres. Slaves were also acquired in this lengthy transaction.

Thomas Mann Randolph's sister, Nancy, embarked on an affair with yet another sister's husband, who was also their cousin. This monkey in the middle was Richard Randolph. At Glynlyvar in Cumberland County, Nancy, visiting at the time, suffered a miscarriage. Richard removed the evidence. He was charged with infanticide. Patrick Henry and George Mason defended Richard and he was found not guilty. The law had spoken and so had everyone who lived in the thirteen colonies. This was gossip too good to be true.

Patsy counseled Septimia that scandals, misfortunes, and "commerce" with slave women were woven into the fabric of society. "People are no better than they ought to be." She quoted her own mother, whom she vividly remembered, as she was three weeks short of her tenth birthday when her mother died.

She made a reference to James Madison Randolph, her eighth child and Septimia's older brother by eight years.

"The more things change the more they stay the same," Harry said out loud. She turned pages wrapped up in notations about the weather harvests, floods and droughts, births and deaths. The death of Medley Orion riveted them to their chairs.

Harry read aloud:

Dear Septimia—

Today in the year of our Lord, Eighteen Hundred and Thirty-Five, my faithful servant and longtime companion, Medley Orion, departed this life, surrendering her soul gladly to a Higher Power, for she had devoted her earthly days to good works, kind words, and laughter. The Graces fitted her with physical beauty of a remarkable degree and this proved a harder burden to bear than one might imagine. As a young woman, shooting up like a weed and resembling my beloved father, not necessarily a benefit for a daughter, I resented Medley, for it seemed cruel to me that a slave woman should have been given such beauty, whereas I was given only some small wit.

Sally Hemings and I played together until such time as our race is separated from theirs and we are taught that we are the master. This happened shortly after my dearest mother died, and I felt I was twice removed from those I loved. No doubt many Southerners harbor these same feelings about their sable playmates. As Medley was younger than Sally and me, I began to watch over her almost as I watched over our dear Polly.

Medley remained at Monticello while I journeyed to France with my father and Sally, who for a year or two was no help at all, being too dazzled by the enticements of the Old Order. How Sally managed to find enticements at Abbaye Royale de Panthemont, I still do not know. When I would visit my father at the Hotel de Langeac on Sundays, I did notice that Sally, a beauty herself, seemed to be learning quite quickly how to subdue men.

Upon our return to our sylvan state, our free and majestic Virginia, I again became acquainted with Medley. If ever a woman was Venus on earth, it was she, and curious to note, she evidenced no interest in men. I married. Medley appeared chaste in this regard until that New World Apollo, Braxton Fleming, the boldest rider, the most outrageous liar, the incarnation of idle charm and indolent wit, arrived one day on the mountaintop to seek my father's assistance in a land matter. The sight of Medley as she walked along Mulberry Row unstrung his reason, and Braxton had precious little in the first place.

He laid siege to Medley, encouraged no doubt by the all too evident fact that Peter Carr had made Sally his mistress and Sam Carr enjoyed the favors of Betsey, her sister. And he could not have been ignorant of the condition of my uncle, John Wayles, a good man in most respects, who took Betty Hemings, Sally and Betsey's mother, as his mistress. The Federalists accused my father of being the sultan of a seraglio. Far from it, but politics seems to attract the coarsest forms of intelligence with a few luminous exceptions.

Medley eventually succumbed to Braxton's flambouyant infatuation. He dropped gold coins in her apron as though they were acorns. He bought her brocades, satins, and the sheerest silks from China. I believe he truly loved her, but two years passed, and his wife could no longer bear the whisperings. He was good with horses and bad with women and money. He drank, grew quarrelsome, and would occasionally take a strap to Medley.

At this time I was domiciled at Edgehill with my husband, but the servants would come and go between Edgehill and Monticello and I heard the tales. Father was president at this time. He was spared much of it, although I do fear his overseer at the time, Edmund Bacon, a trusted and able man, may have burdened him with it.

Braxton decayed daily in a manner we were later to see in the husband of Anne Cary. But I will greet the Almighty in the firm conviction that Charles Lewis Bankhead should have been placed in the care of an institution for dypsomaniacs. Braxton was a horse of a different color. He had not much mental power, as I have noted, but he was a sane man. However, circumstance and the crushing weight of impending financial ruin sapped whatever reserve and resolve he possessed. Upon learning that Medley was to bear his child, he—and this was reported to me by King, one of your grandfather's most loved servants—appeared to collapse in on himself. He was reputed to have gone to his wife and spurned her before their children. He declared the intention to divorce her and marry Medley. She told her father, who conducted a meeting with his son-in-law, which must have been incendiary. The man, now deranged, arrived at Monticello and plainly stated to Medley that since they could not live together they must die together. She should prepare to meet her Maker with a clean breast, for he was going to murder her. He, as the suicide, would bear the stigma for this deed. "Even in death I will protect you," he said.

Despite her love for Braxton, Medley felt she could not save him. She once said to me years later, "Miss Patsy, we were like two bright things caught in a spider's great web."

More, Medley wished for the unborn child to live. When Braxton turned from her, she seized her iron and smote him as hard as she could upon the back of the head. He perished immediately, and while it may be wicked to wish death upon another, I can only believe that the man was thereby released from his torments.

King, Big Roger, and Gideon buried his body underneath her hearth. That was May 1803.

The fruit of that union is the woman you know as Elizabeth Goorley Randolph. You are charged with protecting her children and never revealing to any her odyssey.

After the crisis Medley came to me, and when the baby was born, I recognized the child, even more beautiful than her mother, and a child who bore no trace of her African blood.

I believe no good can come from a system wherein one race enslaves another. I believe that all men are created equal, and I believe that God intended for us to live as brothers and sisters and I believe the South will pay in a manner horrible and vast for clinging to the sin of slavery. You know my mind upon this subject, so you will not be surprised that I raised Elizabeth as a distant cousin on the Wayles side.

Father knew of this deception. When Elizabeth turned seventeen I gave her seventy-five dollars and secured for her a seat on the coach to Philadelphia, where she would be joining Sally Hemings's brother, who made his life in that city after Father freed him. What I did not know was that James Madison Randolph wished to honor the lady with his heart and his life. He followed her to Philadelphia, and the rest you know. James, never strong, surely hoped to live longer than the scant twenty-eight years allotted to him, but he has left behind two children and Elizabeth. I am too old to raise more children, my dear, and I have heard death's heavy footfall more and more often in the twilight of my years.

I will not live to see an end to slavery, but I can die knowing I was an agent of sabotage and knowing, too, that I have honored my father's truest intentions on this issue.

I no longer fear death. I will rejoice to see my father in the bloom of youth, to see my husband before his misfortunes corrupted his judgment. I will embrace my mother and seek my friend Medley. The years that God bequeaths us are as moths to the flame, Septimia, but with whatever time we own we must endeavor to make the United States of America a land of life, liberty, and happiness for all her sons and daughters.

Yours,

M.J.R.

"God bless her soul." Mrs. Hogendobber prayed. The little group bowed their heads in prayer and out of respect.

67

Mrs. Murphy sat beside Pewter in Mrs. Hogendobber's garden. The stakes for the peas and tomatoes all had been driven into place at last.

"*I guess you all are lucky to be alive.*"

"*I guess so. She was crazy behind the wheel of that car.*" Mrs. Murphy knocked a small clod of earth over one of the rows. "*You know, humans believe in things that aren't real. We don't. That's why it's better to be an animal.*"

"*Like a social position?*" Pewter followed Mrs. Murphy's train of thought.

"*Money, clothes, jewelry. Foolish things. At least Harry doesn't do that.*"

"*Um. Might be better if she did believe in money a little bit.*"

Mrs. Murphy shrugged. "*Ah, well, can't have everything. And this color thing. It doesn't matter if a cat is black or white as long as it catches mice.*"

Tucker nosed out of the back door of the post office. "*Hey, hey, you all. Come around to the front of the post office.*"

The cats trotted down the tiny path between the post office and the market. They screeched to a halt out front. Fair Haristeen, bestride a large gray mare and wearing his hunting clothes, rode into the post office parking lot. Mim Sanburne stood out front.

Harry opened the front door. Mrs. Hogendobber was right on her heels. "What are you doing? Vetting a horse on Main Street?"

"No. I'm giving you your new fox hunter and I'm doing it in front of your friends. If I took her to the farm, you'd turn me down because you don't like to take anything from anybody. You're going to have to learn how, Harry."

"Hear. Hear." Mim seconded the appeal.

"She's big—and what bone." Harry liked her on sight.

"*Take the horse, Mom,*" Tucker barked.

"May I pet him?" Miranda tentatively reached out.

"Her. Poptart by name and she's got three floating gaits and jumps smooth as silk." Fair grinned.

"I can arrange to pay you over time." Harry folded her arms over her chest.

"No. She's a gift from Mim and me to you."

That really surprised Harry.

"*I like her color,*" said the gray cat.

"*Think Mom will take her?*" Tucker asked.

Mrs. Murphy nodded. "*Oh, it will take a while, but she will. Mother can love. It's letting someone love her. That's what's hard. That's what this is all about.*"

"*How'd you get so smart?*" Tucker came over and sat next to the tiger cat.

"*Feline intuition.*"

Dear Highly Intelligent Feline:

Tired of the same old ball of string? Well, I've developed my own line of catnip toys, all tested by Pewter and me. Not that I love for Pewter to play with my little sockies, but if I don't, she shreds my manuscripts. You see how that is!

Just so the humans won't feel left out, I've designed a T-shirt for them.

If you'd like to see how creative I am, write to me and I'll send you a brochure.

Sneaky Pie Brown
c/o American Artists, Inc.
P.O. Box 4671
Charlottesville, VA 22905

In felinity,

SNEAKY PIE BROWN

P.S. Dogs, get a cat to write for you!